OUT OF THE BLUE

THE FLYNNS BOOK ONE

KAYT MILLER

THE FLYNN FAMILY

OUT OF THE BLUE

CONTENTS

1

SOPHIE

"**H**ow many times do we have to tell you, *Miss Piggy*, to stay away from the tux area?"

I look up from unpacking boxes filled with new designer wedding dresses and see Ari staring down at me, hands on nonexistent hips. "No one was there to help him," I say defensively. I know *they* don't want me over there, but what else was I supposed to do? Leave that man standing there, staring at me?

"I was in the back doing inventory." That means Ari was doing her usual disappearing act. She does no actual work around this place, none.

I stand up in front of her, the top of my head only reaching her chin. God, I'm so sick of these people I work with treating me like dirt. But I *need* this job. "I didn't see you when I went back to grab the tuxedo order file for that wedding. I wasn't just going to leave him standing around, waiting."

"You could have texted me."

Why would I need to text her if she was doing inventory in the back? Because she wasn't in the back doing inventory. She was probably across the street at the Coffee Bean, taking another break. She spends half her day there.

"I don't know what the big deal is; I know what I'm doing in the tuxedo area." I mean, I'm the one who trained Ari, Brit, *and* Ashley how to do the tuxedo side of the shop. How soon they forget.

Ari sighs like she's getting prepared to teach a child something important—teachable moment, here it comes. "You know you aren't supposed to be over there. The men that come in don't want someone like *you*," she says, using her finger to point at my body, "touching them. We don't want to lose customers because we let you wait on them." She pauses long enough to flip her long, blonde hair back over her shoulder. "Isn't it enough that Brooke lets you work with the brides? You're lucky she doesn't have you steaming and pressing in the back all the time."

Brooke is Brooke Bellamy, owner of Bridal Belles & Tux Shoppe. Brooke *knows* I'm the best sales consultant she has. She'd never relegate me to the back room, although I already do all the steaming of the gowns and bridesmaids dresses too. If it weren't for my consistent sales, she'd be forced to rely on Arianna, Ashley, and Brittany, and those three spend more time gossiping about the brides or at the Coffee Bean than selling bridesmaid dresses and renting tuxedos. I don't think any of them have ever opened a packing box here. Why does Brooke put up with them? Before I say something I'll regret, I pick up the box I was working on and head to the stockroom.

"Hey," snaps Ari, "I wasn't done talking to you!"

I ignore her and continue walking. I'm thirty and have been here over three years. Ari has been here six months, and she's not quite twenty-two. Why she feels she can talk to me like that, or why I let her, I can't say. I know I should defend myself, but it's pointless. Brooke talks to me the same way, so the other employees follow her lead.

Besides, I'm not as hideous as they make me out to be. Sure,

I'm a bit overweight, especially when compared to Ari, Brit, Ashley, and even Brooke. I don't really make any effort with my appearance either. That costs money I don't have, so I never get my hair professionally cut or styled, and the only makeup I wear is lip gloss. I haven't bought myself new clothes for several years, and when I do, I hit the thrift stores or the Old Navy clearance racks.

I know I look a little like my mom. My dad used to tell me how beautiful my mom was and that I was going to grow up to be just like her. I should probably take Dad's words with a grain of salt because Dads are supposed to tell you things like that. It's the law. I giggle to myself.

Even though the other women at this shop are the vilest creatures I've ever known, I've got to remember why I'm here. *I need this job.* I need to stay here until I can get the major home repairs done on my grandmother's old Victorian house, and *then* I can quit. My estimate is eight months—one year, tops. This job isn't so bad, right? *Yeah, keep telling yourself that, Sophie. Think of Grandma Sophia's house.*

I know when Gran left the house to me in her will, she wouldn't have wanted me burdened with huge bills like the astronomical taxes. But it's been in my family since my grandfather built it in 1936. I want to hang on to it if I can. Sure, the taxes alone are killing me at almost $7,800 per year, but that's not uncommon for Chicago. One good thing is that my tenant, Willy Gibbons, helps cover that portion of my expenses. He's been renting our garage-turned-carriage house for ten years, and that income helps immensely.

The surprising part of home ownership has been the cost of the repairs. The electrical work nearly broke me, but it was a fire hazard. The roof is next. The old Victorian has a fairly complex roofline, so it's going to cost me twenty grand. The contractor was a friend of my father's, so I trust him. He's even given me his family discount. It has to be done because water is slowly making its way into the attic. Any water damage now will cost me more money further down the road. I'd love to quit this job, but I make good money. Money I'd never make doing a job related to my degree. I'm pretty limited there until I earn a higher degree so I'd be stuck being an entry-level research assistant or even administrative assistant. No. Right now. This is where I need to be. All of these thoughts make me sigh loudly. I've forgotten about Ari altogether, but once out of my fog, I hear her screeching voice.

"Are you sighing at me, you fat bitch?"

Wow, that's nice.

"No, I was sighing thinking about all of the work I need to get done before my next bridal appointment. Don't you have something you need to be doing?" I know I should take offense at the name-calling, but I just can't go there. If I let it bother me, I wouldn't be able to get out of bed each morning.

"It's none of your business what I need to do around here," she squeaks. "I think I'll call Brooke and tell her about your attitude problem today and your little attempt to grope one of the male customers!"

"Go ahead." I don't care. I really don't.

Ari stomps away toward the tux area. It's not long until I hear her on her phone. Yep, she called Brooke. God, I *hate* this place. If it weren't for the brides, it would be unbearable. But I love my brides. They come into the store searching for their dream dress, and I make it my mission to give them what they want and help make their wedding day perfect.

Heck, I don't even mind the Bridezillas. I tell myself those brides are just misunderstood. I snort at that notion because, in reality, they're just as they seem—bitches. But bitches need dresses too, and those brides tend to have the biggest budgets. Since I need the commission, I can put up with a lot for a sale.

The rest of the day, Ari stays on her side of the store, and I stay on mine. I sell two beautiful gowns, earning myself hefty commissions. Yay! I've almost got the roofing money. At closing time, I notice that Ari has snuck out early, which leaves me in charge of doing all of the closing duties. Truthfully, I'd rather do it by myself than spend any more time with her.

I double-check to be sure the front of the store is locked up. Then I clock out, grab my things from my locker, and head out the back, making sure I enter the code into the keypad to secure the store. I shiver thinking about Brooke Bellamy. She would kill me if I ever forgot to turn on the alarm.

On the ride home on the "L"—Chicago's aboveground, or elevated, transit system—I look around me at the packed train. I've somehow secured a seat for myself. It's not a great seat, as the guy next to me is so bulky that his massive, muscled arm is smashing my body into the outside wall of the train. His legs are spread so wide they're pressing into mine.

There's a seat facing me. In it sits a pretty young woman with a mass of auburn hair twisted up on top of her head—she's spent the entire time texting on her phone—and a young man in nerdy glasses next to her doing everything he can to get her attention. It's sort of adorable that he's working so hard to get her to look up from her phone. *Good luck, dude.* I giggle to myself. Who knows? Maybe they're destined to be together. Perhaps it was fate they sat next to each other on this train?

Ah, who am I kidding? Life doesn't work like that. *Fate, schmate.* Love is elusive to the majority of us mere mortals. If it weren't, I'd start to fantasize about that guy who'd come into the shop today.

Sighing, I lay my head back on the bench seat and squeeze

my eyes shut, recalling what he looked like. He was tall, really tall, muscular, and absolutely gorgeous, with blond hair that looked strategically tousled. He had a little bit of a scruff of a beard on his square jawline, which seemed to draw my attention directly to his soft, full lips.

I'd done my best to pretend I wasn't checking him out. *Why?* The reason is simple. A guy like that would probably laugh right in my face if he thought I was checking him out. Because people like Henry Flynn don't go for short, plump, broke, bridal consultants like me. But dang it, I couldn't seem to help myself. He'd smelled so manly, like musk and wood. I wonder if that had been aftershave or if that was just him? His scent had only added to his overall appeal.

As we approach the next stop, the man next to me—who I've dubbed "Hulky"—gets up from the seat in anticipation of our stop. The young couple facing me are now both on their phones, completely engrossed. It appears that the young nerd-man has given up. Too bad. Since they're distracted, I decide to call my best friend, Tracy. I don't think they'll mind if I talk on my phone for a minute if I'm quiet.

I hit Tracy's contact information on my old flip phone and wait. I love my best friend. It's too bad she lives so far away. Sure, Iowa City, Iowa isn't across the country, but it's too far for me right now. I sure do miss her, though. Trace and I met in high school and were roommates in college. She's married now with two young boys, but she's still there for me whenever I need her. I could call anytime, day or night, and she'd stop whatever she's doing to listen. And if needed, she'd jump in her car and drive to Chicago if I asked her.

It rings several times. Where is she? She should be home by now; it's almost eight o'clock. When she picks up, I hear her say, "Well, it's about time, bitch. You haven't called me for two months!"

"The phone rings both ways, Trace," I say, laughing. She always gives me a hard time about keeping in touch. She has the excuse of her family. I only have work and my house. "I know. I'm sorry. I've been trying to work as many hours as possible to get this house in shape."

"I wish I could be there to help you out, hon."

"Me too. I'd just love to see you. The fact that I could put you to work on my house is just a bonus."

"I'd love to help. Home renovation is my new favorite hobby. Not. So, what's up?"

Tracy knows I don't call unless I have a story to share or I need to vent about the women at work. "Nothing. Same old."

"So, how was your day, dear?" Tracy asks sarcastically.

"Well, now that you mention it...."

"Yeah? What?"

"I helped a man order his tuxedo today. He was hot as sin."

"Wait. Was the tux for his own wedding?"

"Nope. His brother's."

"Phew! What happened? Tell me everything." I can tell she's excited.

I tell her how Henry came in and acted all sexy and macho, and about Arianna and her reaction to my helping Henry. I left out the part where Arianna called me names. If Tracy knew what those women said to me on a daily basis, she'd drive over here and beat them senseless. She's kind of a badass that way.

Not getting the information she wants, she asks impatiently, "What does he look like? Sheesh, woman. I need deets!"

"All right. His name was Henry, as I said."

"Henry? What does that mean?"

Tracy knows I have a thing about proper names and their meanings. My background in linguistics, specifically onomastics —the study of the origin and history of proper names—and literature makes me a nerd about that sort of thing. Call it a hobby now, since my college career ended four years ago when my father died from a sudden heart attack. That meant no more money for school, and I instantly became the primary caregiver for my grandmother on the same day.

Honestly, it was no burden because my grandmother, Sophia Kincaid, was sweet, gentle, and funny as hell. I miss them both every day. I'll never, for one second, regret giving up my research and dissertation, "The Origin and Meaning of Literary Names from Fiction," to help Gran.

"It's Germanic for 'ruler of the house.' He seemed interested in the meaning of his name, too."

"Cool." She laughs. "What else?"

"Well, he was tall."

"Everyone is tall to you, shorty." Tracy snorts.

"Funny. He's probably six three or six four."

"Wow! He *is* tall!"

"He has sandy-blond hair that needed a trim. But it was sexy all mussed up. He had a scruff of a beard on his chin, and his eyes, Trace, his eyes were so blue they were almost aquamarine."

"He sounds flipping gorgeous. What else? You said he had muscles? How were his teeth?"

Tracy is obsessed with teeth. She always wanted to be a dentist, but she met her man, Tommy, in college, and the rest was history. She's a dental hygienist now, so....

"Straight and white. You'd approve," I assured her.

"Thank God. There's nothing worse than a guy with crooked Chiclets."

Chiclets is her name for abnormally small teeth. "Nope. He has nice teeth that are surrounded by full lips. I'm telling you, Trace, the man was gorgeous. Henry is one of those guys you'd only think exists in fitness magazines or on the cover of erotic romance novels. Think Hemsworth, only better."

"Oh my God. You're joking! Chris or Liam?"

"Chris. Definitely Chris Hemsworth when he was Thor. Henry's built like Thor."

"You're making that up. There's no way a guy like that exists." She giggles. "When will you see him again?"

"Never. He's *that* hot. He was only there to get measured for his tux."

"He'll be back to pick it up, right?"

"Yeah, but you know I'm not *allowed* over there. I need to forget about Mr. Henry Flynn."

"Ah, babe. If it's meant to be...," Tracy says, attempting to reassure me.

"I know. I know. If it's meant to be, it will be." Tracy is uber-optimistic. I need some of that positivity in my life. I'd be happier. "But I can't think of any reason I'd ever see him again. I'll just use him as fodder for my active fantasy life. I needed some new material." I snort at my own humor.

"Sophia, you are so beautiful. I'm sure your prince will come. You deserve someone who'll watch out for you and give you amazing orgasms."

The word *orgasm* surprises me to the point that I have a coughing fit on the L. It even makes the two in front of me look up at me—but only for a second. The other people around me look at me strangely. No doubt they're annoyed that I'm on the phone while on the train. *Sorry, folks, I needed to talk to my Trace.*

"Well, I should hang up. People are staring at me, and my stop is coming up next. I'll call you soon. Or you could call me."

"I will. I'm sorry I haven't. I miss you so much, Sophie. I wish you'd sell that house and come to school here at U of Iowa and finish that degree of yours."

"I miss you too, Trace. I'll give that some serious thought. Things here aren't great. I'm a little depressed about everything, to tell you the truth. A change would do me good." On that, we vow to keep in touch and hang up. Damn, I miss my best friend so much.

2

———

HANK

I fucking hate weddings. Why the hell my brother thinks he needs to marry that harpy is beyond me. No amount of talking will get him to change his mind. You'd think he would have learned from my mistake. My being legally tied to that spiteful gold digger, Angela, for a year should have been enough for every guy in my family to stay the fuck away from marriage.

Even after ten years, I'm still pissed about her taking me to the cleaners. It's a good thing I'm resourceful and recouped my money, or my bitterness would be far worse. She even tried to get alimony out of me! My attorney laughed her out of divorce court with all the proof we had of her many infidelities.

Groaning, I mourn the loss of my little brother. No, he's not dead, but his soon-to-be-wife will likely kill his spirit. She's a clone of Angela. Fucking idiot.

Walking into the tux store, I'm reminded of my own wedding day. Everything was over the top. Angela spent thousands on a wedding dress, and for what? Her daddy paid for most of the circus we called a wedding, thank Christ.

Okay. That's enough. Instead of making my mood worse, I've got to do my best to focus on the task at hand: getting measured for my tux. As best man, I'm expected to do whatever my bro needs me to do to make his wedding day pleasant. You never know, his marriage could last.

I clear my throat, attempting to get the attention of the kid unpacking a box on the floor. Customer service must not be this store's forte.

"Excuse me? I need a little help here," I ask in my demanding cop voice.

"Oh, um, I'm sorry?"

The person I mistook for a kid turns out to be one of the tiniest women I've ever seen. She can't be more than five feet tall, which puts her more than a foot shorter than I am. As a detective, I catch things like that right away. Like the fact that she's small—while also lookin' like her curves would feel soft against me. She's got nice tits for a petite gal. Her hair is so shiny it could be silk. It's brown, but the color reminds me of dark chocolate. It's pretty short—cut bluntly above her shoulders— and she's got both sides pulled back behind her ears, with a pen resting above her right ear. I prefer a woman with long hair, but shorter hair seems to suit her. I suspect her diminutive body would get lost in long hair.

My eyes move from the pen to her face. Goddamn, she's pretty. I'd guess her age at about twenty-two. She has a fresh-ness to her face. It could be the freckles she's got sprayed across her nose. I tend to think of kids as only having those. She's cute with her turned-up nose and her full, rosy lips. I could picture her doing some amazing things to my dick if she weren't so young. Damn, that's a shame. I continue my perusal and catch a sparkle in her big, brown eyes—the color of melted milk choco-late with specks of gold around the irises. I must be hungry. Everything about this little honey is making me salivate.

She's wearing black from head to toe—a long shirt and those legging things the ladies are wearing these days. Some guys hate those tight, stretchy, pant things, but I love them. They show off a woman's legs and, if I'm lucky, her ass. I love a plump rump, and this angel looks like she'd have ass for days.

I decide to play with her a bit. "You're not sure?"

"Sure? What?" She blinks like a scared doe. She's fucking precious.

"You're not sure if you're sorry?"

The brown-eyed beauty flutters her long, dark lashes as she peers up at me. I seem to have confused her. Maybe she's not very bright. That would be a shame. I like my fuck buddies to have something going on upstairs. Nothing is more tedious than hooking up with a bimbo. I mean, I'll do it, but it annoys the fuck out of me. This girl, though, I don't get the impression that she's dumb. She's just spellbound by me. Yeah, that's it. I can be intimidating.

"I'm sure."

"Sure about what?" Okay, now it's me who's confused.

"I'm sure I'm sorry. I didn't mean to ignore you. I thought Ari was up front greeting customers."

"Well, there's no one here but the two of us," I say in my sexiest voice as I walk closer to my peach. Her name tag reveals her pretty name. *Sophie*.

"Sophie? Is your name Sophie?"

She peers down at her name tag and then up at my face as she touches the tag with her left hand.

No ring.

"Yes, I'm Sophie. How can I help you today?" She's now in sales mode.

"I need to get a tux for a wedding."

"Oh, um, that's not my area. I'm bridal."

"Well, there's no one else here, and I need to get this done. I've got to get back to work."

"Um, well, okay. Follow me."

I can tell she's reluctant to help me. Am I making her nervous? Usually the ladies fall all over me. "Are you sure? Do you know what to do?" Her hesitation makes it seem like she might be new at this.

"No, that's not it. I know what I'm doing. I'm supposed to stay over on my side of the store, but I'd be happy to help you." A fake smile spreads across her sweet face, but she sounds unsure.

This little thing is likely frightened of her own shadow. We walk to the other side of the store, where mannequins wearing suits in black, gray, and navy mark the perimeter of the men's area. There's even a tux with a camouflage design. Who would wear a camouflage tux on their wedding day? If a guy finds a woman who lets him wear camo on his wedding day, he's one lucky bastard. His woman will be putty in his hands. Either that, or she's an idiot like her future husband. Camouflage? God, it's fucking hideous.

Sophie leads me over to a small table surrounded by stools. "Um, is it *your* wedding?"

I wonder if she's asking for herself.

"God, no! My little brother's getting hitched. I'm the *best* man." I puff my chest out proudly for some inexplicable reason. Before this moment, I gave two shits Dave chose me as the best man.

"What's the bride's name and the wedding date?" she asks, getting professional on me.

"Jen, and it's in about two weeks, Saturday the twenty-third."

She waits like she wants me to say more. "Does Jen have a last name?"

"Probably." I'm just not sure what it is.

"Well, let's try this. What is your brother's name? Hopefully you know *his* last name," she smirks.

Cute. Now I see a spark to Sophie. "David Flynn." See, *I knew.*

Sophie walks into a back room and comes back with a file folder. "Okay. They've got everything chosen, so I'll just need to measure you to make sure we get the sizes you need."

"Which tux did they pick? Please tell me it's that one." I point to the display of the camouflage tux.

She stares at me as if I've lost my mind.

I chuckle, knowing I've shocked her.

"No, they've chosen from the *Downton Abbey* collection."

I groan loudly. Fucking pussy. My brother let Jen pick some snooty British shit?

"Well, wonderful," I say sarcastically. "Which one of these is the suit?" I'm cringing already, and I haven't even seen it yet.

Sophie points to a tux prominently displayed near the door. It must be a popular choice to garner that spot. I walk over to see the suit close up, and I've gotta say, it ain't bad. Thank fuck. It's navy and black. The jacket has a subtle pattern of black and dark blue plaid. The pants are black, and the vest is blue. It's cut higher in the chest, with four buttons instead of the usual three. It's not bad at all. I suspect I'll look great in that style. Yeah, I'm a bit full of myself—nothing wrong with being confident, is there?

"Okay, what do we need to do to get this tux thing ordered?" I watch her pull out a sheet of paper from the folder and pick up a ballpoint pen.

Touching the end of the pen to her full bottom lip, she says, "I need your name so I can write down your measurements on this order form." She holds up a white sheet of paper.

"Henry."

Sophie's head pops up from her worksheet. "Henry?" She blinks. "Hmm. Yeah, that suits you."

"You think? Everyone calls me Hank."

"Why? Henry is a very strong name. It's Germanic for 'ruler of the house.'"

I puff my chest out again when she says my name is strong. What am I now, a peacock? "Really? That's cool. How do you know?"

Sophie shrugs and returns to her worksheet. "Phone number?"

"312-530-1037. I am the oldest in my family, and I'm usually pretty bossy." I wink. Hopefully she gets my innuendo.

Setting the pen and worksheet onto the table, she turns to face me. "If you'll stand up and take off your jacket, we can get started."

Okay. We're apparently changing the subject from my name to the task at hand. She's all business as she reaches into a wooden box in the center of the table and pulls out a long tailor's tape. She grips the tape in her right hand, and I can't help noticing her tiny hand shaking as she wraps the tape around her neck. Either I'm making her nervous, or....

"Have you done this before?" I ask.

Her head jerks up, and she looks into my eyes. "Of course."

"Well, you seem a little nervous. Do I make you nervous?" I whisper. A part of me hopes I'm eliciting this reaction from her. No, I'm not a creep to women. I don't want to scare her, but I like the notion that she feels the same sexual tension I'm feeling right now.

"No. It's just that, well, you're very tall. But I've got this."

She walks away from me. I watch her round bottom as it swishes from side to side. When she reaches an open doorway, she walks through it, bending at the waist to pick something up. Yep, she's got a stellar ass. When she stands, I see she's got both arms wrapped around a step stool. I'm surprised it doesn't have her name stamped on it—Sophie's step stool. I chuckle at my joke.

She stops in her tracks, clutching the stool. "Are you laughing at me?" Her face is suddenly pink, her shoulders tense, and her eyes angry slits.

"No, sweetheart." What should I say? *Think, idiot.* "I was thinking about my idiot brother and his *Downton Abbey* tuxes." I hope she believes me.

I watch her shoulders relax. "Oh, okay." She sets the stool down right in front of my feet, sighs, and steps up. Now the top of her head is lined up right with my chin. "Lift your arms straight out, please."

I lift my arms out like I'm a giant letter T. Taking a deep breath, little Sophie reaches around my chest, holding the tape with one hand as she attempts to grab the other side of the tape behind my back.

I may have mentioned this earlier, but I'll repeat it. I'm a big guy. No, I'm not fucking fat, asshole. I work out, a lot. I'm a cop, so I need to stay in shape. Not only that, but I'm naturally broad. I'm not sure her tiny arms will make it around me. I can sense frustration. She's trying not to touch me, but it's not working.

"Um, can you come a little closer to me?" she asks nervously.

"Sure thing, sweetheart." I know, probably a tad too familiar, but we're so close we're practically fucking right now. I step closer—so close that our chests are touching. I can feel her perky breasts against my abs. Nice. I can smell her hair too— jasmine. Beautiful. Her hair looks so silky that I want to run my fingers through it, maybe grab some of her hair in the back and pull her in for a sweet kiss. Jesus, I need to get a grip. She's twenty-two, for fuck's sake.

Her face is turned to the side and pressed up against my chest now. Her breathing a little labored, and I hope it's me that's making her breathless. Her quiet grunting sounds are adorable. Holy hell. She's giving me a woody.

"Shit," she whispers. "I've almost got it."

It's then I hear a woman's voice that makes my ears bleed. "Sophie! What on earth do you think you're doing?"

Sophie's head jerks up and pulls away from my chest abruptly as she turns toward the screeching voice from hell. Her tiny hands are resting on my chest now. They look perfect there. I'd love to move my arms down and around my pocket-sized Sophie to protect her from the evil that just walked into the room, but I resist.

I look up from Sophie's hands to see the origin of the squawking voice. No surprise. Her voice matches her appearance—tall, blonde, beautiful, and bitchy. I know this woman. Well, not her specifically, but I know women like her. She's narcissistic and vapid.

"Um, I'm measuring this customer for a tuxedo, Ari."

Duh. What did it look like she was doing?

"Well, *Sophie*," she says in a condescending voice. Her arms are crossed over her fake chest, one expensive-stiletto-clad foot tapping on the floor. "You know you're not supposed to be over here. You need to stay over in bridal."

The woman says Sophie's name like Sophie's an idiot child and then smiles at me with a false grin that makes my skin crawl. She points a red talon toward the wedding dress area as she looks back at Sophie. "How many times do we need to tell you? Men don't want you to touch—I mean *measure*—them."

What the fuck? Is there something wrong with Sophie? I look at her and then at the bitch chastising her. She's too fucking skinny, and she's fake everywhere. Typical. She got one look and wanted me for herself—I know the type. Before I know it, Sophie is down from her stool, has placed it near the back door, and is rushing back to her bridal area. What the hell just happened?

"I'm so sorry about her. Sophie has no business dealing with the men—er, tuxedos," she whispers like we're friends. "We've had complaints."

I highly doubt that but remain silent.

"Now, where were we?" She picks up Sophie's order form from the counter. "Your name?"

"Henry," I say with pride. Sophie made me feel like it's a great name. No reason not to use it.

I hear Ari the Blonde snort out a laugh. "Henry? Really? You do *not* look like a Henry. That's such an old man's name."

As it happens, it was my grandfather's name. I scoff at her comment. "It means 'ruler of the house,'" I say defensively.

"You're too gorgeous to have that name. You should be Dirk or Mitch but *not* Henry." She giggles.

"I'll be sure to tell my mother she fucked up." I sigh. "Can we move this along? I need to get back to work."

"Let me get you measured." She grabs the measuring tape Sophie left on the table and wraps her arms around me. Ugh. "You know," she coos, "I think I measured the other groomsmen from this wedding. Any relation to you?"

"Not sure." Yeah, I know who they are. They're my brothers. Like she didn't know that. We all look exactly like my dad, so the resemblance is frighteningly similar. I'm the oldest, so I'm the best looking. I'd laugh at my joke, but then she'd want to know what was so funny.

"You don't know the other groomsmen? That's weird."

"My brothers," I mumble. I have a big family—three brothers and two sisters make up the bunch. I love them all, even though they can be pains in the ass. But a family is like that sometimes.

My focus returns to the task at hand when Blondie wraps

herself around me, lingering too long. It's obviously intentional. Her hair doesn't smell like jasmine. It reeks of cigarettes. When she goes down onto her knees to measure my inseam, I get the urge to flee. Instead, my thoughts return to Sophie. I can picture her on her knees in front of me. But with her height, I'd probably have to sit in a chair for her. Damn. Thinking about Sophie's lips on me is making me hard again. I hope bitch face here can't tell.

I lower my eyes at her as she looks up at me. "About done down there? I need to get back to the precinct."

"Precinct? Ooh, you're a cop? That's so *hot*."

"Sure. The murder investigation I'm working on is pretty sexy. Ever seen a guy garroted? Blood everywhere." That should shut her up.

"Eww, that's disgusting."

"Yeah, it was. Now, let's get a move on."

She gets a move on, and I'm finally measured and out the door. Forty-five minutes of my life I'll never get back. Well, except for the fifteen I spent with Sophie. It's a damn shame. I would have preferred to spend all those minutes with the pretty Sophie.

WHAT A LONG-ASS DAY. After my clusterfuck of a tuxedo fitting, the day went further downhill. Chicago has become a hotbed of homicides this summer, and I'm getting sick and tired of it. Why can't people just get along? I laugh at that thought. I'd be out of a job if that were the case, but it would be worth it.

It's ten o'clock, and I'm finally on my way home. Twelve hours of typing out reports and hunting down leads has made me dead tired. I laugh again. God, I'm so funny tonight. I'm dead tired, and just as I think I'm making a clean getaway, my phone rings.

"Flynn," I say with practiced succinctness.

"Where you at?" says my partner, Kent Jones.

"Almost home. What the fuck do you want?" I know I sound irritated, but the guy can be a little intense and annoying. He's decent at his job, though.

"Get your ass over to Edgewater."

"Why? I'm almost home." Now I'm whining.

"Body discovered in a garage apartment. Got a call from the uniform first on the scene. He thinks it's a professional hit. I'll text you the address."

"Fuck!" I shout. "On my way." I hate professional hits. We can never nail those guys. They're in the wind before we even get to the scene, and they're impossible to trace because they leave no evidence. Whatever. It's my job. I gotta try my best.

I whip my car around and head northeast. Edgewater is a funky, old neighborhood. In its prime at the turn of the century, it was where the wealthy lived. Named Edgewater because it's situated close to Lake Michigan, it's now kind of dilapidated. I searched there when I was house hunting, but many of the old Victorians needed too much work. While I've got the cash for that, the time it would have taken to renovate one of the monstrosities was not something I could afford.

Fifteen minutes of driving like a bat out of hell, and I'm at the scene: 1511 West Highland Avenue. I find a spot a block from the house and park on the street. Jumping out of my sleek, black BMW i8, I hit the lock, making it chirp then see a uniformed officer standing in front of the home.

"Around back, garage," he says, using his thumb to point me in the right direction.

I turn and walk through the narrow area between two homes, making my way toward the back. Kent is standing near the alley talking to the medical examiner, or ME as we call them. I nod to the examiner and ask Kent, "What've we got here?"

"Male. Name William Gibbons. Age forty-two. Gunshot wounds—head and heart."

"Yep. Sounds professional."

"Yeah. It looks like the place was turned over too. Hard to tell, though; the guy was a slob. The owner is in the big house," he says, pointing to the old Victorian home. "One Katherine Kincaid discovered the body. She's waiting to answer questions. I thought I'd give you the honors since you took your sweet-ass time getting here."

"Jesus, you called fifteen minutes ago."

"Yeah, I was already here. Don't you ever listen to dispatch?"

No. I don't. I figure if I'm needed, someone will call me. "Whatever, asshole." I turn toward the garage.

I want to walk through the crime scene before I question the old lady. I need my ducks in a row. When I stand in the open doorway, I see crime scene techs everywhere, and I sure as shit hope they aren't fucking anything up. The CSI department here does a good job, but every once in a while, they blow our case for us. If this is a professional hit, we need all of the evidence we can get.

I step over the threshold and stop just inside the door. There's a box of rubber gloves and shoe covers sitting on the floor. I reach down and grab two of each. I slide the light-blue paper shoe covers over my size thirteens first and then snap the gloves on my hands.

The garage has been converted into an efficiency apartment. I'd bet my Beemer that this little renovation was never granted a permit by the city. If that's the case, the owner is going to be on the hook for some nasty penalties and taxes. Poor bastard. The place wasn't badly done, though. Whoever did the work spent some money making sure it was livable. It's nice and cool in the room, thanks to the window air conditioning unit, thank God. July has been hot as hell. To my right is a small kitchen with full-sized appliances. Not much counter space, but there's a small island with one stool to help with that. The apartment is decorated in man-cave chic. You know the kind, right? It's when a guy gets all of his crappy furniture from family members, thrift stores, and garage sales. Nothing matches, and it's all falling apart.

The walls are white, or they used to be. Beyond the kitchen is a small area with a nice flat-screen television and a love seat. There are several video game controllers on top of the small coffee table. The vic was a gamer. A relatively substantial desk sits against the far wall. I can see a dust outline on the top from —a computer. Another doorway lies between the desk area and the bed—the bathroom, no doubt. The bed is up against the wall on the left side of the open space. It's there that our victim lies.

I approach the bed slowly, making sure I'm not treading on anything of importance. "Is this all clear here?" I ask one of the techs.

The crime scene tech dusting for prints on the other side of the room replies absently, "Yep." Without skipping a beat, she returns to her work.

I approach the deceased and look down into his gray face.

The ME walks up and stops just out of my line of sight. "Been dead about forty-eight hours, I'd guess. Obviously died from gunshot wounds, probably in his sleep. There's minimal blood splatter. I'm guessing the killer held the pillow over his face. I'll know more once we do the autopsy."

"Okay. Call me when you have the results." Duh. Jesus. Why do these medical examiners have to do that? There's a pillow sitting next to the guy's face with two bullet holes in it.

Any idiot could surmise that the pillow was involved in some way. Best to stay on his good side, though. He can delay the autopsy results if I piss him off.

As far as assuming Gibbons was murdered in his sleep, I'm not so sure, but there's no defensive wounds, at least at first glance, so it's possible. I take a closer look at our vic. He's lying on his back on top of his bed covers. It's been pretty hot the last few days, so I can see why he'd be on top of the covers, but they hadn't been turned down yet. That is curious. He's not wearing a shirt, only his tighty-whities. Damn, those things do look ridiculous. Boxer briefs are the way to go, gentlemen.

I look down his short legs to his toes. Pink? Are his toenails painted pink? I take a quick photo of his feet with my phone. A fetishist? One thing about murder, especially a hit like this, is there are only two real motives: sex and greed. My eyes move back up his body to check out his fingers. Not painted. I examine his face—eyes closed, mouth slightly open. Because of the air conditioning unit, the smell is minimal. I'm a pussy when it comes to the odors associated with death. Ten years at this job, and that's something I've never gotten used to.

I make a quick sweep around the room again, peeking into the bathroom for anything that seems odd or out of place. Experience has taught me that the little things matter. Hopefully, the old lady in the big house can tell me more. I spend extra time looking at the large desk. Dust outlines tell me that there were two computers on this table.

"Did the techs take the computers or were they already gone?" I ask the woman closest to me.

"No computers found at the scene. Either the perp took them, or they were gone prior."

Another comment deserving my silent *duh*. Hopefully, these crime scene techs are like this for everyone and not just because they think I'm a fucking idiot.

I slide open the three drawers on the left side of the desk. There's nothing out of the ordinary in the first one—stapler, pens, pencils, ruler, scissors, and staples. The second drawer is filled with printer paper, and the third, hanging file folders. I run my fingers over the tabs but don't see anything out of the ordinary, just folders labeled Utilities, Credit Card, Electronics, Pay Stubs, Personal Correspondence, and Miscellaneous.

"Hey," I say to the tech closest to me. "I'll be back after I talk to the old broad in the big house, so don't bag these up yet. Got it?"

"Aye, aye, Cap'n," says the female tech with a limp salute.

"Smart-ass," I grumble.

When I reach the alleyway, Kent is gone. Bastard. I guess I'll question the lady all by my lonesome. It's okay; I prefer that. Kent tends to interrupt the witness and me during questioning because he thinks he's the Jedi Master of interrogations. Master of nothing, more like. Plus, he ruins my detective mojo.

I walk the narrow sidewalk to the back door of the old Victorian. The place has character, but I can tell from the peeling paint on the wood siding and the broken concrete steps that the house is falling apart. Shame. I knock three times on the back door and wait. And wait. I knock again.

A woman says, "Just a second." I hear her groan and curse as she wrenches open the door. "Damn thing sticks," she mutters.

Without looking up, I start my spiel. "Hello, I'm Detective Flynn with Chicago PD. I'd like to ask you a few questions." I lift my head and peer right into the eyes of my little Sophie from the tux shop. "Katherine Kincaid?"

"Yes," she murmurs.

"May I come in and ask you a few questions?"

"Yes," she repeats softly.

She holds the rickety old back door open for me and steps to the side. "Would you like to sit here in the kitchen or the living room?"

"Here is fine."

"Can I get you a cup of coffee? I just brewed a pot."

"Sure. Coffee would be great. Black."

Sophie, or I guess it's Katherine, makes her way over to the small counter area that holds her four-cup coffee maker. She's wearing sleepwear that includes some tight yoga pants with something printed on them. Miniature slices of pizza? Those are paired with a tight, pink, V-neck tee. There's some sort of logo or character on the front, but I didn't get a good look at it. I'll check it out when she turns around. I remember those perky little breasts pressed up against my chest earlier today, though. That's hard for a man to forget. As she turns around, I can't help but notice how they look even better in her tight tee.

I clear my throat. "Katherine? I thought your name was Sophie?"

She looks up suddenly.

Did she think I could forget her? It's only been twelve hours. Seriously, everyone must think I'm dense. "I remember you from the tux shop," I add.

"Of course. Um, well, my full name is Katherine Sophia Kincaid. I'm named after my mother, Katherine, who died in childbirth. My dad started calling me Sophie, after my grandmother, because hearing my mom's name made him sad."

"I'm sorry. I can see why that would be hard for your dad. Is your father here?" I hope there's another witness. The more people we can get to add to the story, the easier my job is.

"No, he died about four years ago."

"I'm sorry." Jesus. This girl's life sounds damned tragic.

"Does anyone else live here?"

"Nope. Just me. My grandmother died a little over three

years ago. She left this place to me, so besides Willy, I'm here by myself."

"Willy?" Who the fuck is Willy?

"William? You know, the guy...," she says, pointing out the kitchen window toward the backyard.

"Oh, right, William Gibbons."

"Uh-huh. But we called him Willy."

"Okay, Sophie. Can I call you Sophie, or do you prefer Katherine?"

"Sophie."

"Sophie, how long has Willy lived in your garage?"

"Carriage house." She corrects me as she sets the steaming cup of coffee in front of me.

"Sure. Sorry. Carriage house." I lift the cup and sip. "Good coffee. Thanks, Sophie. So, how long has he been your tenant?"

"Well, my father did the work to the garage to help Gran out with some of her bills. He did it about, let's see...." She taps her chin with her tiny finger. "I was a sophomore in college, so I'm going to say it was about ten years ago."

"Okay." What? "How old are you?"

"Twenty-nine. I'll be thirty in a couple of months."

"Shit. I thought you were early twenties, tops."

Chuckling, she explains, "Being fat helps me appear younger."

"You're not fat."

Sophie rolls her eyes. "Yeah, well, anyway, Willy's been the only tenant."

What's with the fucking eye roll? I'm going to move on, but I've got to say, I don't like Sophie's self-deprecating attitude one damn bit.

3

—————

SOPHIE

Why do people think they need to correct you when you openly admit your own flaws? I'm fat. I know it, and Henry knows it. Actually, I'm probably average weight for a woman my age. Heck, I may weigh the same as Arianna does. But she's at least five nine; I'm barely five feet tall. My height-to-weight ratio makes me rounded and plump. It's just the way I'm built.

"Okay, that's good, Sophie. So, now, can you please start at the beginning? Tell me everything you can think of that could help me here. What time did you get home from work?"

"I already told the other officer all about it." *I don't want to relive this.*

"I know. But tell me too. Okay?"

I sigh. "Okay. Well, let's see. I got home from work at about eight forty-five."

"That's a long day, Soph."

Soph? "It's a normal day in retail. Besides, *you're* still at work. Your day has been longer."

He chuckles quietly. "It has been a long day. But murder won't solve itself."

I gasp at that comment. It was obvious Willy was murdered, but hearing it out loud like that is a shock.

"I'm sorry. That was rude. Willy was your, what? A friend?"

"Um, not really. I saw him occasionally. He did his laundry in my basement, but we didn't hang out or anything. He was nice but a little odd."

"How so?"

"Well, he wasn't very social. I don't think I ever saw anyone visit him. He was into computers and video games, you know?"

"What did he do for a living? Do you know?"

"Yeah, he worked for Luciph Corp. You know, the huge company just west of the city?"

"I know it. What did he do there?"

"I'm not sure. I'd guess it had something to do with computers, though."

"Anything else about him you found out of the ordinary?"

Hmm, I need to think for a second. I walk over to the counter to grab my own cup of coffee. I take a sip as I walk back over to the table. "Well, he usually stayed up super late. His lights were always on at night. He may have slept with his lights on. I'm not sure."

"How do you know they were on late?"

"I have a hard time sleeping, so I sometimes read late at night. His lights were always on. That's why I went to check on him."

"Why? What do you mean?"

"His lights were off two nights in a row. I thought it was odd. At first, I assumed he was gone, but his bicycle was still leaning against the back of the garage."

"His bicycle?"

"Yeah, he rode it everywhere. He rode it to the train every morning and left it there while he was at work, and then he rode it home—even in the winter. So, the lights were off, and his bike was there. Red flags for me."

"So, what did you do next?"

"I was worried about him, so I walked out and knocked on his door."

"And what time was this?"

"Probably nine fifteen or so."

"What did you do next?"

"The door was ajar, and when I knocked, it opened slightly. I leaned into the doorway and yelled his name, but there was no answer."

"Then what?"

"I remembered the light switch was at my right, beside the door, so I flipped the light on." Henry remains quiet, so I keep going. "I pushed the door open farther so I could see into his place without actually going in. I didn't want to do anything that would make him angry with me. You know, tenant and landlord rules."

Henry nods. "Please continue."

"Once the door was open and the light was on, I saw him on the bed. I could see blood underneath his head. I ran up to him to see if he was okay, but as soon as I got to him, I could tell he was, um, dead." Recalling all of this is getting to me, and tears burn in the back of my eyes. Willy was a bit strange, but he was nice enough. Plus, he always paid his rent on time. What am I going to do now? I need that rent money. Oh, shit, I'm going to cry. God, I'm such a bitch for only thinking of myself after the poor guy was murdered.

"Shh, Soph, it's okay," Henry says as he reaches out to me from across the table.

Big, warm hands wrap around my upper arms and pull me out of my wooden kitchen chair. Before I know it, I'm standing between his legs, and he's pressed his hand to my back until I'm against his hard, warm chest. He's hugging me. Damn, Detective Flynn smells so good as I take a deep breath. Is this appropriate?

"Um, I'm okay." I press my hands against his hard chest, trying to push away from him.

"No, you're not," he says, holding me in place as his hands run up and down my back in a reassuring way. "You've just seen a dead body, babe. That's traumatic. You've been holding it together surprisingly well. You were bound to let go. It's good I was here with you when it happened." He gently pats my lower back one, two, three times. "Speaking of which, is there somewhere you can stay for a few days? A friend's house? A boyfriend's?"

"No."

"No boyfriend? An aunt? Cousin? Coworker?"

I snort at the last one. "No. I've got no living relatives. My only friend lives in Iowa. I can't go away; I have to go to work." I leave out the coworker option. I don't think he needs to hear about that train wreck.

"It's not safe for you to be here, Sophie," Henry whispers. "We don't know what we're dealing with here. The person may come back. We don't know."

"I'm fine. I'll be sure to lock up tight."

"Sophie...."

"I'll be fine, Detective. I have nowhere else to go."

"How 'bout a hotel?"

"No. It's not in my budget. I'm fine here." Jeez, can't this guy take a hint? He's confusing the hell out of me too. *Babe?* He called me *babe?* Does he do that to all of his witnesses?

"You can't stay here, Sophie."

"I can, and I will. The crime scene is out there," I say, pointing out the window again. "Besides, I can't leave my house."

Henry brings his hands to my upper arms and leans back, I guess so he can look me in the eyes. He takes a deep breath. "Fine. I'll see if I can get a uniform over here to keep an eye on things, but tomorrow, you need to have an alternative place to stay for a couple of days at least."

"I'll try," I say, knowing full well that I won't be staying anywhere but here.

Henry rolls his eyes and then stands up. Damn, the man is tall. I look up and smile. "Thanks, Detective."

"You're welcome, Sophie. And call me Henry, please. If you think of anything else, will you call me?" he asks, handing me his business card. "My cell is right there. Don't hesitate to call, Soph, day or night. Whatever you need. If you think of *anything*, or if you just need to talk, call me. Got it?"

"Got it," I say, saluting him.

"Smart-ass," he mutters.

I giggle. He's kind of funny. A gorgeous man with a sense of humor? Pinch me.

4

HENRY

Damn, she's got a sweet giggle. I can imagine hearing her laugh in my bed as I'm teasing her. Fuck, what is wrong with me? She's not my type. At all. I'm usually interested in the leggy, blonde variety of women. Not the petite-brunette-with-freckles-and-a-turned-up-nose kind of girl. But that's just it, she's not a girl; she's a woman—a twenty-nine-year-old woman.

Sophie's a twenty-nine-year-old woman who may or may not be in danger. I hate the thought of her being in this house alone. She's got no friends? What the hell is up with that? No boyfriend, but that's good. Wait. What? Why do I care if she's got a man in her life or not?

Damn, I've gotta get laid. It's been too long—three weeks feels like three years. Maybe I should stop at Murphy's pub to see if there's anyone worthy of a night in my bed—just a night. I don't do relationships or anything more than a night—two if she's extra special.

A woman like Sophie is a relationship kind of girl. I couldn't treat her like my usual hookups, so that leads me to the conclusion that thinking of Sophie as anything other than a witness to a crime and my tuxedo salesperson is a bad idea—a terrible idea. Then why can't I get the feeling of her small body against mine out of my fucking head? *God, knock it off, Hank. Women are bad news.*

Shaking off my errant thoughts, I take a step back and look down at her with my most serious cop face. "I'm heading back out to the crime scene. I've got to check things out. Please stay in the house. You're safer in here."

"I will." She nods.

"Oh, one more thing. Did William have any family nearby?"

"I only know of one sister, but she lives in Seattle."

"Can you get her address for me?"

"If I have it, it'll be in my office," she says as she leaves the kitchen.

Mesmerized by her round ass, I follow her. I should stay put since I wasn't invited to tag along, but I decide against reason.

"How old is your house?"

Sophie jumps, startled by my comment.

"Oh, sorry. I thought I'd follow you. Faster."

"Of course. Right. Um, the house was built in 1939." Sophie leads me through the long, narrow living room toward the front entrance. We cross a small hallway into an office about the size of one of my walk-in closets. "I should have his original rental application in here. My dad kept great records."

While she digs, I look around her office. Books. There are books everywhere. From the floor to the ceiling, she's got books. "You must like to read."

"Love it. It's my favorite hobby. Okay, let's see what we've got here."

She opens the top drawer of a tall filing cabinet. She can barely see over the top, so I walk up behind her, close enough to feel her heat and smell her scent. Her ass is barely touching the front of my legs, but it's enough to make my dick twitch. This girl is making me crazy.

"Um, I can get it," Sophie whispers.

I ignore her. "That's late for a Victorian, isn't it? What's the file name?"

Sophie's breathing speeds up. Is she feeling the same heat?

"It was late, yes, but I understand my great-grandfather wanted it to fit in with the other houses in the area, so he chose this style. And the file should either have his name on it or something about a rental agreement."

I reach above her head to run the fingers of my right hand along the handwritten tabs of the files. I've let my left hand rest on her hip—for balance. Yeah, for balance. Sophie is standing stock-still, since I've got her caged in against the front of the file drawer.

"That makes sense. About the house that is. Aha! I've got it." I pull a file out that titled *William Gibbons Rental Agreement*. "You're right. Your dad was very thorough."

Without moving, because I'm a fucking pervert, I set the file down on top of the open drawer and flip it open. Moving in closer, I hear a tiny squeak out of her and look down. She's facing the front of the file drawer—eyes closed.

Yeah, I know. I'm acting fucking unprofessional. But I like being close to her, touching her. I want her to feel safe. Yeah, that's it. Not to mention, I met her *before* this murder occurred, which makes it feel like we're already friends. So what if I feel a bit protective of her? Sue me.

"You're right. He has a sister. But she lives in San Diego, not Seattle. This thing is old. What do you think the odds are that she still lives there?" It's more of a rhetorical question.

She has squeezed out of her spot between the drawer and me and stands a couple feet away. "The odds aren't in your favor. She lives in Seattle."

"It says San Diego."

"Well, she lives in Seattle *now*. He gets mail from her—you know, cards for his birthday and holidays. I've received them by accident before, noticed the sender and return address."

"Ah, okay. When I get back to his place, I'll look for some of that. Thanks, babe. Can I keep this file?"

"Sure. Anything else, Detective Flynn?" she snaps.

Wow, is she pissed? Her face is bright red. "Please call me Henry." I mean, I had her up against a filing cabinet. We should be on a first-name basis. "Are you angry with me?" I smirk.

"No. Oh, um, don't you need to go investigate or something?"

She's trying to get rid of me? That's a first. "Yes. Yes, I do. I'll be in touch, sweetheart."

I turn and head back to the garage—er, I mean carriage house. By the time I enter the vic's apartment, Kent is back. That's good news. I want to get to bed sometime tonight. I slip on a new pair of shoe protectors, grab a pair of gloves, and meet him near the desk.

"The ME took the body," Kent explains.

"Thank God. I saw the empty bed and thought, 'Shit! Someone stole the body!'" Jesus, these people are dead certain I'm a fucking idiot. "Come on. Let's get started, asshole."

5

———

SOPHIE

I wake up Tuesday morning with a headache that rivals the time Tracy and I shared a bottle of Mad Dog 20/20. But there was no alcohol involved this time. I tossed and turned all night long, thinking about Willy's murder and Detective Sexy. Yeah, I had a very nice dream about Henry. He was wearing only a shoulder holster and a smile. Can you picture it? Trust me, it was a great dream.

Dang, that guy is trouble. I have no business dreaming about him. He's flirty and annoying. He probably teases and touches everything with a vagina. Not to mention, a guy like that would never go for someone like me—you know, fat, ugly, and broke. He's just, well, I don't know what his game is, but I've got to stay away from Henry Flynn before my heart breaks into a million pieces.

It's happened before. I had a thing for my lit professor at the University of Chicago. He was a flirt too. It was only a crush; the guy didn't even know I existed. It still hurt when I discovered he was sleeping with one of my classmates. No, *hurt* isn't the right word. I was devastated. Shit, that's been ten years ago, and I still remember how it felt when I saw them outside of his office, kissing each other like their lives depended on it. God, I'm pathetic. *Forget about Professor Dickens.* See? Even his name was literary and perfect.

I drag myself out of bed and walk to the one and only bathroom in the house. It needs work like everything else. But this bathroom is all original. It's got a claw-foot tub, no shower. I have one of those handheld shower things attached to the nozzle so I can still stand up in there, and I've rigged up a shower curtain around the tub, so I don't flood the place. There's a pedestal sink and a toilet on the opposite wall. The flusher is even one of those pull chains. It's unreliable, but it's so cool and authentic. I hate to change it, but the plumbing and fixtures are in disrepair and will need replaced at some point.

The floor of the bathroom is covered with black-and-white mosaic tiles, while the walls are white subway tile. This place was built to last. I fear I'll have to tear everything out, tile and all, to get to the plumbing, but I can't think about that right now. I'll be lucky if I can afford to keep the house. Willy's rent helped me out. Without it, I'll have to choose between eating and paying my taxes and utilities.

I START the water in the tub. It takes a while to get it hot enough to bathe. Even then it's just warm. A new boiler system is also on the list. I sigh, thinking I may never get to leave Bridal Belles. I shower, doing the best I can with my hair and makeup, and dress in all black—the required uniform at the shop. Brooke goes ballistic if you wear anything other than all black. She lets us wear shoes and accessories with some color, but not much. I've been called into her office several times because I've worn gray instead of black. Ari, Ashley, and Brittany, the three other consultants, seem to get by with adding color to their outfits, but that's the way things go there. No need to get my panties in a twist. My goal at work is not to be summoned into Brooke's office for something stupid.

I finish getting ready in time to brew coffee, grab my favorite Starbucks travel cup, and exit my back door. It's then that I remember the crime scene in my backyard. There are still several police cars in the alley. People in lab coats and uniformed officers are walking around too. I guess I should have gone out the front door.

Turning to go back inside, I hear, "Ma'am?"

I turn toward the voice and see a guy in a suit walking toward me. "Yes?" *I hope this doesn't take long. I will be late for work.*

"Mind if I ask you a few questions?"

"I only have a minute. I've got to get to work."

"Just a few questions." He reaches his hand out to shake. "Name's Kent Jones."

"Sophie," I reply as I shake his rough, dry hand.

"I know you talked to my partner last night, but we had a couple more questions for you."

"Okaaay." *I'm not sure I can help them any more than I already have, but I'll try.*

"So, you've known the vic—er, the victim, for ten years?"

"I guess. He's lived here for ten years, but I haven't always lived here."

"How long have you lived at this address, ma'am?"

God, I hate *ma'am*. It makes me feel old. "About four years. I moved in to help my grandmother after my father died."

"So, would you say you and the victim were close?"

"No. I told Henry"—I look up and see a peculiar expression on Kent Jones's face. I correct myself—"I mean, Detective Flynn, all about this last night. Can this wait? I'll be late for work."

"Just a few more questions, ma'am."

This guy is annoying the hell out of me. "Let me text my boss. If I'm not there on time, she'll kill me." Note to self, bad time to say *kill*.

Me: Brooke. Running late. Emergency at home.

I wait for a response but get none. I see the notification pop up on my screen that she's read my message. Still no response. Yep, she'll be pissed.

Kent clears his throat.

I sigh and look back up at him.

"Ready now?" he asks, annoyed.

"No, I wasn't close to Willy. He was a nice guy, and we were pleasant to one another. He'd do nice things for my grandmother and then for me after she died."

"What *kind* of nice things?"

Why does he make it sound like something sordid? "Like shoveling the sidewalks after it snowed or making sure the lawn back here was mowed in the summer. He'd drag the garbage cans out to the street on garbage day, that kind of thing. He was a decent guy."

"Sounds like he was a keeper."

This guy is a tool. I much prefer getting questioned by Henry. Henry is much easier on the eyes too. This guy looks like a detective. In his fifties, he resembles Columbo from that old television show, but without the trench coat and cigar. It's not legal to smoke on the job anymore, and it's too hot for a trench coat, but I wouldn't be surprised if he had that coat in his police car.

"Is there anything else?" Damn. I'll be so late.

"One more thing."

I sigh. "Yeah?" I know I sound impatient.

"Where were you Saturday night between ten o'clock and one in the morning?"

Huh? "Am I a suspect?" I squeak.

"We can't rule anything out, ma'am."

What was I doing Saturday night? The same thing I did every night. "Nothing. I was home. Alone." *Shit, that sounds bad, doesn't it?*

"Alone? Did you talk to anyone that evening?"

"No. I was tired from work, so I got into bed early. I read until I fell asleep."

"What time was that?"

Shit! "I'm not sure. I don't remember hearing anything, you know, like a gunshot, so I may have fallen asleep before ten." I got up in the night to get a drink of water, but I will not admit that to this guy.

"Mm-hmm," Kent mumbles as he jots down notes in his tiny, stereotypical detective spiral notebook. Just like Columbo.

I'm getting worried here. I have no real alibi, no friends, no family, and no way to prove I was in my bed at the time of the murder. "Can I go? I'm late for work."

"Sure. Sure. Just don't leave town."

I practically guffaw at that. Where would I go? How would I pay for it if I did go? "I won't," I deadpan. Turning, I race through the house to the front door. I unlock it, wrench it open, and step out onto my broken and cracked front steps. I turn, lock the door, and rush to the L. Brooke is going to kick my ass.

6

HENRY

I wake up in a fog. My head hurts like the time I drank half a bottle of Macallan single malt. *That* was a shitty day. Wait, did I drink last night? No. I didn't get home from that crime scene in Edgewater until after six this morning, and it's ten o'clock now. That means I got a whopping four hours of sleep. Hell, who needs sleep?

I trudge out of bed and into my en suite bathroom. My place is classy, if I do say so myself. I've got a large brownstone all to myself, with three bedrooms and three and a half baths. It's in a great neighborhood called the West Loop, in the River North part of the Windy City. The area is a bit hipster for my taste, but the benefits outweigh that annoying aspect.

The place has an industrial feel. My little sister, Sandy, helped me decorate because she was worried the entire place would feel cold and sterile. Thanks to her, my home feels warm and inviting. If I had any free time, I'd definitely spend more time at home. If only....

I turn on the shower nozzles, adjusting the temperature to 105 degrees. The electronic controls for my steam shower are fucking awesome. Once under the spray, it takes only minutes for the pounding headache to calm the fuck down. I wash my hair and scrub my body. Normally, I shower as soon as I get home from a crime scene, you know, to get the stench of death off me, but last night I was too wiped. So I scrub extra hard to remove the memories of William Gibbons's gray face. It's part of the job I hate. I do my best to forget about the corpse and concentrate on the evidence.

With that, my mind turns from the investigation to Sophie. Why would I think of Sophie? It's because she's a woman alone. I hope she finds a place to stay tonight. Thinking of her in that big house alone makes me nuts. It also makes me rock-hard. I consider taking care of that with my soapy palm but decide against—too much to do today. I rinse off and hop out of the shower, grabbing my towel from the towel warmer. Yeah, I'm a pussy, but I love a warm towel when I get out of the shower, even in the summer.

I skip the shave for yet another day. It won't be long until I have a full beard. Pulling on jeans and a light-blue dress shirt, I grab a tie to make me look more professional. What I'd like to wear is my Black Sabbath T-shirt, but I'll be questioning people today and need to look the part. I attach my badge to my belt loop and slide my wallet into my back pocket. Searching the ground, I spy my shoes near the door. After slipping those on, I grab my sport coat, and I'm ready for my day.

First stop? Check on Sophie.

7

———

SOPHIE

The minute I step into the shop, I see Brooke at the bridal counter and hear her shout, "My office. Now!"

Hells bells. I hate this job. I follow her into her office and watch as she plops her boney bottom into her chocolate-brown, leather executive chair. I turn to shut the door. She stops me.

"No, keep it open." That's so the others can hear. It's like Brooke, Brittany, Ashley, and Arianna are all from the same sorority house or something. They are all tall, thin, beautiful, and evil. The only one who's halfway decent is Ashley, but she jumps on the bandwagon as soon as the others start to pick on me.

"Sophie, you're late. Again!" Brooke shouts.

Again? I'm *never* late. Hell, I've only called in sick twice in three years. And I called in then because I had walking pneumonia. I couldn't wait on brides when I was that ill. Attempting to defend myself, I say, "Brooke, I've never—"

"Save it. I'm so sick of your drama."

Drama? I'm not dramatic.

Brooke leans forward in her chair, placing her elbows on her desk. She rests her chin on the top of her hands and arches one brow like she's some kind of Doctor Evil. She continues her rant.

"If it isn't one thing, it's another with you. But that's not why I'm angry with you, Sophie." Standing up from her comfortable perch, she walks to the front of her desk and leans on the edge. She's above me, looking down at me with a scowl. "It's because the new Vera Wang is missing. I looked at the inventory sheet on the computer, and it shows that *you* checked it in late last week," she says, pointing a red-tipped finger at me. "Now, where is it?"

"I don't know. I steamed it, tagged it, and hung it out in the showroom. It should be there." That's the third dress in as many months that has gone missing. They weren't ordinary dresses, either. They were some of our highest-priced gowns. The Vera Wang was brand new, just off the runway. It was quite a coup that Brooke got a sample in the store so soon. She'd planned to use it to draw in more brides. Now, it's gone.

"Well, it's not, and your appointment that you missed this morning came here to try on *that* dress! Thank goodness I was here to make sure the bride left my store with a happy face. I have to do *everything* for you, Sophie."

That is such crap. I bend over backward to make sure everything runs smoothly here. I've taken on a lot of Brooke's duties over the last three years. So much so that Brooke spends as much time at the Coffee Bean or getting her hair and nails done as the others. I remain silent because this whole thing is upsetting me.

"You need to find that dress, Sophie! If you don't, I'll have no other recourse. I'll have to let you go. I can't trust you."

"Me?" I squeak. "I had nothing to do with that missing dress." *She can't fire me. I need this job, damn it.*

"You're the only consultant, besides myself, who works with

brides. You checked it in, and you claim to have hung it in the showroom, but it's not there. Where is it, Sophie?"

"I'll find it," I mutter. I can't decide if I want to cry or punch something. Maybe I'll punch something and then cry.

"That's all. You may go."

I turn and walk out of her office, almost bumping into Ari and Brittany, who are standing outside Brooke's door.

"Looks like your days are numbered here, fatty," sneers Ari.

"Yeah," mimics Brit, Ari's little lapdog. She does whatever Ari tells her to do. It's pathetic.

I ignore the evil twins, walk out into the bridal shop, and then stop.

Henry.

Henry is here? What the hell does he want now? Oh, maybe he's here to remind me that I'm a suspect in the murder of my neighbor. Great. Just great!

8

———

HENRY

When I first walk into the bridal shop, it looks empty. There are no salespeople around anywhere. I walk over to the side with all the fancy dresses and peek around corners. Does anyone work here? Where is Sophie? I poke my head into one of the huge dressing rooms in the store and even walk over to the tux area, fearing a run-in with that blonde from the other day. Walking back over to the front desk closest to the bride area, I wait.

It's not long before I hear voices and see movement coming from the back of the store. Sophie enters first, and it's obvious—to me at least—that she's about to cry. Either that, or she's so angry she wants to punch something. Her face is pink with emotion. She lowers her head as she hurries toward me. I'm not sure she sees me yet.

When she looks up, she spots me at the desk. Her eyes brighten, but then they suddenly look dark and irritated. She's not happy to see me?

"Hey, Soph."

"Henry. What are you doing here?"

"I needed to ask you a few more questions."

"Oh, yeah? Like 'Where were you Saturday night, Sophie? Did you murder your neighbor, Sophie?' Things like that?" She mimics the words with a terrible impression of a man's voice.

"No. Why would I ask you those things?"

"You wouldn't because Detective Kent somebody-or-other already did. He said he was your partner."

That asshole. "Sophie, you're—"

I'm interrupted by someone's throat clearing. I look up and see three women, including the blonde woman from the other day, Ariel or whatever. My eyes slide to Sophie, who looks terrified.

What is it with this place?

The woman standing closest to us, a tall redhead with serious cleavage, speaks. "Sir, I'm so sorry to interrupt," she says in a syrupy-sweet voice. "But do you mind if I grab Sophie for just one sec? One of the other girls can help you."

Just as I'm about to refuse the help, Red grabs Sophie's arm with slightly too much claw and drags her into one of those huge dressing rooms. Two tall blondes, the one from the other day and a new one, follow them. Luckily, there is only a curtain separating me from their discussion.

Another slim woman, a brunette, slinks over and asks, "What can I do for you, sir?"

"Nothing. Shh," I say, waving her away. I want to hear what's going on behind that curtain, so I lean in close enough to hear some loud, pissed-off whispering.

"Sophie! How many times do I have to tell you not to wait on the male customers? You're not attractive enough. We have a reputation to uphold here. The brides don't care who they work with, but the men deserve better."

Is this bitch for real?

I hear Sophie start to speak. "But—"

The brunette tries to stop me from listening in, but I wave her off again. I think I've frightened her.

"No buts, Sophie. First, you're late with some bogus excuse about an emergency, and now you're disobeying us again?"

Us?

"Yeah, *Miss Piggy,* I told you the other day to stay away from the men. But you're too stupid to listen." Those hateful words come from the blonde from the other day. I'll call her Blondie One. It's easier.

That's it! I walk over, grab the edge of the curtain, and rip it open. My Sophie has tears running down her cheeks, and those three hyenas are standing over her with their hands on their hips.

"Excuse me. I couldn't help overhearing because you're loud as fuck! What's going on? I came to speak to Sophie."

"Sir." Red interrupts.

That woman has *no* manners. I step closer to Sophie and rest my hand on her shoulder.

Speaking quietly, I say, "Sophie, maybe we should talk to the store manager or owner. Do you let your coworkers talk to you like that all the time?"

Sophie gazes up at me, attempting to blink away the tears in her eyes. She swipes her hand across her left cheek.

I move closer and bend down so I can look into her big, beautiful, sad eyes. In a whisper, I continue, "Because I'm pretty sure the store owner wouldn't want you to be talked to like this—especially in front of a customer. Where is he or she?"

Seconds tick away with no one saying a word.

I look up to see that Red is opening and closing her mouth like a damn fish.

I look back at Sophie. "Soph?"

Sophie raises her hand and points at Red. "That's the store owner," she says in a whisper.

"Red? You're the store owner? You treat your employees like that?" I turn to Sophie. "Why do you work here? These women are bitches."

I get no response from my girl. Seriously? What is the deal?

"Henry"—that's Blondie One again—"you don't understand."

She's talking like we're on a first-name basis. Fucking bitch.

"Maybe I don't, but I can tell you what I've observed. One, you, Red, are letting other employees like Blondie One and Blondie Two here, along with a customer, observe you reprimanding Sophie. That should be a confidential discussion with Sophie behind closed doors. Real doors." I point to the flimsy curtain.

Sophie looks like she's going to be sick. She's a shade of green I've only seen after a night of debauchery.

"Two, you are berating one of your employees about something you know nothing about. Three, you need to check yourself—all of you. I'd much rather have Sophie's hands on me when I'm ordering my tux than any of yours," I say, pointing to all three women.

Sophie looks at me in shock.

"And four"—I hold my hand up, showing four fingers—"Sophie's tenant was murdered last night. She's been through enough. You bitches need to lay the fuck off." I turn to my girl and ask softly, "Sophie, why do you work here? This place is toxic."

"I need the money," she whispers.

"Sophie?" Red gasps. "Your tenant was *murdered*?"

Sophie nods.

"Yes, I'm Detective Flynn, and I came to ask Sophie a few more questions."

"Sophie. Are you..." Blondie One begins, and then turns to me with a gleam in her eye. "Is Sophie a *suspect*?"

"You'd like that, wouldn't you?" Ugh, these women are the worst kind of people.

"No!" Feigning shock, Blondie Two adds, "Not our little Sophie!"

I grab Sophie by the arm and pull her toward me. "Let's talk outside."

"I c-can't! I-I...," she stutters.

"Just give me five minutes. That all right with you?" I glare at Red.

"Of course, Detective, take all the time you need with our little Sophie."

Grumbling, I pull Sophie out the front door and to the left of the building, away from the large store windows and prying eyes of the other women. I move her until she's got her back to the wall and I've got my arms on either side of her head—caged in.

"Sophie, seriously, why do you work there?"

"I need the money. The house repairs are expensive."

"Sell that old house."

"No! It's been in my family since 1939. I can't be the one that loses it." Her weak tone of voice concerns me.

"Baby," I whisper, "I know we just met, but I already know you deserve better than to work at *that* place," I say, pointing to the building. "Those women are terrible. Horrible."

"I make good money. The commissions are keeping me afloat."

Damn, I wish I could give her the money, but that would be inappropriate.

"Why are you here, Henry?"

"I stopped by to see how you were doing. I was worried about you in that big house all alone."

"I was perfectly safe. There were twenty police officers swarming my house all night."

Yeah, I was one of them. "Just so you know, you aren't a suspect. Kent, my partner, is just an asshole."

"He sounded pretty convinced I was a suspect. I don't have an alibi. I was home alone that night."

Of course you were. Shit!

"I need to get back to work, Henry. I have a bridal appointment in a few minutes."

"Okay, sure," I say as I run my thumb across her cheek. I can't seem to help myself. I need to touch her. I brush a few strands of her silky hair back behind her ear. "I need to get back to the scene. I'll be in touch. Remember to call me if you need me. You still got my card, right?"

She nods. "Right."

Why don't I believe her? Next time, I'll just program my number into her phone. Then I'll know she's got me on speed dial.

9

SOPHIE

Why? Why is he checking on me? What the heck is going on? He called me *baby* again too. He's making me think he likes me—you know, *likes me* likes me, and that's impossible. Men who look and act like Henry do not like women who look like me, who work in bridal stores and allow people to treat them like dog crap. Nope, a guy like Henry goes for tall, confident, beautiful woman. I need to keep any stupid hope from creeping in because I'll just end up disappointed—or worse, brokenhearted.

"Oh, before I forget," Henry says, breaking into my thoughts, "I talked to William's sister last night, and she's making arrangements to get here as soon as she can, so you won't have to deal with anything relating to Willy and his belongings."

That's a relief. Willy was a pack rat. He loved to go to thrift stores and auctions. I'd say he was getting to the level of hoarder, but he hadn't made it that far before... Oh, poor Willy.

"Yeah, well. Anyway," he says, looking reluctant. "Remember to call me if you need me."

I nod. "Right." *Now, where did I put that card?* "But you

don't need to check on me. I'm fine. You need to find the person responsible for Willy's death."

His hand slides down my arm until he clutches my hand, giving it a reassuring squeeze. "I am. We are."

He lets me go, and I watch Detective Henry Flynn stride to the curb toward the coolest car I've ever seen. It looks like a Ferrari or something like it. It's expensive to have a car in the city. Maybe he lives in a suburb, which makes owning a car more practical. Heck, that car is not practical. It's shiny, black, and it's got two doors that open like it's got wings, instead of four. That thing is 100 percent sports car. See? Not practical.

He revs the engine, making it purr. When I peer into the passenger window, Henry waves. I wave back and then make a beeline for the store. My bride will be here any minute, and I need to pull dresses for her to try. I hope she doesn't want to try on the new—missing—Vera Wang. I've got to find that dress or my career as a bridal consultant and my hefty commissions will end.

It's already been a long and stressful day. Brooke won't speak to me, and the other girls just give me dirty looks from their side of the store. I work with five brides through the day, which is good for a Tuesday. My last bride purchased a beautiful Monique Lhuillier gown. My commission will be amazing, which means I'm only a few hundred away from the roof. At closing time, I'm alone. Again. Brooke left at three thirty, saying she had a hair appointment. Ari took off at three thirty-one, as soon as Brooke was out the door. Brit and Ashley both took off at four o'clock, after their last appointment with a group of bridesmaids. That left me to watch the store until six.

Closing the shop alone is quiet, and I can relax a bit. At seven o'clock, I wipe down the counter in the bridal area, drop the paper towels in the waste bin, grab my phone and my travel coffee cup, and head out the back door, setting the alarm as I go.

Nearly to the "L," I realize I don't have my purse. Therefore, I do not have my "L" pass or my wallet. Shit! I sigh and turn around. The walk to the shop is only fifteen minutes, but I'm beat, so it takes closer to thirty to get there. The sun has gone down, and the streetlights glow. It's a warm July night in beautiful Chicago. The walk is good for me.

I don't have a key to the shop, only the security code to get into the rear of the building. I round the corner to the back and stop in my tracks. There's a compact car I don't recognize parked near the back entrance. I can see a person sitting in the driver's seat, and the back door of the shop is ajar. Without thinking, I pull my phone out to take a picture of the license plate when I hear voices.

"Hurry the hell up, Brit," hisses the voice.

Almost automatically, I flip my phone from photo to video and hit record. I have a feeling I know what's going on, and I want proof. I hide behind the smelly dumpster behind the shop. I'm not tall enough to be seen, but I make sure by squatting down farther.

"Jesus, Brit. What is taking you so damn long? Do I have to do everything myself?"

My camera zooms in on the figure exiting the car. It's Ari! She leaves her car door open and then yanks the back door wide just as Brittney comes out carrying a dress bag with a large white dress inside. I'm not sure which one it is, but my guess is it's a new design.

"What took you so long?"

"Ari, I was trying to bag it up. I didn't want it to get dirty. We'll never be able to sell a dirty dress."

"Fine. *Whatevs.*"

"How much do you think we'll get for this one?"

"It retails for twelve thousand, so we'll get at least ten.

That's good because Mama needs a new pair of Jimmy Choo's." Ari cackles.

I know I look ridiculous standing here with my mouth agape, but I would never have guessed that these two were the masterminds behind the thefts.

"Are you sure there aren't any cameras around?" Brit nervously glances around the alleyway.

"I'm sure. Brooke's too stupid to put any kind of real security in this place. She trusts everyone with the codes. She's a fucking idiot."

"If you're sure. I like Brooke. I feel bad stealing from her."

"Well, if she'd fire that fat bitch and let us sell bridal instead of only selling bridesmaids and renting tuxedos, we'd get real commissions and wouldn't have had to resort to selling this shit online. It's her own fault."

"I guess," Brittany says, resigned. "I wish the online account wasn't in my name. Why didn't we use your name again?" Brit places the bag in the trunk. It's a big ball gown, so it barely fits.

Brittany is such an idiot. Ari will pin this whole thing on Brit in a New York minute.

"Because your name is common. Mine isn't. I've told you that like a million times. Now, shove that thing in the trunk and get in the fucking car, Brit. We need to get outta here."

I watch Brittany slam the trunk lid down and race to the passenger side of the car. I get the license plate in my video. I'm not sure what to do about all of this yet. Should I call the police? Brooke would be upset if I got the police involved. Bad publicity.

I think about it on my way home. I think about it while I eat a bowl of cheap ramen noodles and when I shower. I lie in bed, watch the video I took of Ari and Brit, and think about it some more. It's unbelievable. Honestly, part of me isn't surprised that

Ari and Brit are thieves, but there's a part of me, the one that wants to see the good in people, that's shocked.

I can't believe they'd do that to Brooke. She treats them like they're her daughters. Actually, when I think of the dynamic at the bridal store, it's more like the fairy tale *Cinderella*. I'm Cinderella in this scenario, while Brooke, Ari, Brit, and Ashley would be my evil stepfamily. Cinderella prevails in that story, thanks to the handsome prince. I snort aloud at that notion. I'm no Cinderella, that's for sure. A happy ending isn't in my future. But perhaps Ari and Brit will earn their comeuppance like they do in the story. That is, if Brooke decides to do something about this video.

I roll over to my side, facing the window. It's still aglow from the lights on and around the carriage house. The police are still hard at work in there looking for clues. I wonder if Henry is down there. Now, there's a sexy addition to my little fairy tale. If I could choose, right now, I'd pick Detective Henry Flynn to be my prince. *Get over yourself, Sophie. He's too hot for you.* You need to look for an average guy, a nerdy man—someone like Willy. I inhale sharply.

"Poor Willy. He didn't deserve that fate."

In the morning, I feel like I had zero sleep. I know I slept some, just not enough. I shower again, hoping it wakes me up. Dressed in all black, I pull my hair back into a low, short ponytail. No time to fix it. Brooke gets in early on Wednesdays to do the schedules and prepare for our weekly staff meeting, held at ten o'clock on the dot every hump day, thirty minutes before the store opens. I want to catch her before anyone else gets there. I slap on some eye shadow and lip gloss and call it good. Grabbing my favorite Starbucks travel mug, I step out of my front door into the heat. Jeez, it's only eight in the morning, and it's at least eighty degrees already.

I speed walk to the "L," hoping to beat the crowd of people who show up at this time every morning. My plan works. I'm able to be one of the first to squeeze onto the train. It's too full to grab a seat, but that's okay. I'm too nervous to sit. The jostling of the "L" and the chattering of the morning commuters are just the distractions I need right now.

At my stop, I squeeze my way out of the mass of passengers, walk the normally fifteen-minute trip to the shop in less than ten, and open the back door that Brooke has unlocked already. Dumping everything except my phone into my locker, I step in front of Brooke's office door and take a deep breath.

Knocking, I hear, "Come in, Sophie."

"How did you know it was me?"

"Who else comes in early?"

True.

"Brooke? I need to show you something." I am overeager about this. Nothing good comes from being too optimistic.

"I'm busy. Can't it wait?"

"No. It can't. I know what's been happening to the dresses."

She gives me that expression—the one-eyebrow-raised expression. I know the look. It's one of disbelief. Brooke thinks I've been stealing them.

Sighing, she says, "Fine. What is it?"

I pull my phone out of my pocket, bring up the video, hit play, and then set the phone in front of her and watch her as she views the video. Her eyes grow larger the longer she watches. When she hears Ari say, "Brooke's too stupid to put any kind of real security in this place. She trusts everyone with the codes. She's a fucking idiot," she flinches. I think she had high hopes for Ari. Ari was her favorite.

When the video stops, Brooke's head slowly rises. She looks angry—at me. "Did you suspect them? Is that why you have this on video?"

"No. I forgot my purse last night. I needed it to take the 'L,' so when I walked back to get it, I saw a car parked and the back door ajar. I was just going to take a photo of the license plate, but I heard voices and thought a video would be better."

"Did you call the police?"

I know why she's asking me. "No, I figured you'd want to handle this yourself. But I think you should call the police."

"Don't tell me what to do, Sophie. This is *my* shop," she says, patting her chest. "I'll handle this. Do not breathe a word of this to anyone, especially your little detective friend. You know, the protective one who treats you like his little sister?"

"I won't." I wince at her words. She's probably right. He's overly protective. Just like a big brother.

"Get to work," she mutters.

I'm an hour early for work. I haven't clocked in, so I'm not technically working yet, but I decide not to argue the point. There are always things to do, so I clock in and start my opening duties. I turn on the rest of the lights in the store and set the thermostat so it will cool down the store before the staff meeting. I run the vacuum in the dressing rooms, turn on the satellite radio to a mellow station, count and open the register for the day, and brew a pot of coffee. When I look at the clock, I've still got some time, so I reorganize the wedding veils and neaten up the belts and other accessories on the display wall. I finish in time to see Brittany walk right past me to her place in the tux area.

I can tell she doesn't suspect a thing because she acts like she normally does. She completely ignores me as if I don't exist. Fine by me. Ari strolls in as though she owns the place at five minutes to ten—just in time for the staff meeting. We gather around the small table in the tuxedo area the way we do every week. Brooke seems to be taking her time. I hope she handles this all quickly. No time like the present.

When Brooke steps out of her office, she's pale. She's the color of oatmeal. Not a good look for a redhead. She steps up to the table and clears her throat. "I have news," she mumbles.

"News? What kind of news?" Ari says in her perky voice. "Are you finally firing fatty over there?" She points her thumb at me.

"Well, someone is fired, but it's not Sophie. This time, anyway."

Huh? This time, anyway?

"Sophie has brought something to my attention. Last night, she videotaped two people stealing a dress right out of the back of my store." Brooke clears her throat again, obviously trying to hold back her emotions.

Why the hell did she tell them I videotaped it? Shit! I look over at Ari, and she's glaring at me. Brittany looks as if she's wet herself.

"The video is clear, as are the voices on the tape."

I clutch my phone in my left hand. Ari looks right at it. She has to know the recording is on it. Little does she know, I emailed it to myself in case my phone went missing. Still, I need my phone, so I bring it around to my back and hold it as far away from her as I can.

"Ari, Brit, clean out your lockers. You're fired," Brooke says in a sad voice.

She's firing her minions, who, sadly, have no respect for her. I know I shouldn't feel the least bit gleeful, but hell, ding-dong, the witches are gone. I can't help myself.

"You!"

I turn to see a red-faced Ari lunging for me. I quickly move back to avoid any contact. I'd never win in hand-to-hand combat with someone like Ari. She's got claws.

"You fucking fat cow. You're the one who should be fired. It's your fault I had to do it. I make nothing renting stupid tuxedos and selling bridesmaids dresses. You get all the commissions. It's not fair," she whines, and then her voice rises as she continues. "You'll pay for this, Sophie. You'll regret getting your nose in my business. Watch your back, you fucking bitch!" she spews.

Brittany is crying. Bawling is a better way to describe it. "Are you going to ca-call the po-police?" she asks Brooke.

"I should, but no, I'm not. I don't want the negative publicity. But you need to go before I change my mind, Brit. Ari, go!" Brooke shouts.

Fuming, Ari stomps toward me and rams her shoulder into me as she passes. I nearly fall to the ground but catch the edge of the table with my hip. It'll leave a bruise. I look at Ashley's shocked expression. I don't think she suspected a thing.

Ari and Brit take forever to leave. I hear Ari pleading with Brooke for an hour to give her another chance, but Brooke won't budge. If Ari hadn't called her an idiot, I bet Brooke would have let her stay. Brooke *is* that stupid. After the drama is over, Brooke leaves early. Not a surprise.

Ashley makes her way over to my area, and I take a step back out of reflex. With everything that has happened in the last few days, I'm a bit skittish. I'm not surprised by her question, though. "Did you suspect them? Is that why you videotaped them?"

"No. I came back for my purse and saw it happening. I taped it for my protection. Brooke threatened to fire me over the missing dresses."

"I see." She starts to make her way back over to the tux area but stops. "I'd watch my back if I were you, Sophie. Ari is M-E-A-N, mean. I wouldn't put anything past her."

For the life of me, I can't figure out why Ashley would bother warning me. While she's not as bad as the other two, she's not that good either.

"I'm not afraid of Ari. She's too self-absorbed to spend any more time on me. She'll find a new job and a new person to bully."

Shrugging, Ashley says, "If you say so."

I say so. I've got other things to worry about.

10

HENRY

Before leaving the carriage house for the station and our briefing, I check on Sophie. I noticed the lights in the big house turned on a few minutes ago, which means she's home from work. I walk up the back sidewalk and tap on the door. When she doesn't appear, I try the doorknob. It's open. Damn it, she needs to lock her doors. She probably isn't concerned since there are so many cops swarming around here, but still.

I turn the knob, and the door doesn't budge. Ah, I remember. This door sticks. I use my shoulder to push the door and then step into her small kitchen. It's dark. Maybe she hasn't made her way to this part of her house yet. The living room light is on, though, so I walk through. Hearing footsteps coming from the upper level, I take the steps two at a time until I'm at the top of the stairs. At three steps to the top of the landing, I watch as Sophie steps out of a bedroom.

I'm standing about ten feet from her, but I'm pretty sure she hasn't seen me yet because she's reaching around trying to unhook her bra. She looks up and squeaks, "What the hell, Henry?" Jerking away, she turns her little body so the front of her is facing the wall. "What are you doing up here?"

She needn't bother. I already glimpsed the goodies, and let me tell you, she looks soft and sweet. But damn, the back view is even better, and I can examine her from head to toe without her catching me. Boy, I like what I see. She's a compact thing—soft arms and legs, beautiful back with porcelain skin. But, by far, the best feature is that plump ass.

"Damn, Sophie. Your bottom is just as luscious as I imagined." Her head rises, and she stares up at her ceiling. She won't look at me?

"Wha-what? You imagined my bottom?" Her beautiful skin turns a lovely shade of pink—all over.

Oh yeah. "Baby, are you blushing?"

"I'm embarrassed. Can you please go? Jeez, Henry. How did you get in here? I didn't give you a key."

Still perusing her cute little body, I can just picture her on top of me in a reverse cowgirl. The thought makes my cock twitch. That, coupled with her blush, is making me harder by the minute. Thinking about all the ways I'd like to have her is killing me.

"Back door was unlocked. You should be careful, Soph. Someone could come into the house."

"You mean like *you*?"

"Nah, I'm the good guy."

"No, you're not. Get out, Henry. God!"

I'm not about to leave when this is getting good, but I hear footsteps and my jackass of a partner yell, "Hank, you up there?"

He's coming upstairs. Shit. I move closer to Sophie to shield her from prying eyes. She's mine, and hell will freeze over before I let Kent see her. *Jesus, I sound like a caveman.* I move in close, pressing my front against her sweet behind. My dick is rock-solid now. I'm sure she can feel me.

"I'm busy. Get the fuck back downstairs, asshole. I'll be there in a few."

"You're a fucking dick, Hank. Hurry up. We need to get back to the station for the briefing."

"I know! Five minutes!" *Jesus.*

"Um, Henry? Can you move back, please?" she whispers.

"No. I like it here." I let my eyes move from her shiny hair all the way down her back. Her skin looks so fucking soft. "Are those cupcakes on your panties, Soph?"

"God. This is so humiliating."

"Now, I don't know what I should call you—Cupcake or Sweet Cheeks? I'm leaning toward the second one. What do you think?"

"I think I want to die," she murmurs.

"Shh, beautiful." I chuckle. Damn, I want to touch her. But I know it's not the right time. I watch her chest rise and fall. She's as turned on as I am. I know it. I'm so close, I see right down the front of her. She's clutching her breasts to keep her bra in place, but the fact that her tits are getting pressed out above the top of her hands hasn't escaped me. I lean down and whisper in her ear, "Everything about you is beautiful, Sophie."

"Henry," she breathes.

I step back and turn. "I'll be in touch, Sweet Cheeks."

"Oh, God," she groans. "That was so embarrassing."

I chuckle again as I rush down the stairs. It's time to get to that briefing, because the more officers that get a listen at our preliminary information the better. I'm sure they'll think of things we haven't.

BACK AT THE STATION, I've got all of William Gibbons's files sitting in a box in front of me. They've already been fingerprinted, and I've been through them twice. I don't know why, but I know there's something in these files that can help us. I've already summarized my preliminary findings and copied the pertinent information for the rest of the officers assigned to the case, along with the squad cap, Captain Cooke.

"Hey, everyone, let's get this started. Hank, why don't you tell us what you've got so far," announces Captain Cooke.

"Thanks, Cap. Okay, I'll talk about these files, and then Kent will take over with information from the scene." I take a deep breath. "First off, when I looked through the files, I didn't notice anything out of the ordinary. Each file was labeled, and nothing stood out. Utilities folder had old receipts of his bills and payments for electricity and cable. I read through his cable bill for the added packages William bought, and the only added stations were some porn sites."

Someone in the peanut gallery snickers and says, "At least the guy had something to do in his spare time."

"Yeah, so remember to wash your hands after handling his stuff." I chuckle. Only one guy laughs. Yeah, bad joke. "Okay, back to the bills. He only had an electric bill and a cable bill, so Ms. Kincaid must have paid his water bill. I'll double-check that. Next was Electronics. Here he's got every brochure and warranty information for every piece of equipment he's purchased in the last twenty years, I swear. There's one in here for a Sony Mavica camera. Remember those? You used a floppy disk to store your photos."

"Yeah, and they only held about ten pictures tops," adds Detective Matt Hampton.

"True," someone else agrees.

"He's also got information and receipts for his computers. He recently bought a MacBook Pro. It's gone. We're assuming the perp must have taken it, along with an HP desktop, but we're still checking. My guess is they're long gone, but we'll keep looking."

Kent adds, "His computer at work is gone too. According to Janet McClenney, the Human Resources director at Luciph Corp, it's not uncommon for the IT department to remove the computer and wipe it clean when someone leaves the company."

"Or dies," I add.

"Anyway, as I was saying"—Kent scowls at me—"it had already been done by the time we talked to them."

"Fuck. That sucks," mutters someone in the back. It sounds like Hampton.

"Yeah, it does. Okay, personal correspondence like cards and letters from his sister are in this one. There were quite a few of those. It appears he kept every card she ever sent, but I'm not sure why. They were only signed with her name. No sentimental brother-sister stuff."

It's weird. I always put a note in my birthday cards to my family, and we all live in the same city. We're all close and see each other whenever we can, and I still tell them how much they mean to me in my cards. It's just what brothers and sisters do.

"I glanced through a few other cards—Christmas, congratulations for his new job, and more birthday cards. All just signed 'Julia.'"

Kent speaks up. "One other interesting tidbit about Ms. Julia Gibbons is that she's *very* eager to get her brother buried so she can get to his will. She's called me multiple times to see if his body has been released yet."

"Yeah, I called the vic's attorney, and he wouldn't tell me anything other than he won't do a reading of the will until his body has been released. Not sure why, but he's holding steady on that," I say.

"Interesting," agrees Captain Cooke. "She got an alibi at the time of death?"

"Yeah. She was in Seattle. But that don't mean she couldn't hire someone," grumbles Kent.

I scan the nods of agreement around the room. I don't like Julia Gibbons for this one. Sure, she may inherit, but enough to murder her own brother? I've seen people kill for less. I guess it's possible, but I don't think so.

"Alrighty then, back to the files. Credit Cards. Now, this is interesting. Again, he's kept every bill since the beginning of time, but they show he rarely used the cards. I lined them all up in order and by card. He's got two major credit cards and one Macy's card. From the statements, he only charged small items, and then paid off the balance each month."

Why have credit cards? Just pay cash.

"I've contacted the credit bureau, and they'll fax me his credit report and credit score information. I'm also checking to see if he's purchased anything major in the last five years and if he's got any student loans or outstanding debt somewhere else."

"He must have been living pretty inexpensively to have everything paid off," says Cap.

"Either that or he's been doing something he shouldn't be doing. It could explain the professional hit," adds Kent.

Several of the guys grumble in agreement. It could be the case.

"Next up was his Miscellaneous folder, which held receipts from the last few months. Grocery store, Target, Craft-mart, and Gamerz were the primary places he shopped, at least recently. The final folder, labeled Pay Stubs, was empty, which I thought was strange. But when I opened it up completely, I discovered writing on the inside of the folder, down near the fold. I've made copies for each of you. It's in your packet."

The rustling of papers interrupts my flow, but I continue. "He's written the notes in different colored pens, but I don't think that's significant—at least not at this time." I move to the center of the room. "Here's what the notes said." I list off the years, amounts, and other information as everyone looks at their copies.

2009: --$20.15 x 108,001 emp

2010: --$19.39 x 110,170 emp

2011: --$22.84 x 111,184 emp

2012: --$18.68 x 110,875 emp

2013: --$19.75 x 112,984 emp

2014: --$17.88 x 110,548 emp

2015: --$22.95 x 109,150 emp

____

--$141.64 x 110,416 ave emp = $15,639,322.20

(estimated average)

2016: --$11.13 to date. (108,998 emp to date)

Officer Pete Peppers snipes, "What the fuck does any of that mean? Emp? Almost sixteen million?" He looks from me to Kent and then back to me. "Was this guy some kind of savant? *Rain Man* kind of stuff?"

I scoff at Pepper's comment. That guy can be an idiot. Savant? Jesus.

"I'm not sure what it means. I assume that emp means employees. When I checked out the number of people employed by Luciph Corp, it was around that number." I peek at my notes. "The most recent employment numbers for Luciph Corp are 108,987 worldwide."

"So, the sixteen million is related to the hundred-thousand-plus employees?"

"Not sure yet. But his math makes us think he was tallying something that relates to Luciph employees," I clarify. "Okay, but there's more. When I went to place the folders back in the box, I found a slip of paper at the bottom. It was a pay stub from January 2015. A copy of the stub is in your packet. It's not enough, but it's a start. I've requested copies of all salary and retirement information for William since he worked for Luciph Corp."

"What's with this part that's highlighted?" asks Captain Cooke. "Retirement withholding: $286.94."

"It's the amount of money he had going into his retirement account that month. William highlighted that amount himself. I'm not sure how it all fits in. It could be nothing, but it was important enough for him to mark the area on his pay stub. That's why I included retirement data in my request with his HR department."

I look at Kent, cueing him that it's his turn to talk. "He is—well, *was*—forty-two. Maybe he was keeping track of all that because he wanted to figure out if he could retire early. The HR director didn't make it easy to get this shit. But we're supposed to get more stuff in a day or two," Kent adds gruffly.

"The a-hole—Christopher Collins, chief financial officer—said he wouldn't release any financial docs without a judge's signature. So, we got a judge's signature. It delayed us, but we'll get what we need," I add.

"Kent, what'd you find at the scene?" asks the cap.

"The guy was a pig. He never picked up any of his shit. It made going through his crap a nightmare."

"And?" Apparently, the captain isn't impressed with Kent's comments.

"So far, I've gotten nothing that can help. He collected a ton of junk from thrift stores and secondhand shops. He had a particular interest in crappy paintings and furniture that's falling apart. It all needs to go to the dump, but that's not my problem."

Cap sighs. I think Kent has lost his touch.

I say, "He had a lot of stuff but kept it all organized. He had about a million old floppy disks and an equal amount of flash drives. The techs are going through those now. It'll be a while."

"Okay. If you two need help, grab Peppers. His case is cold as an Arctic winter. The rest of you, let's meet again when new information comes in. Sound good?" adds the cap.

"Yeah," the group agrees.

When I get back to my desk, the old landline telephone on my desk is ringing, pulling me away from my thoughts. "Flynn," I answer.

It's the ME assigned to our case. I listen as he jabbers on and on. All I want are his results, not small talk. When he's finally done, I spot Kent across the room and yell, "Yo, asshole. I've got information from the ME. Get over here."

Kent grumbles and pushes himself out of his old office chair, circa 1973, mumbling to himself as he makes his way to my desk. I know he thinks I'm on the wrong track, that none of the info from the files has any bearing on the investigation, but I'm going with my gut on this one. I'm right more than I'm wrong when my gut gets involved, and he knows it.

Stomping up to my desk, he growls, "What?"

"The ME says what we thought he'd say."

"Which is?"

"Cause of death, two gunshot wounds, head and heart."

"Duh. Jesus, Hank. You're wasting my time."

I ignore him because if I didn't, I'd want to punch him in his ugly, smug face. "He thinks first shot was heart."

"So? Who the fuck cares? He died from a gunshot. Why do I give two flying fucks which came first?"

"Never mind. Jesus, you're such a prick, Kent."

"Love you too, Hanky," he says as he stomps off.

Fuck. I need a new partner. On second thought, I could end up with Peppers. I'll take my chances with the surly asshole I've got.

11

SOPHIE

This has been a long week. The good news is that I now look forward to work since Ari left—er, was fired. The police are still working in the carriage house, and I haven't seen Henry since the embarrassing incident in my hallway. Willy's sister is flying in tomorrow night. She'll come by the house so she can see to Willy's belongings. I hope we'll be able to get into his place by then.

I wonder what Henry is up to. Most likely, he's busy solving crime and saving the city from evil. I giggle at the thought of Henry as a superhero. He'd look good in tights.

Damn it. I've got to stop thinking about Henry.

His brother's wedding is next weekend. He'll be in to try on his tux soon. Maybe I'll get a glimpse of him in his tuxedo. I bet he'll look fantastic. What would it be like to be his date to the wedding?

Stop it, Sophie! You will only end up disappointed. I'm sure Henry has a date who could stop traffic. Maybe he'll take a model from that famous lingerie company. I can just picture him with a willowy, blonde supermodel—not with short, fat, old me.

After work on Friday, I stop and pick up a pizza from Giordano's—the best Chicago-style pizza on the planet. A small pie will last me the rest of the weekend. I order the veggie lover's and wait in the bar. It takes a while to get your food, but it's worth it. I grab a beer and stand near the bar, watching the Cubs play on the nearest flat-screen. They're having a great season, but I don't hold out any hope of it finishing as well as last year. That's just the way it goes. If you're a true Cubs fan, you have to accept disappointment.

When my Giordano's handheld buzzer zings, I set my empty glass down and walk to the hostess station. She brings out my steaming-hot pizza, and I head out the door toward home. Why does food make me so happy? I should feel guilty about pigging out on pizza tonight, but I'm excited about going home, getting my jammies on, and watching Netflix. I wish I were more adventurous, but I'm not. Ashley is probably out with her friends dancing the night away at a hip club or something.

My mind turns to Henry again. Is he out on a date with that lingerie model? Is he whispering sexy things in her ear, kissing her, touching her? I'm in my own world, not paying attention to my surroundings, when I hear someone yell, "Watch out!"

I look up just in time to watch a car as it speeds through the intersection veering toward me. In shock, I can't figure out how to move until I feel myself being pulled back. Dropping my pizza and purse on the ground, I fall backward. The front passenger side wheel of the car rolls up the curb and misses me by inches and gets my pizza instead. *Damn it, I was hungry!* The car pulls back out into traffic and is gone before I can even think to look at the driver.

"That car almost ran you over!" exclaims the man behind me. "If I hadn't pulled you back, you'd be like that pizza."

"Did anyone get that asshole's plate number?" an older woman asks, but the nearest onlookers shake their heads.

I'm in shock. "Th-thank you." Since my mind was on Henry, I didn't catch a license plate. I knew it was a bad idea to think about him.

"You okay?" asks my hero.

"Y-yeah. I'm okay. Thanks." I stand up and sweep the dust and dirt from my clothing. I've torn my leggings. It's okay; I have a million more pairs. There's blood seeping out of one hole, but nothing a Band-Aid won't fix. After picking up my purse, which made it through the ordeal with only a few scratches, I limp the few remaining blocks home, knowing I'll be sore tomorrow.

Instead of eating delicious pizza, I spend my evening tending to my bumps and bruises, watching a sad movie on Netflix, and feeling sorry for myself. Sighing, I grab my bag of microwave popcorn and pour it into a big bowl. It's fine. I'm perfectly happy here by myself. I'm used to it. What else could I possibly need? Friends? Sure, I could use a couple friends. A cat? Maybe cats, plural, would be a nice addition to my life. It may be time to do that cat thing. They'd keep me company when I'm depressed. God, I'm pathetic.

12

HENRY

First thing Saturday morning, the team meets up in one of our larger conference rooms. While I hate working Saturdays, I need to because the investigation is moving along at a snail's pace. I've written out everything we know about the vic on the wall-mounted whiteboard, so we can all look at it at the same time.

William James Gibbons Jr.:

- Date of birth: February 15, 1974
- Place of birth: San Diego, CA
- Parents: William Sr. and Janice

Professional life

- Current employer: Luciph Corp.
- Years at current employer: 10 years, 2 months
- Current annual salary: $125,000.00
- Previous employer: AT&T, San Diego, CA
- Years at AT&T: 5
- Previous annual salary (AT&T): $95,000.00

- Current paid vacation: 4 weeks, but he's only taken 1 vacation in 10 years—Acapulco, alone, in 2011.
- Job description: Computer programmer specializing in Fortran and Cobol languages. (Note: Rarely used anymore; some older institutions still use these languages.)

Personal life and finances

- Spent little money on household items and clothing. Ate mostly processed foods.
- Spent serious green on electronics.
- Paid his bills on time, paying more than the minimum balance on credit balances if applicable.
- No outstanding debt. No student loan debt. No current loans. No major purchases in last five years.
- No close friends and only one sibling: Julia. Friendly with coworkers but spent no time outside of work with them.
- Porn enthusiast. Subscription to PornCast Network, Digitalplaytown Network, and Pornproz Network.
- Collection of video games and equipment: Xbox and Nintendo devices, both handheld and console for the TV. May have played multiplayer online games. Tech investigators looking into this aspect of his life.
- Owned large collection of DVDs and old VCR movies—primarily science fiction and fantasy flicks. Each movie is listed on the inventory sheet.
- Retirement fund: TBD—still waiting.
- Other information from pay stubs: TBD—still waiting.
- Resent the warrant to Luciph Corp for copies of all

of William's payment records, including his retirement account documents, but still haven't gotten them.

THE TEAM GATHERS TO review the pertinent information about our vic. From the meeting, we have a new list of leads to check out, including making a personal visit to Luciph Corporation to put some pressure on them to comply with the court order. That means I'll have to sit in a car with Kent for over an hour. That's gonna suck because, for one, he drives like he's eighty and, for another, I'll have to talk to him.

The cap also wants us to dig a little deeper into Gibbons's life. He's got a hunch there was more to him than video games and porn. Besides that, our plan for the next few days is:

Meet Julia Gibbons at the carriage house when she gets into town for a chat. (Kent)

Visit Luciph Corp personally if we don't get requested docs by Tuesday. (Kent and Hank)

Get with tech investigators to see if they found anything on the flash drives or disks. (Peppers)

Contact vic's attorney. The body will be released to Julia Gibbons in seven to ten days. (Hank)

ON MONDAY, I head straight to the tux shop as soon as I'm up and ready. I need to pick up my tux. In truth, I want to check on Sophie. This time, I'll *demand* that she wait on me. *That should piss off those women.* I chuckle at the thought.

When I walk into the shop, the brunette approaches me. "Well, hello again," she flirts. "What can I do for you?"

"I need to pick up a tux. Where's Sophie?"

"She's not allowed to—"

"I want Sophie to help me. Get her." I know. I'm an asshole.

"Sir, I need to be the one to help you."

I glare at this one. "I. Want. Sophie."

"Sir, she'll get into trouble. Just let me help you," she whispers.

For fuck's sake. At least this one seems like she's looking out for Soph. "Fine," I mutter as I walk over to the tux area.

"Bride's name?"

"Jen."

Pause. "Last name?"

"Just search for David Flynn. Wedding is this Saturday," I mutter.

"Right. Be back in a sec."

I walk over to the bridal area and scan the room. That's when I see a round bottom peeking out from under a row of wedding dresses. I walk over. "Sophie?"

She squeaks and hits her head on something behind the dresses. "Shit!" she says quietly. It's cute coming from my little Soph. She peeks her head out, rubbing it with her right hand.

"Henry?"

"Hey, babe. Came to get my tux. I wanted to say hello, see how you're doing."

"I'm fine. You'd better get over there. I'm not allowed to help you."

"Well aware, babe. Well aware. You need to quit this place. I also noticed that you still haven't found another place to stay. I'd suggest you stay with someone from work, but I think you're safer at your house." I smirk. "I'll stop back before I leave," I say as I give her a tiny salute and head back over to tuxedos when I hear my name called.

Trying on tuxedos is invasive. I swear the brunette woman is trying to get in the dressing room with me. I barely get the shirt on when she's pulling the curtain open on me. When I slide the pants up, I nearly piss myself. They're about ten inches too short and tight as hell. Everyone will know *everything* about me, if you know what I mean. How the fuck did this happen?

I can barely get them buttoned. I step out into the tux area. "Yeah, these aren't right," I say, pointing down to my feet. "I look like Angus Young."

A giggle erupts, but then the clerk gets serious. "Um, I think the wrong measurements were taken. Either that, or they sent the wrong pants."

"Ya think?" I ask sarcastically.

"Hang on. Let me get Brooke."

Not Red. Fuck! Three minutes later, Red and the other girl have closed in on my pants and me.

"Oh, dear," says Red. She picks up the folder with our names and measurements and then looks down at my pants. "It looks like the wrong measurements are listed here."

I'd add "ya think?" to the conversation again, but I want this over with.

"Damn, Sophie," snipes Brooke.

"Excuse me, but that other blonde woman took my measurements, not Sophie."

"It has Sophie's initials right here." She points.

"Sophie started to help, but the other blonde chick berated her and made her leave."

Sighing, Red assures, "Let me get the right measurements. I'll call this in and get you the correct pants. It will take a day or two, but you'll have it by the wedding."

The wedding is in five days; I hope she's right. "Fine." I go back into the dressing room and change into my street clothes so Red can take my measurements again.

As I head toward the front door, I look back, searching for

Sophie. She's peering at me, so I give her a small smile. She smiles back and limps toward the back of the store.

Limping? I walk back toward her. "Sophie, why are you limping?"

"Oh, I fell on my way home the other night. Just some bumps and bruises. I'm fine."

Did she roll her eyes at me? Again? "You should see a doctor. You've got quite a limp there. Maybe you really hurt something."

"No, I'm fine. I've just been on my knees working on bridal gowns. It'll be good as new in a day or two."

"All right. Well, take care, Sophie." I turn and walk out the door. I need to get over my crush on Sophie, and picturing her on her knees isn't the way to go about that. Besides, she's too good for the likes of me. Plus, I don't do relationships. Thinking of Sophie as anything other than a person of interest in a murder investigation is as far as I should go with her, and I need to stick to my guns on that.

13

SOPHIE

I think I know why it's called a crush. Because when you realize the guy you want doesn't want you back, it feels like you're being pressed down into a flat nothing by a large garbage truck—crushed. No good comes from fantasizing about a guy like Henry. I need to get over my crush.

After he leaves the store, Ashley wanders over to my area. "Did you see Hank?"

"Henry."

"Yeah, well, he wanted you to wait on him, but I told him you'd get into trouble. He seemed to understand. What's the story with you two?"

That's nice that he wanted me to wait on him. "No story. I met him last week when he came in to order his tux, and he showed up at my house to investigate my neighbor's murder. It was all coincidence."

"He defended you over there. Brooke tried to blame you for the error in the measurements, but he made sure she knew Ari did it. I think he likes you, Soph," she whispers excitedly.

"Ash, there's no way a guy like *that* likes a girl like me."

"What? Why not? You're cute."

"I'm short, fat, and plain. He's used to people who are like you. Gorgeous. Maybe *you* should go for it."

"I'd love to, but Mike wouldn't like that." She giggles.

Mike is Ashley's boyfriend of two years. He's kind of a douche; at least that's how he seems from the stories she tells. I've never met the guy. "Well, it may be time for a trade in." I snort out a laugh.

"Ha, ha, hilarious. Mike's been doing much better lately. I'm not giving up on him yet. Besides, Hank—er, I mean, Henry—didn't glance twice at me. It was all Sophie all the time with him."

"He acts like he's my big brother, all protective and stuff. It's nothing more than that."

"If you say so. But I know guys, and it was more than that."

I huff out, "Whatever. Guys like Henry don't date girls like me, Ash. It's how the world works. But I appreciate that you think it's possible. I also appreciate that you aren't treating me like a sack of dirt. I hope we can be friends now that the evil twins are gone."

"Oh, Sophie. I'm sorry about that. Ari was a bitch, and she was very controlling. That's no excuse for letting her say nasty things about you, though. You've always been nice, and I hope we can be friends too. I'm sorry."

"S'okay. No worries. I need to get back to work, Ash. My next bride will be here soon."

"Right. Let's go out sometime soon. I'll take you to one of my favorite clubs and introduce you to some of my friends."

"Sure. Okay. Thanks, Ash." *Not gonna happen.* She's nice enough, but I can't see myself clubbing with a bunch of twenty-year-olds.

Afterward, Ashley and I close the shop—yes, that's what I said, she stayed and helped me close. It was fun. We turned up the satellite radio and sang as we counted out the drawer, cleaned mirrors and the front windows, and vacuumed. It was the first time in a long time that I enjoyed my job.

As I make my way to the "L," I feel like my steps are lighter than they have been in a long time. After my dad died so suddenly, I had to quit graduate school. It was too expensive to pay for, and I needed to be around for Gran. It was such a sad time for both of us. We mourned together. By the time things felt normal again, Grandma Sophia's health took a turn for the worse. She fell and broke her hip and ended up in the hospital and then contracted pneumonia there. Gran didn't make it out of the hospital.

Gran had a good life, though, surrounded by people she loved, who loved her back. A person can't ask for more than that. Besides, neither my dad nor Gran would want me to be sad over their loss. They always wanted the best for me—to be happy and to live out my dreams. So, that's what I'm trying to do—at least that's what my goal is.

I'm also sure that Gran would have wanted me to sell the house and move on with my life, but I can't do it. I have so many happy memories there. We spent every holiday in that house—Thanksgiving, Christmas, Easter—shoot, even the Fourth of July was spent there. I stayed at least one night a week with Grandma Sophia. She was so much fun, always baking and making crafty things and always buying extra of everything so I could work alongside her. Those were happy times. I need to believe there will be happy times again, with a house full of people I love.

By the time I reach my home, I'm exhausted. As soon as the door is unlocked, I kick off my shoes, and drop all of my stuff at the bottom of the steps. In the kitchen I get a glass of water and see what there is to eat. A loud crash startles me, and I bash my side against the refrigerator as I let out a small scream. "What the hell was that?" My breath is labored, and my heart is beating double time.

Mustering as much courage as I can, I step away from my fridge leaving the door ajar. Creeping toward my living room I round the corner and see it. Glass everywhere. My eyes catch on what used to be my large front window. Jagged edges protrude from the perimeter.

What the...?

Pounding on my back door almost has me screaming again. Cautiously, I inch back toward the kitchen. "Open up, Sophie!"

At the sound of that familiar voice, relief rushes through me. It takes both hands on the doorknob and my foot on the door-jamb for leverage for me to yank the door open. Damn sticky door. With the door open, I peer out at Henry. He's looking amazing in his dark jeans, light-blue shirt, and pink tie. *Pink?* A uniformed officer is right behind him.

Henry's expression is fierce. I don't know any other way of describing it. It's part angry, part concerned. "What was that noise? Did you scream?"

"Um. Yeah. Well—"

"What happened?" Henry demands.

"My front window broke." What else can I say? It's broken. I can't change that now, and life's too short to make a big deal out of a broken window. It could have been worse. Yes, I'm doing my best to keep myself under control. The window breaking *is* a big deal, but what's done is done. "I don't know how. I was in the kitchen when I heard it break."

Henry and the officer stride past me into the living room. "Got any lights in here, Soph?"

I reach around the edge of the wall and flip the switch. This room has an old light fixture hanging in the center of the room. It's not very bright, but it illuminates the mess enough for me to see just how much glass is there. A lot!

"Jesus," mutters the cop.

"*Jesus* is right." Henry walks through the glass, looking around.

"What are you looking for?" I step toward Henry.

"Stop!"

At his loud demand, I stumble backward, and a sharp pain shoots up through my foot. Perched on one foot, I lose balance, but just as I'm about to hit the ground, strong hands wrap around me.

Henry lifts me into his arms and pulls me close. "I've got you," he whispers.

He carries me into the kitchen and sets me down in a chair before taking the chair next to mine and lifting my injured foot up into his lap. "Damn it, Soph," he mutters.

"Is it bad?" I'm afraid to look.

"Where's your first aid kit?"

I try to stand, but he grunts, "No! Sit still. Tell me where it is."

"Upstairs. In the bathroom cupboard."

He jumps up, and glass crunches underneath his shoes as he makes his way toward the stairs. His big feet make loud clomping sounds as he goes up. A few minutes later, he's stomping back down. With the first aid kit in hand, he sits back down and lifts my foot into his lap.

"You've got several pieces of glass stuck in your foot. Let me pull those out first. Then I'll doctor you up, okay?"

"Okay." I wince and suck in a deep breath, preparing for more pain because this hurts now. Getting things plucked out of my foot is only going to hurt more. I need to let him do his thing. He pokes away with a small set of tweezers from the first aid kit. I squeak in pain when he has to dig in with the little pointy things.

"Shh, I need to get one more," he assures. I hold my breath

until he says, "Got it!"

Thank God.

The antiseptic wipe he uses stings like hell, but the Neosporin he coats over the wound is soothing. The last step is to cover the cuts with bandages. Thankfully, I have every size and type in there.

"There, good as new." Henry smiles at me, proud of his work.

"Thanks, Henry," I whisper giving him a smile because he was sweet to take care of me.

The uniformed cop steps into the kitchen. "I think I found the culprit."

Culprit? Between his gloved fingers, he holds up an object about the size of a baseball. A rock.

"A rock? Someone threw a rock at my house?"

"Apparently."

"Damn it." The fierce look has returned to Henry's eyes. "This is not good. Will you bag and tag that thing? Then head back out and keep doing what you were doing. I've got this from here."

"Sure thing, *boss*," grumbles the uniformed officer. He sounds a bit sarcastic, but I can't be sure.

I turn to Henry. "What? It's fine. I'm sure it was neighborhood kids. There are some ruffians living around here." It's true. Something is always getting vandalized in this neighborhood. My neighbors grumble about it but what can you do? Sure, it's gotten worse in recent years. I'll just have to learn to adapt to the changes. I've got nowhere else to go.

"Ruffians?" Henry laughs.

"Yes! They're always vandalizing stuff around here."

"I suppose that's possible." Henry sounds relieved.

It's not a relief, though. The cost of replacing that huge window will set back my roof repairs by weeks. I could see if my homeowner's insurance would help me out, but my Gran always told me to avoid making claims on insurance—it just makes the premium go up. Now what am I supposed to do about the gaping hole in the front of my house? Maybe dad's contractor friend could come over and board it up. Immersed in my own thoughts, I miss what Henry is saying. "Huh? What?"

"I said..." He grasps both my small hands in his huge ones, pulls me toward him, and then grabs my waist and lifts me slightly so I'm sitting on his lap. "I'll call my brother. He'll have a piece of plywood large enough to cover your window. Some of his guys can come clean up this glass, too. He can order your window, get it at cost."

"Why?"

"Why what?"

"Why would you do that? Why would he have wood and a crew?"

"Baby," he coos, "you can't stay here with a broken front window. It's not safe. And my dad and brother are contractors, so they have lots of materials sitting around and a big crew of guys who can help clean this up."

"I can't afford—"

"Shh, Soph. He won't charge me. Believe me, he owes me. I've saved his ass on more than one occasion."

"But I can't—"

"Babe, I've got this. Let me do this."

"Henry, why?" Being pressed up against Detective Sexy with his arms wrapped around me has my heart pounding.

"Why what?" he whispers into my ear, his breath touching my neck.

"Why are you helping me?" My voice is so soft that I'm not sure he can hear me.

14

HENRY

Why *am* I helping her? Why did I pull her onto my lap? I don't know, but it feels fucking perfect. This tiny beauty was made for my lap, among other places. Her round little bottom has enveloped me in such a way that I'm busy concentrating on other things just so my cock doesn't get any harder.

"Why am I helping you?"

She nods shyly.

My Sophie isn't used to having any help. She's unfamiliar with the idea that there's someone out there who cares about her, wants to protect her.

"Yeah. I know you think you're like my big brother, but—"

"Big brother?" I chuckle. "I've got enough siblings; I don't need any more. Besides, I don't put my sisters on my lap. That would be creepy as fuck."

"You have two brothers, right?"

"I have three brothers and two sisters. I'm the oldest, and then there's David and Keith—you'll meet him tonight, along with my dad, Declan. Then there's my sister, Sandy, my brother, Mick, and the baby, Emily, is ten years younger than me."

"Wow, that must be amazing. I always wanted a brother or sister. I can't imagine what it would be like to have so many."

"They're pains in the ass. I've cleaned up so many of their fuckups." I chuckle. "But I love them. My mom—her name is Sarah—and dad make a big dinner for us on Sundays. I try to make it most weekends, but it's hard when I'm knee-deep in a case. I like to spend time with them."

"So, you're the fixer in your family?" Sophie asks. "You really are the ruler of the house, as your name suggests," she adds. "You take care of all of them, don't you? Do you all get along with everyone? I can't imagine all the different personalities at your dinner table."

She sure is curious. Not a surprise, since she's an only child with no living family to speak of. It's normal she'd have questions.

"We're all close, but I'm closest to Keith. He's my confidant. He's got a girl now. Keith's happy, his business is thriving, and it's cool to see him settled. He's stopped doing dumb shit."

She giggles. "Why? Did he get into trouble?"

"Not legal trouble, thank fuck. But I've saved his ass a couple of times. He had a period when he made terrible choices." I laugh, thinking about all the shit he's pulled over the years. I pull Sophie even closer. "I'll introduce you to them sometime. You'll like my mom and sisters. They're cool."

She turns her head so we're face-to-face and nods. I don't think she believes that she'll meet them. I'm not sure either, but right now all I can think about is the fact that she's so close I can feel her breath on my lips as she peers into my eyes.

This close up, I can see her big, brown eyes so clearly. There are golden flecks around the outer edge of her irises. That's why they sparkle. I slide my hand up until it's at the back of her neck, at the base of her skull, fingers in her silky hair. I nudge her, pulling her forward. *Time to kiss my girl.*

Her mouth opens, letting out a quiet gasp, and that's when I go in for the kill. My lips meet hers, and the second they touch, I feel fucking light-headed. They're as soft as I imagined. Maybe more so. A faint taste of cherry makes its way into my mouth. It's the sweetest thing I've ever tasted. I know, right this second, I'm screwed. At first she stiffens in my arms, but as I slide my mouth over hers and lick her bottom lip, she begins to relax. With a soft moan, her mouth opens a bit more and her lips latch onto my bottom one, sucking just enough to make me hard as a fucking rock. Damn. She'll feel that under her lush little ass.

Sure enough, Soph wriggles around in my lap, feeling my erection, but she doesn't seem to mind. Tangling my fingers in her hair, I turn her face just enough so I can go deeper. My tongue sweeps into her sweet mouth, drawing another moan from Sophie, and I'm a fucking caveman. Without releasing her lips, my hands go back under her arms, and I lift her so she's straddling me. I know this is wrong, but I've never been this turned on in my life.

At first, I think she'll make a move to jump off of my lap, but she surprises me. She slides in closer and grinds her pussy into me. If only we were naked. I'd love it if we were naked. It's my turn to moan. I'm gonna toss my stuff into my pants, and that's not cool. Jesus, I should have more control than this. I grab her hips to halt her movement, but I don't try very hard because fuck if it doesn't feel amazing.

I pull my mouth from hers. "Soph. You'd better stop. I'm gonna come in my pants."

"I don't.... Um, I'm almost...."

My sweet girl is going to come? I slide my big hands around to her ass touching her the entire way. When my palms meet her round backside it's a perfect fit. Holding her in place, I thrust upward, helping her along. If I lose it in my pants, so be it.

"Oh, God. Henry...," she pants.

Hearing her say my name in that way is sexy as hell. "I've got you, baby. Let go."

"I'm gonna... ahhh, oh shit," she moans. "Henry...," she says with a breathy voice.

I wrap my left hand into her hair again and pull her in for a deep, frantic kiss. Watching her lose control like that is absolutely, hands down, the hottest thing I've ever seen. She's so innocent and pure that seeing her dirty and wanton makes me feel proud—proud that I made her writhe like that in my lap. Damn, this woman will be my undoing. Ah fuck, I'm so screwed.

She tries to jump out of my lap, but I hold her in place. I suspect she's either embarrassed or regretful. Maybe both.

"Soph?"

When her only response is to push my hands away, I let her go. I won't hold her captive if she doesn't want me to touch her.

"Soph?"

"Um, Henry. That was...."

I'll help her out. She obviously regrets what we did. "That never should have happened. I'm sorry." I stand up from her kitchen chair and turn to walk out the back door, saying, "I'll call my brother. He'll be here before the night is out to get you squared away. Call me if you need anything."

I hesitate in the doorway for just a second. Am I doing the right thing? With my hand on the doorknob, I turn to look at her. Yeah, I'm doing the right thing. She needs space.

"Okay?"

"'Kay," she whispers, not making eye contact with me.

15

SOPHIE

Wow. How could something that felt that good make me feel like utter crap two minutes later? I wanted to tell Henry how amazing it was, but before I could get it out, he's telling me how much he regretted it. I made him do that. I was acting like a damn slut. Jeez. He felt sorry for me because those hoodlums broke my window. My life is a hot frigging mess. He gave me a sympathy orgasm. At least he gave me an orgasm, a first from anyone other than myself. I should be thankful, not humiliated beyond imagination. But humiliated I am.

An hour later, there are about ten men roaming in and out of my house, two of whom look like Henry. One of them is an older version, and one is about the same age as Henry. The older guy directs the crew as the younger Henry hammers and nails the boards into place. By ten o'clock, my front window is boarded up and my living room is glass-free.

Before the two Henry look-alikes leave, the man himself steps in the front door and introduces me to his father, Declan, and his younger brother, Keith. He explains to them about the murder that occurred in my carriage house. That was the only explanation he gave as to why he asked his family to help me. He didn't stand near me. He didn't touch me.

Keith told me he'd order my window. "It'll take a couple of weeks to get in. It's a big window, so it'll be a special order."

"Thank you so much! Please be sure to send me the bill, okay?" *A special order? That will be expensive.*

Keith and Declan wink at me as they follow Henry out the door.

Three full days pass without word from Henry. Why would he want to see a hussy like me? When I do finally see him, it's at the bridal store on Friday. He opens the door to Bridal Belles late in the afternoon—to pick up his tuxedo, no doubt. Working in the back of the store, I see his reflection in the mirror as he enters. He doesn't even look over to my side of the shop as he walks straight to the tux area.

Just to punish myself, I sneak into the back room so I can listen to Henry and, hopefully, see him in his tuxedo. He's got a body made for a tux.

"Well, hello, Henry. We've got your tux right here, and I'm positive it will fit you like a glove," preens Brooke.

"It'd better. The wedding is tomorrow."

As soon as he exits the dressing room, I gasp. Damn, I hope he didn't hear that. He looks amazing. The bride chose the *Downton Abbey*-style tux. It suits Henry and makes him seem so debonair and sexy.

"Wow, you're amazing in that tuxedo, Hank," coos Brooke. "Too bad I couldn't get you to model for us. You'd really draw the brides into our shop."

"No thanks. I've got a job," he grumbles.

Just then, I hear Ashley's voice. "You should show Sophie how you look in your tux. I can get her. She's here somewhere."

"Nope. I'm good," he says, sounding annoyed.

Oh, hell. Tears start to burn in the back of my eyes. When he says he doesn't want me, it hurts way more than I thought it would. A small part of me was hoping he was just trying to be gentlemanly. I guess not.

I tiptoe back over to my area, so he won't catch me listening. That would make me even more pathetic than usual. I can still hear them over there, though. He thanks them, and when the front door opens, I watch his reflection in the mirror at the back of the store. He doesn't even turn back.

I race to the bathroom and shut the door. The last thing I need is for Brooke to catch me crying. Once I've stopped sobbing like a damn baby, I wash my face with cool water to diminish the red blotchiness. I use my hands to tidy up my hair. As I exit the employee restroom, I nearly run in to Ashley.

"I'm sorry, Sophie. I was just trying to nudge things along with him since I saw you hiding in the back room. I thought for sure he'd jump at the chance to talk to you."

"It's fine, Ash. I told you he wasn't into me." I turn and walk back to my area. She doesn't follow me. She can tell heartache when she sees it, and heartache doesn't like company.

On Saturday afternoon, I think about Henry and the wedding. I bet it's beautiful. I also bet that Henry's date is lovely and confident. I can imagine him dancing with her right this minute. I sigh at the thought. What would it be like to be Henry's date? His girlfriend? It's not in the cards for me. It's for some other lucky woman to get that honor.

After work on Saturday, I trudge home. It's hot and muggy outside. My black work ensemble is sticking to my body by the time I make it home. I've turned off my window air conditioners because the plywood window lets in a lot of heat. That would mean the thing would run all day long without shutting off, and I can't afford that utility bill. It also means my house is a sauna.

I pull off my clothes as soon as I shut the door. No one is around to see me in my bra and undies, since the police have stopped hanging out at the carriage house. There's still yellow crime scene tape here and there, but it has been cleared for me to sort through his things.

When Willy's sister Julia came to town, she peeked into his apartment through the barricaded door and shook her head from side to side. "No way. I want none of that stuff. Get Goodwill or whatever to come and get it. It's not my problem, anyway. He was *your* tenant."

What kind of sister would not want to go through their brother's things? What if he had something sentimental in there?

She had interrupted my thoughts by saying, "I'll be back in a couple of weeks, as soon as the police release his body. I'll make arrangements for him then, and I'll meet with his attorney for the reading of his will. In the meantime, if you find anything of value in there, please hang on to it for me."

Like I work for this woman? "Um, I'm not—"

"It's your job as his landlord," she snapped.

Is it?

"Besides, what else have you got to do?" she said, looking down at me and then around the house and yard.

"Okay," I whispered. I'd have agreed to anything to get rid of the woman.

I might as well get the apartment cleaned up, so I won't have to deal with Julia again. On the plus side, if I clean it out, maybe I can get a renter in there to help offset some of my bills—like the one for the new window, which is going to cost me a fortune. Surely there will be someone who didn't read in the papers about the murder that happened here.

16

———

HENRY

I fucking hate weddings. My brother's is no exception. It's hot as Hades outside, and this church is not air-conditioned. I hope to hell the reception hall is air-conditioned. I'm sweating straight through my stupid tuxedo. David can't feel any better, but it's his own damn fault.

It's a small wedding party with just David, Keith, Mick, and me, but it's a big-ass wedding. As I stand up front, waiting for this stupid ceremony to be over, I notice the packed pews. There's got to be five hundred people in this sweltering church. I see fans flapping around all over the place as I scan those in attendance. I pay special attention to the interested looks from several lovely ladies. One of them even winks at me. If I play my cards right, I'll have a date tonight. Well, *date* is the wrong word. I'll have a quick fuck tonight. That's what I meant. A quick fuck, and I won't think of that cute woman in Edgewater for one second of it. No way.

The wedding ceremony lasts over an hour. Part of the reason is that David's bitch wife makes him recite his own vows to her. I'm pretty sure she wrote the shit for him because in my entire life, I've never heard my baby brother utter such bullshit like: "I give my heart. I promise, from this day forward, you shall not walk alone. May my heart be your shelter and my arms be your home."

When he finished that up, I literally snorted with laughter. My brother, Mick, jabbed me in the ribs to make me stop, but when I looked over my shoulder, I saw Mick and Keith laughing their asses off too. Needless to say, Jen was pissed. Better get used to that, though.

Sure, I laughed at my brother being forced into saying that shit out loud, and while I can't imagine David meaning one fucking word he said, I can somehow picture myself saying those words—to Sophie. When that window broke and she cut her foot, the only thing I wanted to do was wrap her up in my arms and protect her. I wanted to be her shelter, her home. I shake my head. *No.* Sophie Kincaid is not for me. I'm never settling down again, and she deserves way better than this jaded asshole.

After the ceremony from hell, we're forced to stand around for pictures. I swear to fuck it takes another two hours. The entire time, I'm fantasizing about beer and hooking up with one of the single ladies in the audience. I know that's an asshole move after I made my Sophie come on my lap a few days ago, but like they say, the best way to get over someone is to get under someone else, and that's what I intend to do.

The reception hall is blessedly cool and huge. This place must have cost a fucking fortune. Luckily, David's got the green to afford such a place. What a waste, though. He could have put a down payment on a house for the cost of this venue. And the decorations? Over the top. His wife has the place decorated in purples and reds, for some odd reason. There's also a shitload of sparkly glass shit hanging from the ceiling and on the tables. It looks like a fairy threw up in here.

As soon as I walk into the place, I'm granted permission by

the high priestess—the bride—to take off my jacket, vest, and tie. Finally comfortable, I grab a drink and a plate full of food and sit down at the head table next to the maid of honor, Jen's best friend, Kimberly. She attempts small talk with me as I scan the room, looking for my lay for tonight. When her hand slides over my thigh, I get the distinct impression that she'd like to be a contender.

I ignore her hand and find the winker from the wedding sitting at a table in the center of the large ballroom. In her mid-to-late forties, she's a bit older than my usual, but she takes care of herself. Her dress is red and sexy. Her shoes and nails are red too. Maybe she's a little too desperate—she has clinger written all over her, so I make a mental note to avoid her.

By the time dinner is over, I've cleaned my plate and had three bourbons. I'm finally feeling good, festive. Hell, I even dance. First with a redhead who acts coy, but I can tell it's just that, an act. Her dress is expensive, as is her perfume. She's a clone of Angela, my ex-wife. *No. Thank. You.* The maid of honor was a contender, but when I figured out she's Jen's whipping dog, running around like a crazy person doing Jen's bidding, I decided she'd be too tired to fuck after this whole thing ends.

My final choice is a petite brunette who reminds me of *Sophie.* She barely looks legal, so I ask my brother, Mick, if he knows anything about her. He was chatting her up earlier. "Bro, you're crazy. She's not your type, like, at all."

"She's cute."

"Sure, she's cute. If you like that sort of thing."

Mick is an asshole. He's the best-looking one of the Flynn bunch and tends bar at a swanky club downtown, so he's used to getting whatever pussy he wants. He's five years younger than I am—almost thirty and still acts like a frat boy. I should set him up with Blondie One or Blondie Two at the bridal shop. He'd love them.

"You're such a dick, Mick. Grow up," I snap as I walk away, heading toward the brunette. Close up, I can tell that she's pretty, but she's wearing too much makeup. Her dress is expensive, probably made just for her. Her hair is long and curled perfectly. She's nothing like my Sophie—too polished. As I approach, I overhear her speaking to another young woman.

"God, did you check out her dress? Hideous. She's *so* fat."

She's definitely *not* my Sophie. Sophie would never say something mean about another person. She's too good—too sweet and kind. The only similarity between Soph and this bitch is their height. I pivot and make my way to the bar. Time to get stinking drunk with my brothers.

AT ONE IN THE MORNING, my phone buzzes next to my head. I blink to clear the haze left over from too much bourbon. The insistent buzzing won't stop. I pick it up and gruffly say, "Flynn."

"Henry?" says a shaky voice.

"Yeah," I grumble. I hear the crackle of a storm outside my bedroom window. There's nothing like a storm after a hot day. It's lightning-packed and loud with thunder.

"Um, I'm sorry it's so late. But—"

"Sophie?" *She sounds scared.* "What's wrong?" Something has to be wrong if she's calling me.

More lightning illuminates the window beside my head.

"Um, I thought I saw something. Someone...," she says, tentatively.

"What do you mean you saw someone?"

"Haaanky," a whiney voice says behind me.

Fuck!

"You woke me up, Hanky. Did you want to do it again?" she says in a husky voice.

Fuck!

"Oh, um, I'm sorry to bother you. You sound busy." Sophie rushes the words out.

Click. The phone goes dead. She hung up on me.

"Sophie? Sophie!" Goddamn it. I roll over to find out who the hell is next to me. My memory of the reception isn't great right now, but I think it's the lady in red. Looking around my bedroom floor, I spot a red dress and red shoes. Fuck! The clinger. I don't remember bringing this woman home, and I sure as hell don't remember fucking her. I hope to hell I wore a condom.

"Time to get dressed and get out." I know I'm a rude asshole, but I've got to check out what's going on at Sophie's place. She wouldn't have called if something weren't wrong.

"But, Hanky," she whines.

"I've gotta go. Emergency. You can't stay." The truth hurts.

Pouting, Red picks up her shit and slowly dresses.

I pull on my jeans and a T-shirt. As I'm bent over to grab a sock, I peer into the trash can near my bed. Hell, yes—condom. I've never fucked anyone without a rubber, not even Angela, but I was pretty trashed. I jog downstairs to grab my waterproof jacket and car keys. Red takes her sweet-ass time coming down the stairs. I hold the door open for her, and then I'm out the door.

"Aren't you going to give me a ride, Hanky?"

I hate being called Hanky. "Call an Uber," I mutter.

I jog to my garage door and enter the code, hit unlock on my key fob, jump in, and in less than twenty, I'm standing in front of Sophie's house.

Knock, knock, knock.

Nothing. I knock again. Waiting, I decide to text her. She may already be asleep, but her phone should wake her up.

Me: Soph, I'm at your front door. Open up.

Sophie: ...

Those little dots moving back and forth as she types her response taunt me.

Sophie: Go home.

Me: Open the damn door. I'm getting rained on out here.

Sophie: I'm asleep. Go home, Hanky.

Fuck. She heard.

Me: Please, Soph. You worried me. You saw someone?

Sophie: ...

Me: Let me in. Please.

Sophie: It was just a bad dream. I'm fine. Go home, Hank.

Me: Soph, open the fucking door!

No response. Not even the scrolling dots. She won't let me in. *Damn it.*

17

———

SOPHIE

I saw someone in my backyard. I woke up when a huge drum of thunder sounded. Lightning followed it closely, and then more thunder. I got up and used the restroom and grabbed a glass of water. As I passed my window, lightning struck again, and that's when I saw him. A silhouette, standing at the edge of the garage. It wasn't a bad dream.

I quickly crouched down so the dark figure couldn't see me standing there. My room was dark, but I didn't want to take any chances. My first thought was that I was just imagining it. The storm was raging out there. Storms that come off of Lake Michigan can be strong. The thunder sounded again, and I waited for the lightning just to be sure I was mistaken. But when the sky lit up, I saw him again, and this time, he was closer to my house. I panicked. I had Henry's number programmed in my phone, so I grabbed it from my nightstand and hit his number.

When he answered, I knew he'd been asleep. I felt terrible about waking him, but he'd told me repeatedly to call him if I need anything. This was definitely a good reason to call a cop. There shouldn't be anyone lurking in my yard at this time of night. But when I heard the feminine voice in the background calling him "Hanky," I was hurt. I was more upset about that than about a potential killer on my property. In that split second, I didn't care what happened. *Do your worst, psycho guy in my yard.*

When he had the gall to show up at my door, I wasn't about to let him see me with red, puffy eyes. I'm honestly not a big crier, and crying over him is a waste of time, but I can't help it. I'm probably just overtired and emotional thanks to everything that's happened between Willy and work. That's it. I'm stronger than this. If I can get through the drama at work and Willy's death, I can live through Henry Flynn. Peeking through an upstairs window, I watch Henry's car pull away from the curb and drive down the street. I sigh as I crawl back beneath my sheets and lay my head on my pillow. I know sleep is going to be impossible, but I've got to try; otherwise, work is going to be a real B-I-T-C-H.

My alarm sounds early for a Sunday. I drag myself out of bed, take a long shower, and prepare for work. I fill my favorite travel mug to the brim with coffee, and then exit my house, locking the door and clomping down my front steps. As I turn toward the "L," a figure steps out from between two cars parked along the street and shouts, "Sophie!"

Startled, I drop my cup and watch it split right in two, pouring the nectar of the gods on the sidewalk. I look up and see Henry.

"Jesus, Henry! You scared the crap out of me. And you made me break my favorite travel mug!" I reach down and pick up the pieces, seeing it's unsalvageable. When I stand back up, Henry is right in front of me, so close I can smell his aftershave. Or is that just eau de Henry?

"Sorry, babe. I thought I'd stop by to see how you were this mornin'. Where are you going?"

I attempt to walk around him, but he touches my arm. Hesitating, I answer, "Work. I've gotta go. I'm running late."

With his hand still on my arm, he walks around to face me. "Work? You don't work on Sundays."

"We're shorthanded. Brooke needed me to cover."

He steps closer. "Babe, before you go, tell me what that phone call was about last night."

"Nothing. Just a bad dream."

"Soph, I know you wouldn't have called me unless it was important. What happened? What spooked you, sweetheart?"

Sighing, I look up at his beautiful blue eyes, and my heart stops because he looks worried. Heck, I'll just tell him. "I saw someone in my backyard last night."

"What? Who?"

"I don't know. It was raining hard, and when the lightning hit, I saw someone standing next to my garage."

"It could have been a uniform. They're still checking on you from time to time."

"Well, maybe, but I watched, and when the lightning hit again, the figure was closer to the house. I couldn't make out a face or anything else, but it freaked me out. That's why I called."

"I'm sure it was nothing, but let's walk back and check out your yard. We might see footprints since the yard is still wet."

"Okay, but I've got to get going. I can't be late. I'm the only one working today, and it has to be open right on time or Brooke will kill me."

We walk between my house and the neighbor's and into the backyard. He motions for me to stay near the edge of the house as he checks things out. He first walks over to the carriage house and then takes the sidewalk up toward my house. "Here? Is this where you saw them standing?" He points to a spot in the middle of the grassy area.

"Yeah. I think so."

"There are muddy footprints here."

The tracks stop on my back door, and there's a piece of paper stuck into the crack between the door and the jamb. He stalks up to the door, but before reaching for the paper, he pulls out a white cloth, using it with his first finger and thumb to pull the paper out of the crack. Careful not to touch the note with his actual fingers, he lets the folded paper drop open.

"Fuck!" he shouts.

"What? What is it?" Henry is freaking me out.

"I shouldn't show you this, but you need to know."

I step up to him and lean over his open palm. It looks like a ransom note, but not.

Your next, you fucking bitch. Your D E A D.

"They spelled *you're* wrong. Twice. It should be *Y-O-U*-apostrophe-*R-E. You're.*"

"That's all you have to say? They misspelled two words on your death threat note?" Henry chuckles coldly. "That's it! You're not staying here anymore, Soph. Did you find another place to stay?"

"I'm not going anywhere. Someone is just trying to scare me. Nothing will happen to me, Henry." I turn and walk back to the front of the house.

"Where are you going? This is serious," he says, following close behind.

"I've got to get to work. I'm late. I need that job. Jesus, don't you ever listen?" *No. He doesn't.*

"Sophie, I need to make a report about this. You'll need to come down to the station with me."

"I can't! I've got to go to work!" I shout, jamming my hands on my hips. "You can do the report yourself. You were here too."

"Come on, baby—"

"And stop calling me 'baby'!" I scream as I stomp as fast as my short legs will take me away from him. He's exasperating. He probably calls all women *baby*—like the woman from last night. God, such a chauvinistic thing to do!

"Katherine Sophia Kincaid. Stop right there!" he shouts.

I spin around to face him. "You did not just say my entire name. I'm not a child. I'm not *your* child. I'm—what the—" I'm lifted off the ground and thrown over a large shoulder. Henry is carrying me in a fireman's hold. "What the hell, Henry?"

"Fine. I'll take you to work, but as soon as you're finished, you must fill out a report. I'll start it for you." He carries me over to the passenger side of his car. I hear it chirp and then see his fancy space-age car doors rise. He sets me on the ground and points to the seat.

"I can take the 'L.'"

"Get in the fucking car, Sophie," he grumbles.

"I want to take the—"

His arms wrap under my legs as he lifts me up. After setting me in the seat, he reaches across and buckles me in. "If you so much as move from this car, I'll turn you over my knee, bare your ass, and spank you until you're red as fire. Do you understand, Sophie?"

I swallow deeply and whisper my response. "Yes."

"Good. Now," he says, leaning menacingly over the open doorway above me, "I'll take you to work if you promise to meet me after work to fill out the papers."

"Yeah. Okay," I grumble in defeat.

He shuts my door and jogs around to the driver's side, slips inside, buckles up, and presses the start button. Sliding it in gear, he pulls away from the curb. I remain silent, looking out my window at the sights before me. I refuse to be the first one to speak. Before I know it, Henry is pulling into a Starbucks.

"What do you want to drink?"

"Nothing." I stare out my window, unable to look at him.

"Sophie," he whispers. "What kind of coffee do you like? I'd like to replace the cup you dropped. You've had a long night. You need the caffeine. If you don't tell me, I'll just get you what I like."

"That's fine. Just whatever." I know I sound like a complete brat, but I'm reeling from everything. His lady friend from last night—I can still hear her squeaky voice. *Haaanky, do you wanna do it again?* Sickening.

"Fine," he mutters and then stomps onto the sidewalk.

I should hop out and run away, but I don't feel like it. The ride to work is a nice change. I'll be early.

When he comes out of the store, he's holding a travel mug just like my old one. *That was nice, I guess.*

"Here. I got you café mocha. It's my favorite."

It's my favorite too. "Thank you, Henry."

I call a truce with the man; that's my only olive branch because I have no intention of going down to the precinct after work.

His car stops in front of the shop, and I open my door. Before I can step out, he reaches an arm over and says, "Soph, be careful."

"I will. Thanks for the ride, Henry. See you later."

"You'll see me after work, right?"

"Right." I smile sweetly. *Not a chance, Hanky.*

The shop is dead all day. Sundays are never great anyway. I have two no-show brides. They must have purchased their dresses elsewhere. A lot of them neglect to cancel their appointments with other shops if they find their dress. It sucks, though.

My third bride comes with two friends. When it's just the bride and a couple of friends, it almost never means they are there to buy. Now, if a bride brings her mother along, then I know they're serious. I've even had a woman or two who weren't even engaged yet. They *knew* it would be soon, though. They were probably right, but it's still a waste of my time to play dress up with these women.

It's hard work being a wedding dress consultant. Every appointment lasts about an hour and a half, to give the bride enough time to try on ten to fifteen dresses. Each dress weighs a ton. I carry gown after gown back and forth between the showroom and the dressing room. Not only that but cinching a bride into each gown with industrial-sized spring clamps is difficult. My hands and my grip are strong now because of that.

When I first started this job, my hands ached from using those silly clamps. But they help me tighten a gown at the back of the dress so the bride can see what the dress would look like in her size. We only keep one dress of each style in stock, and those samples vary in size. So, if a tiny bride likes a dress, and we only have a size fourteen, I have to cinch the heck out of the thing so that she looks good in the dress. Getting it to fit takes time and practice. I'm good at it now. But I think my best skill is adding a veil and accessories to their favorite dress so a woman can see what she'd look like on her wedding day. That's when the tears fall. I love that part because its romantic, and it means a sale.

My commissions make this job bearable. I make anywhere between 5 and 10 percent commission depending on the designer. I don't try to push my brides toward those 10 percenters. I let her choose. I may slip in one worth more but never pressure a bride to pick that one. It's her day. Brides usually have a vision for their wedding, and I refuse to place pressure on them about the dress. My rule? She has to *love* her dress. She has to be emotionally attached to it, or I don't like to sell it to them. Not every bride has that tearful moment, but many do, and it's my job to know the difference.

After work, I close the shop and head out. Payday was Friday, and since I had done no shopping over the weekend, I decide to treat myself to some decent food. I rarely splurge on anything like that, but I think I deserve it.

Stopping at the market in my neighborhood, I pick up a bottle of red wine, a small steak, and a heat-and-eat, twice-baked potato from the deli case. I grab a few necessities, and when I check out, I ask for paper instead of plastic like a good human. I pay my hefty bill and begin the short walk home.

The route to my house is a little strange. I have to walk down steps to the lower street level to get there. As I make my way down the steps, I notice there are several others moving up and down; it's busy for a Sunday night. About halfway down the stairs, I feel pressure on my back and then a big push. I fall forward at a rapid pace. I can't grab the rail because my hands are filled with grocery bags. I try to scream, but it comes out a painful screech instead. There is no one in front of me, so I free fall down and down until I hit the concrete sidewalk below. I land hard, right on top of my bags. I hear the crack of glass before the pain hits. Red fluid, like blood, runs out of the bag and onto the concrete. My wine. The bottle must have broken on contact and cut my hand open.

"Honey? Are you okay?" asks an older woman.

Shaking, I say, "Uh, I think so."

"Someone pushed you, darlin'," says a man nearby.

"Huh?"

"Someone pushed you. I didn't see their face, but that was deliberate. Do you have enemies?"

"Me? No. Not—I don't think so," I mutter. I know I sound confused. I *am* confused.

"Do you need help getting up? Do you want me to call an ambulance?" the older woman asks as she sees the blood dripping from my palm to the ground.

"No. I'm fine." I stand up and realize that I've reskinned my knee, tearing holes in another pair of leggings. My arm is sore, and my hand is bleeding a lot.

I grab the roll of paper towels from my bag, tear it open, and wrap my hand in several sheets. I sift through the bags to see if anything is salvageable. Not much, at least nothing worth dragging home now. I toss everything in a nearby garbage can and limp home.

When I approach my house, I gasp at the sight of someone sitting on my broken front steps.

Walking toward me, he says, "Sophie. I thought I told you— What the hell happened to you?"

Henry! I run to him, desperately needing someone to hold me for once. *Damn it. I'm scared and tired and in pain.*

He wraps his big arms around me as I cry. *Crying* isn't the right word for it. I bawl in his arms. I'm sobbing so hard I'm shaking.

His arms pull me in tightly as he whispers sweetly in my ear, "Shh, Soph. It's going to be okay." It helps, but I can't stop crying yet. "Baby? What happened? Tell me. Let me help."

After listening to him reassure me, I pull away and show him my hand. "Someone... somebody pushed me down the steps over on Malcolm Ave."

"Pushed you?" He examines the gouge in my hand.

"There were witnesses. I didn't see anyone, but I felt a hand on my back and a push that sent me down the steps. I was holding grocery bags. My bottle of wine broke, and I cut my hand on the glass."

"This is serious, Sophie. First the rock, the person in your yard, the note, and now this."

"Well, there was one other thing."

He looks at me with fear in his eyes. "What other thing?"

"Remember that day I was limping?"

"Yeah."

"Well, it was because I was nearly run over by a car. I thought it was just a strange accident, but in retrospect—after the warning note in my door and seeing that guy in my yard last night—it got me thinking. They gunned the engine and headed straight for me. Maybe all these events are linked."

"Jesus. I'll need to talk to Kent. This may have to do with William's murder. You aren't safe here, Sophie." He looks at my hand. "You need stitches. There may still be glass in the wound. Let's get you over to the hospital," he says, sounding distant.

I pull away from him. "I can't afford the emergency room. My insurance isn't great."

"A walk-in clinic? You need a real doctor for that cut. I'm good, but not that good."

He leads me to his car and opens my door for me. I slide into the seat. He buckles me in and runs around to hop behind the wheel. Since it's Sunday, there's no traffic, and the walk-in clinic is relatively quiet. I'm in luck and get in to a physician's assistant in less than an hour. Thirteen stitches later, I'm out the door.

"We're stopping at your house so you can pack a bag. You're coming home with me."

"Henry. No. I'm not staying with you."

"Please, Sophie. Don't argue with me. I've got two extra bedrooms. I need to get you to a safe place so Kent and I can figure this out."

I sigh. "Fine." I don't have the energy to argue. Besides, I'm scared. Feeling safe is exactly what I need right now.

18

———

HENRY

When we pull into my attached garage, I turn to see that Sophie's dozing. The events of the evening have worn her out. She needs one of her pain pills, but the doc said not to give them to her on an empty stomach. I'll need to ask her when she last ate, but something tells me it was a while ago, since she was carrying groceries home when she fell—I mean, when she was *pushed*.

Damn, this is not good. I just can't see all this being about William's murder. William was murdered by a professional, a hired gun. If a hired killer wanted Sophie dead, she'd be dead. That thought gives me shivers up my spine. *My Sophie.* I can't let anything happen to her. She's too special. She's different than the other women I've dated. She's definitely different than Angela. If I really think about it, I'd say she's my ex-wife's complete opposite—and not just physically, but there is that. Angela was tall and willowy; Sophie is petite and thick. Angela was manipulative, bitchy, and a gold digger. Sophie is sweet, kind, and a bit naïve. See? Opposites.

I turn off my car and hop out. I open her door and whisper, "Sophie, wake up. We're home." *We're home?* As in *we* are home? Sophie and I are home. It is strangely comforting thinking about Sophie living with me. I've never wanted a woman sharing my space, not even my wife. I snort at that thought.

Startled, Sophie jerks upright and blurts, "Are we there yet?"

"Yep. Come on, let's get out of this heat." Even late in the evening, it's still damn hot. "I'll grab your things. Just go in through that door there." I point to the one and only door.

I pop my trunk and grab her small carry-on bag and smaller makeup bag thing. You know the kind? Chicks always have them. I follow her in through the kitchen, stopping just behind her at the edge of the massive living room area to watch as she stares in amazement at my place. *Yeah, it's pretty fucking awesome.*

"Wow, Henry. This place...." She spins, taking it all in. "This place is amazing. How can you afford a place like this on a policeman's salary?"

"It's a long story. I'll tell you about it later. Here, follow me." I lead her upstairs to the bedrooms. I'd love to take her to my room, but I'm not sure I'm ready for that. I take her to the room right next to mine. The bathroom is next to this room, so she can easily get there when she needs it. "Here's *your* room." I lead her in and set her bags on the floor. "Go ahead and put your things in the dresser or closet. They're empty."

I step out the door again. "Here's your bathroom," I say, pointing at the door next to hers. She pops her head out of her room to see where I'm pointing. "There's a shower and a bathtub in there. You're not supposed to get your stitches wet, so a bath might be best."

"I'd love to take a shower. I only have a bathtub at my house. It would be a nice change."

"I can get a baggy and wrap your hand up for you. Give me

a second." I run back downstairs to my pantry and grab a large Ziploc bag, along with a sandwich size. I also pick up the roll of duct tape I keep in my junk drawer. This should keep the water out. I run back upstairs and see Sophie pulling sleepwear out of her bag. "Here, let me wrap up your hand."

"Okay. Thank you, Henry," she whispers.

"You shower, and I'll change, and then I'll order us some food. You need to eat before you can take a pain pill—Doctor's orders. How does pizza sound?"

"Good."

She hasn't looked me in the eye since we got up here. As a matter of fact, I could swear she's doing everything she can not to look at me. What? She's acting shy with me now? I go out of my way to look at her face to test my hypothesis. Damn it if she doesn't pretend to take a keen interest in her fingernails. "Babe, what kind of pizza do you like?"

"Any kind is fine."

"Anchovies?" I snicker. I hate anchovies, so I hope she does too.

Her face squishes together. "No. Gross."

I chuckle. "Then tell me what you like, sweetheart." I like the sound of that question.

"Veggies. I usually get a veggie lover's, but I like pepperoni or Canadian bacon too. Anything—well, except anchovies."

"All right. Let me get changed, and I'll get that ordered."

"Okay."

I watch her walk into the bathroom, clutching her clothing and girly products. I step into my room, pull off my clothes, and slide into a pair of sweatpants. Finally, time to relax. As soon as I'm dressed, I hear my name being called from the bathroom.

"Yeah, babe?" I step out and see her head peeking out of the bathroom.

19

SOPHIE

"Um, I can't figure out how to turn on your shower. It's like a little computer or something. It's beeping angrily at me."

Henry laughs. "Oh shit, I forgot. It is a little complicated."

"Oh, no, um, Henry?" He's about to walk into the bathroom, and all I've got on is the tiny towel that was hanging in here. It's larger than a hand towel, but not by much. My important bits are covered, but there's still a lot of flesh showing. I'm sure I'm pink with embarrassment.

As he steps into the bathroom, his eyes fall to my breasts and then travel down to my knees and back up again. It was almost so fast I could have missed it if I weren't so self-conscious.

"Here, let me show you how it works." He motions to the control panel that could have come from the movie *2001: A Space Odyssey*. It matches his sleek bathroom, with its slate tiles in the shower and gray granite around the vessel sink basins. It's masculine but not in a bad way.

Henry rests his left hand on my left shoulder and moves me toward the panel so I'm between the shower and him. His hand is big and warm. His fingers feel slightly rough, callused. I like how it feels against my now overheated skin. He leans over me, resting his other hand on my right shoulder. He's tall, so when I turn my head, I'm eye level with his shirtless chest.

Dang, he's got a great chest. He's got abs you only see on movie stars too.

He squeezes my shoulder. "Okay, this control sets the temperature for your shower. Anywhere between 100 and 110 degrees is optimal," he explains. "Any hotter than that is a bad idea. If you need a cold shower"—he guffaws—"then try in the ninety-degree range."

"Ha, ha. Hilarious, Henry."

His hands slide up my shoulders, closer to my neck, and squeeze.

A moan slips from my lips. It feels so good.

"Your skin is so soft," he says almost absently.

"Thank you." What else do you say to that? Should I tell him about my beauty regime? I giggle to myself.

He squeezes the spot close to my neck. "Wow, you have knots. Not surprising. You've been through so much. Let me give you a little massage."

I don't argue with him. He uses his big, warm hands to loosen those muscles. I let my head fall back onto his chest and moan again. A chill brushes my back, and I realize he's pulled away from me. I whimper with the loss, but when I feel his lips on my neck, the whimper turns into a sigh.

"Baby, you need to stop making those little noises. You're making me crazy," he whispers in my ear. He kisses and then licks my neck right below my ear, and my nipples get hard.

How does he do that? I let out a shaky breath.

"You like that, Soph?"

"Yeah," I whisper.

He moves to the other side of my neck while his hands move

down to my breasts where I'm clutching the towel for all it's worth.

"Let go of the towel, baby. Let me see you."

"No." *No way.* I clutch the towel tightly to my body. "Henry?"

"Yeah?" he says between soft kisses on my neck.

"That woman..."

He stops kissing but his hands stay put. "Don't Soph. She was nothing. A wedding hook-up." He smiles down at me. "A mistake." He blinks before he adds, "I don't even know her name."

I roll my eyes but nod. It makes sense.

He tugs at the towel, and I let it drop. I have no willpower when it comes to this man.

"You're so beautiful."

"Henry, what are you doing?"

"What I've wanted to do from the first time I saw you. The first time you had your little arms wrapped around me in the tux shop."

His hands slide up to cup my breasts. It feels so good. I arch a bit, so he knows I like it.

"Look how perfectly you fit in my hands, Sophie."

I ignore him because I don't want to look at myself. I want to feel.

"Sophie. Look. We fit like we're made for each other."

I look down and watch him run his thumbs over my hard nipples. I'm trying to keep my sounds to a minimum, but seeing his hands on me is hot as hell.

"Let me help you in the shower, babe. You can't wash with one hand."

"Oh, no. I can do it." Him in the shower means he won't have clothes on either. I'm not prepared for a naked Henry.

He opens the door and nudges me in under the spray. I turn

back just as he's pulling off his sweatpants. My jaw must be on the floor. I swear, I've never seen a more beautiful man. Shoot, a more beautiful person. He's perfect, everywhere. I've only been with one other man, and he was nothing like this.

Henry slides in behind me and reaches above my head for the shampoo. "Put your head under the spray so I can wash your hair for you."

I stand still as he runs suds through my hair. It feels so amazing. Grabbing the bottle of body soap, he pours a liberal amount in his hands. He starts with my breasts and rubs them until they're covered in soapy bubbles and my pink nipples are poking out.

I watch as his hand moves down toward my center, and he brushes over my pubic hair. I don't shave or wax, but I keep myself trimmed up. I'm glad because I wasn't expecting anyone to see me naked today.

His fingers part my folds. "Move your feet apart, Sophie."

I step out so he can have better access. His right hand moves back and forth over my clitoris while his left hand strokes over my ass. It's a strange sensation.

"Do you like this?"

"Yeah," I squeak out.

"God, you've got the sweetest little pussy, Sophie."

At his dirty words, I practically whimper.

He's focused his attention on my clit now. I'm panting and so close to coming. My back to his front, I bring my arms up to wrap around his neck, but the height difference makes that a challenge. This stretches me out and causes me to arch even farther. His left hand leaves my ass and moves to my breast. He pinches my left nipple so hard it hurts, but it's enough to make me come. "Henry...."

He turns me to face him. His mouth is on mine so fast that takes me a second to match his passionate kiss. His tongue sweeps into my mouth with force as he envelops me, his arms wrapping around me as he squeezes my bottom. I feel myself being lifted upward.

"Let's move to a bed." He pushes open the shower door, reaches out, and stops the water by touching something on the control panel. Striding out the door with me wrapped around him, he moves to the bedroom he's designated as mine. He lays me down and falls on top of me, getting right back to that kiss.

"Sophie, I need you. I need to fuck you, baby."

"I need you too. Do it. Take me."

"Oh, God. Say my name. Say *Henry*."

"Henry. Please, I need you."

"Sophie, are you... I mean, have you?"

"I'm not a virgin, if that's what you're asking." It's been ten years since the last time. I'm due.

Henry moves his hand down to my clit and rubs gently as his middle finger moves in and out of me. It feels fantastic, but I want *him*. "Please, Henry."

"You're so tiny, honey. I want to be sure you're ready for me."

"I'm ready!" I growl. He's driving me crazy.

Chuckling, he moves up my body until we're face-to-face. "Okay, tiger. Here we go." He nudges his body closer until he's at my entrance. With his arms on either side of my head, he's hovering over me, his hips between my legs. He thrusts forward until he's inside of me.

Oh, holy crap, he's big.

"Jesus, you're so tight. Hold on, Soph."

I put my hands on his shoulders as he thrusts again. He feels even bigger this time. I feel my channel clutching, squeezing around him. Having Henry inside me, above me, around me is making my skin pebble and frankly, it's hard to breathe.

He pulls out and uses the power of his large body to thrust

back in. His upper body comes closer to mine, and my breasts skim across his as he rests on his elbows. His pace increases, as does the force, and it feels so good.

"Jesus, Sophie, you feel amazing. I've never had a pussy this sweet before."

"Thanks," I mutter.

He chuckles a bit and then gives me a serious look. "This pussy is mine, baby. You hear me? No one else gets this. You got me?"

I'm almost there, so I nod frantically. A few more big pushes, and I'll be over the edge, screaming his name. It feels amazing. The only other time I've had sex was with another virgin, in the dark, and it wasn't good. Three more of his hard thrusts, and I'm done for. I come so hard my eyes roll back in my head. I can feel myself pulsing around him. His arms are shaking as he thrusts several more times. He comes, shouting my name this time.

He stays inside me as he catches his breath. "I swear to God, Soph, it's never felt that good."

"Really?" *Shit, I said that aloud.*

"The best pussy I've ever had, sweetheart."

I wince at those words, but I liked the dirty talk while we were, you know, doing it, so I guess I'll have to accept them outside of that too.

"Sorry, Sophie. I should have said, *you're* the best I've ever had," he whispers in my ear. "You're too sweet to hear me talk like a caveman."

"No, it's okay. I liked it. It felt good. But there's only been one other guy to compare you to so...."

"No need to go looking for other comparisons. You only get me from now on," he says cockily.

I smile, sure I'm blushing too. He pulls out, and I look down and see fluid run down my inner thigh. "Henry? We didn't use a condom."

"That's okay."

"It is?" Surprised by his comment, I don't know what to say. I sure don't want to get pregnant right now. I can barely afford myself. Plus, he was with that other woman. Did he use one then?

I'm about to ask him until he asks, "Sure. You're on the pill, right?"

"No."

"The shot?"

"No. I'm not on birth control. I had no reason to be until now."

"Fuck! What the hell? Every chick is on the pill!" His voice is the loudest I've ever heard from him. He's sitting up now, running both hands through his mussed-up sex hair. "Seriously? Sophie? You're not on anything?" he asks like he's hoping for a different answer.

"No. I haven't had sex in ten years. Why would I spend money on birth control?" It's logical, for me at least.

"Ten years? Fuck! How could you go that long without? Never mind," he mutters. He stands up, walks into the hallway, and comes back a minute later wearing his sweatpants. His fists are clenched at his sides.

His expression is dark. His eyes are slits and his nostrils are flaring. I can't help but feel a little scared. I don't know Henry Flynn, not really. "Henry? Are you angry with me?"

He takes a deep breath and says, "Look, I know it's just as much a guy's responsibility as it is the chick's."

Chicks? How old is this man? Sixteen?

"...But shit, if you weren't on birth control, you should have stopped me." He's still pacing. "I can't help thinking that you did that on purpose. Like you got one look at my place and figured I was an easy target. So, yeah, I've got a little money. You probably assumed you'd settle in here, make yourself at home. Set up house. Get knocked up, you know, like a gold digger."

My head snaps back at that comment. I feel the heat of anger roll across my skin as it turns bright pink. "Um, okay. What?" I pull a loose blanket from the bed to wrap myself in. I'm not having this conversation nude. "Henry, I'm sorry. That's not how I—"

"Save it, baby. I know how this works. I was married to a real piece of work, so I know one when I see one. No worries. We can pick up a morning-after pill tomorrow. No big deal," he says as he walks toward the door. "I'll order the food. You get dressed," he mutters.

God, why in the hell didn't I see this coming? *Gold digger? He thinks I'm a gold digger?* Of all the things that guy could have said in that instance, that's the last thing I would have conjured up. I could imagine words like *fat, ugly, boring, vertically challenged, pathetic, terrible in the sack*—you know, words like that—but not *gold digger*.

Holy hell. What have I done? The thing is, Henry's right, birth control is the responsibility of both parties. For him to just assume I was on the pill is just as irresponsible as me having sex knowing I wasn't on the pill. I can't afford a baby, and I sure as hell wouldn't expect Henry to pay for that, especially not now. If I end up pregnant, then I'm on my own. Just like I've been for the last three years.

With a deep breath I pull some confidence and self-respect from deep down inside me. I'll take this in stride. I don't need an ass like Henry Flynn making me feel like I'm nothing—like some whore. I slip out of bed and slip on some comfy leggings and a T-shirt, and then lock my door and turn off the light. I need to get a few hours of sleep before I sneak out of here to go home. No need to interact with *Hank* again. Ever.

Knock, knock, knock.

I must have dozed off, but his incessant knocking has pulled me from my slumber.

"Soph. Open the door." *Knock, knock.* "Come on, baby. Open up. Pizza's here."

I ignore him. If I pretend I'm asleep, maybe he'll go the hell away. No such luck. I hear a key in the lock and then the door squeak open. Light from the hallway pours into the room. I lay perfectly still, eyes closed.

"I know you can hear me. Come on, it's time to eat. You need to eat something so you can take your pill, babe."

He needs to stop calling me babe, baby, and sweetheart. He's got no right to call me any of those things. It's then that I feel his fingers brush the hair away from my face. He's killing me. One minute, he practically tells me he loves me, makes me swear I'm his, and the next, I'm some kind of money-grubbing slut who's using him for his money. No. Thank. You. I've had enough of this emotional roller coaster that is Hank Flynn.

I feel the tear seep out of my eye and hope he doesn't notice it. He does. He wipes it away with his finger and whispers, "Sophie, come on. Let's eat. You need to eat."

Holding myself still, all I have to do is wait it out. He takes a deep breath. "I'm sorry. I overreacted."

No *duh.* He sighs again and sits on the edge of the bed. I feel it sink down near my knees. I wish I were facing the other way, but no such luck now. I'm not moving.

"Here's the deal. I was married once, a long time ago. You know that." He takes another deep breath. "Let me start at the beginning. When I was twenty-two, I won the lottery. It wasn't a huge jackpot, but after taxes, I won about a hundred and twenty-five grand. My dad advised me to put it in the bank until I knew what I wanted to do with it. I was at the police academy at the time and was focused on that. I listened to Dad and stuck it in the bank."

He stands up, and I can hear his feet pacing. I bet he's running his fingers through his hair. I should just open my eyes and let him know I'm listening, but I can't yet.

"Dad also told me to keep the win to myself or people would come out of the woodwork. Like I said, it wasn't a huge amount, but people would still take advantage. Anyway, when I was twenty-three, I met Angela. She was gorgeous. I thought she was the fucking bomb. I fell in love fast and easy. I was so sure she was the one, I told her about my little nest egg, thinking she'd love the idea of using the money to settle down and buy a place, you know, like you do when you meet *the one*."

He sits back on the bed. "She was eager to get engaged after that. She showed me the huge rock she wanted as we passed a jewelry store one day. I didn't want to touch the money, so the ring I bought her was significantly smaller than the one she wanted. I should have known what kind of person she was when she threw a stinking fit about the size of her diamond. She wanted something big and flashy." He sighs.

The bed moves as he readjusts himself, and his hand touches mine, but I remain stock-still. He seems to be trying to apologize, but I'm not ready. Not yet. Maybe not ever.

"I wish you'd look at me, Sophie," he says with another sigh. "So, our engagement was short. She spent a small fortune on the wedding. Her dress was five grand, but her dad paid for most of her side of things. I paid for a honeymoon in Maui that cost me an arm and a leg. For that, I dipped into my money. I regret that."

I look at him and roll over onto my back. His head is in his hands, and when he feels me move, he turns.

"When we got back, she moved into my apartment. She was a bitch from the beginning. She wanted to spend that money on everything from shoes, clothes, and purses to big trips to Europe. I constantly refused to spend it unless it was on a house or something permanent. It wasn't enough for her, though. Six months in, I knew the marriage was doomed. When my little brother caught her screwing one of his friends in an alley behind the club he frequented, I knew it was over."

I gasped at that. *Who would cheat on Henry Flynn? What an idiot.*

"I knew she was cheating on me, or I had suspected it. To be honest, I didn't care. I always wore a condom with her." He looks over at me. "When I filed for divorce, the true bitch came out. She wanted all of that money I had in the bank. I hired a great attorney, but he wasn't good enough to keep her from some of it. The judge awarded her half. So, after the honeymoon and her half, it left me with fifty grand."

That sounds like a lot of money to me.

"I hated to let go of the money, but I was happy to part with it if it meant I never had to deal with Angela again. So, that's what I did."

He's up on his feet, pacing again. "After the divorce finalized, I gave the remaining money to my brother David to invest. He was just getting started at his brokerage firm, and I thought, fuck it, let's see if he can make back my losses. I was right to do that because David is a genius when it comes to money. Picking women, he's as bad as I am." He chuckles but it's not funny.

I'm not sure he meant that against me, but I take it to heart. It hurts.

"So, there's the story of how I got my money and why I'm so protective of it. It's why I'll never get married again and why I don't do relationships, and I definitely had no plans of being someone's baby daddy. Especially not yo—"

I roll over to face away from him. I know what he's saying. *Especially not yours.* That's what he was about to say. He's saying that he doesn't see me as anything permanent. I was just sex, and that was even screwed up because I could be pregnant, and he can never see me as, well, anything. More damn tears fall.

I hear his steps headed toward the door. I hear my door open, but before it closes, he whispers one last thing. "I'm sorry, Sophie."

As soon as my door shuts, I open my eyes again. Tears flood down my face, and my body is shaking from the sobs. I'm not crying over Henry. I'm crying because this day has been emotionally draining. I've got to let it out somehow.

At just after three o'clock in the morning, I gather up the few items I had taken out of my bag and repack. Opening my door as quietly as possible, I clutch my small duffel with my good hand and my smaller bag and purse with the other and tiptoe down the steps. There's a light on over the kitchen sink. It's just enough to help me see my path to the front door. I unlock the door, open it—hoping there's no alarm system—and I step out and down the steps to freedom. I take a deep breath. The air is hot, and there's only a slight wind, but I don't care. I'll find a taxi a few blocks away and go back to my own home. It's where I need to be right now. It's where I belong.

20

———

HENRY

I wait in my car for Sophie to leave for work. When I woke up and saw her door open and her things gone, I wasn't surprised. It was an emotional day, and I didn't make things any better with my rant about birth control and the story of my fucked-up marriage. How could I expect her to stick around after I unloaded all my bullshit?

I watch as her front door opens and she descends her front steps, clutching her precious travel mug and her purse. "Sophie!" I shout.

Startled, she mutters, "Jesus, Henry, would you stop doing that?"

"What are you doing?"

"I'm heading to work. What does it look like?"

"Why'd you leave?"

She stares at me, fluttering her eyelashes as if she can't believe I asked her that question. She puts her hand on her hip and shifts her weight, trying to look defiant.

I repeat myself, emphasizing each word. "Sophie. Why did you leave?"

"Why do you think? I didn't feel welcome last night."

"Oh, I thought I made you feel *very* welcome last night, babe. Besides, I apologized and explained why I reacted the way I did."

"You know what your problem is, Henry?"

"I don't have a problem." I don't. Well, okay, I've got a few issues.

"Your problem is you run hot and cold. I can't keep up. With everything else—my job, Willy's murder, someone trying to hurt me, now I've got *you* to deal with. It...it's just too much," she says, using her hands to emphasize her current chaotic state. "One minute you want me, the next minute you don't. I can't do it." She takes a deep breath. "You can't say all of those things you said last night and expect me to stay in your home. And you can't say all those things you said and show up here and expect everything to go back to the way it was. I've got enough drama in my life right now. I can't add you screwing with my head to the mix. So leave me alone. Do your investigation and leave me alone."

"Soph?" I walk toward her. I need to get to her. I reach my arm out to show her I have a small bag for her. "Here, take this."

She reaches out and grabs the bag roughly. Opening the top, she peers in. Her face turns three shades of red. "Wow! Gee, thanks, *Hank*." She turns to walk away again.

"Babe?"

"No. No. Stay away. Don't come to my house. Don't come to my work. I need to focus on getting my house fixed up now, so I can sell it and get the fuck out of here."

Damn, she said *fuck*. "But what if you're pregnant?" I ask nervously. If she doesn't take that pill, there's a chance.

She sighs. "You don't have to worry about it. I heard you loud and clear last night. I'd never burden you with something like an unwanted child and *baby mama*." She turns to leave.

"Baby? Come back. Let me give you a ride to work."

She stares at me, her expression fierce. It's kinda hot. "Stop. Calling. Me. Baby. Just leave me alone, Hank."

"Come on, Soph." *Why does she keep calling me Hank?*

"Fuck off, Hank!"

"*Henry*. I'm *Henry* to you. I'm *Henry*." I run my fingers through my hair with both hands. I don't like how this is turning out. I have to try one last time. "Sophie? I'm *Henry*."

She doesn't turn this time, but I hear it all the same when she says, "You're nothing to me."

Goddamn. That felt like a shot through my heart, and it fucking hurt. I'm such a dick.

"Fuck, fuck, fuck!"

I fucked this up utterly. What if I can't fix this? What am I saying? I'm a Flynn. I can fix this! I'll let her go for now, but I'll get her back.

ON MY WAY back to work, I stop over at my brother Keith's place. It's lunchtime. I know he'll be home because he's a cheap ass. He tries to eat lunch at home if his current construction job is close enough to his place. He'd rather eat bologna on stale bread than pay ten bucks a day for lunch. Whatever.

"The best course of action in cases like these is to give the woman time. Time to realize that I was just being a dude. Right?" I ask my brother. He's four years younger, but he's been with the same girl for two years now. He'll have great advice for me.

Keith takes a deep breath. This ought to be good.

"So, you're telling me you fucked your girl bareback and then accused her of trying to trap you with a baby?"

"Well, not in so many words—"

"You called her a *gold digger*?"

"Uh, yeah."

"And you liked this girl?"

Why is that past tense? "I still like her. A lot."

"I can see why; she was a nice girl. Not your usual type. Curvy but tiny."

"So? What's your point, *asshat?*"

"My point is, *douche,* you fucked up. You fucked up so epically that I'm not sure you can rebound." He takes a drink of his milk. "Then you told her about Angela?"

"Yeah. I also may have told her I would never get married again, that I didn't do relationships, and I didn't want to be someone's baby daddy."

"Jesus, Hank. Then, to top everything off with a cherry, you bought her a morning-after pill? And waited out in front of her house like a stalker to give it to her?"

"Well, you're making it sound way worse than it was. She thanked me."

"I think you mentioned that she said, 'Wow! Gee, thank you.' Is that right?"

"Yep."

"That was sarcasm, you dumb-ass."

"She's too sweet to be sarcastic. It's just not in her nature."

Keith laughs so hard he's falling off his chair. "It's in everyone's nature to be sarcastic when it's called for—and I'd say it was called for. You. Are. *Fucked.* Dude."

I know. I *am* totally fucked. "I'm just going to hope that she gets in touch with me once she cools off. What else can I do?"

"Buy her some big-ass jewelry."

"She's not the type. She's more of the wildflowers-and-box-of-chocolates kind of girl."

"Then why the fuck did you call her a gold digger?"

"I. Don't. Know!" I yell. I really don't know.

"I'm sorry, man. I really am. She could have been *the one.*"

Could have been the one? I hate feeling it's over with Sophie. What if she *was* the one? I'll think of a way back into her good graces. Yeah, I'll think of something.

Since my brother was absolutely no fucking help, I head to the office. Kent and I are heading over to Luciph Corporation today to meet with the Human Resources director and, hopefully, the CFO. It's been two weeks, and they still haven't sent over the pay stubs or retirement information. We figured a personal visit is in order.

I barely get in the door before Kent stalks up. "Ready to go? I want to get this shit done."

"I'm ready. You driving?" I know he will because he hates my car.

He scoffs. "Fuck, yeah. I hate your tiny piece of shit."

Whatever.

We make our way back down to the street and hop into his hunter green Ford Taurus, circa 1999. The thing really is a piece of shit, but he loves it. He even named it Penelope. I've learned the hard way that you don't ever criticize Penny. Kent can be a crotchety old bastard on a good day, but say something about his car, and you're as good as dead to him.

I wrench open my door and swear I hear her moan, and not in a good way, like when Sophie moans. That's a good way. Fuck! No thinking about Sophie. *Get your head in the damn game, Henry. Solve William's murder and then figure out how to win Sophie back.*

While we drive west, I figure it's a good time to talk about Sophie's accidents. I tell Kent everything that has happened to her and wait for him to respond. In my heart, I can't see this having anything to do with William's murder, but I also can't figure why anyone would want to hurt her.

Kent finally replies, "I don't think it's related to Gibbons's death. It doesn't feel right because his murder seemed very clean, like a contract. If it was the same going on with Sophie, she'd be dead already. Maybe she's got an enemy."

"It's possible, but that doesn't seem right. She's so sweet."

Kent snorts. "Jesus, you've got it bad, don't you?"

"I have nothing bad, fucker. She's a nice girl. Who would want to hurt her?"

"What about work? Does she have enemies there?" Kent says.

"They're bitches, that's for sure. But they're just mean to her. I can't see them doing this stuff. They might break a nail or something." I chuckle.

"Then I don't know. We need to be diligent about it and see if we can find a tie to the murder."

"I guess." I still hate that Sophie is going back to that big house alone. I should have been keeping her safe at my place instead of screwing her and then turning into a psycho about the birth control. "God, I'm such an idiot," I mutter aloud.

"Yeah. You sure are." Kent chuckles.

He doesn't even know what I did to Sophie. *Asshole.*

21

———

HENRY

Walking into the headquarters of Luciph Corporation, I'm stunned at what I see. I've seen some fancy-ass buildings before, but this thing looks like it's from the future—like a hundred years into the future.

"Jesus. I bet there are robots running this place," says Kent with awe in his voice.

"I was thinking the same thing. It's futuristic." There's glass, chrome, and Lucite everywhere. The chairs in the reception area are clear Lucite, as is the reception desk. It makes sense, I guess. Luciph Corporation's primary business is manufacturing plastics.

When we approach the receptionist, she's on the phone directing callers. We wait. And wait. And wait. I look around. The receptionist is gorgeous. She's got long, brown hair that pours over her back in waves. She's wearing black glasses that are fashionably nerdy looking. I don't get that trend at all. Women and those thick, black glasses shouldn't mix. I can see her clothes through her desk. She's wearing a tight blouse that shows a fair amount of cleavage and a short skirt. Since she's sitting, it's pulled up close to her hips. If she moves just a tad, I bet I'll get a glimpse of her panties.

I wonder if she's dressed like that on purpose. She knows we can see everything. She crosses her legs right then, and sure enough, I see black lace. I look up at her, and she's watching me. She winks. If this had been a month ago, I'd have gone for that. But she's got nothing I care to have. She's got on too much makeup and not enough clothing. She's left nothing to the imagination. It's all out there for me to see. Holy hell, what is wrong with me? What am I saying? The *old* Hank Flynn would have been on that like flies on shit.

Jesus, hurry the fuck up.

After an interminable amount of time, she turns to us, directing her attention to me, and says sweetly, "I'm so sorry for your wait. What can I do for *you*?"

Seems sincere.

Kent takes over, as usual. "Yeah. Finally. We're here to see Janet MacClenny in Human Resources."

"Are you here to fill out an application?"

I pull out my badge and flip it in front of her. "Any day now."

She looks irritated by that last comment but only for a split second. "One moment, please." She turns her back to us. I hear her whisper, "It's the police. They want to see you. Uh-huh. Okay." She hangs up and turns back to us. "She'll be right with you. Just have a seat over there, and she'll come to you." She points to the area with four clear chairs.

They look stiff and uncomfortable. They couldn't put a damn sofa in this lobby?

We both turn and head to the seats. Forty-five minute later —yeah, that's what I said, forty-five minutes later—and Kent is spitting nails. I look up and see the tallest woman I've ever seen approach us. She's got to be six feet tall plus, and she's built like a tight end. She raises her hand to shake, but Kent ignores it. "You MacClenny?"

"Yes. It's so nice to meet you. What can I do for you, um, officers?"

"Detectives," I correct her. "Jones and Flynn. May we speak to you in private, ma'am?" *Or is it sir?* I think I see an Adam's apple bobbing around her throat. She's wearing a man's white dress shirt, wide-legged pant things, and a blazer, both black. They're definitely women's clothes, but on her, they look, well, masculine. Her hair is reddish brown and cut short. It's shorter than mine, but I need a trim and a shave. She's got on no jewelry except for a watch. After my perusal, I tune back into the conversation.

"In private? What's this about?" she asks, acting coy.

"William Gibbons," I answer.

"Oh, right. Poor William. Such a nice man," she simpers. "Follow me."

I find it hard to believe she would even remember William, let alone know he was a nice man. This building is massive, and there are thousands of employees. But who knows? Maybe she remembers him.

She leads us into a conference room made of glass from floor to ceiling. Everyone can see us, and we can see everyone else. Hell, even the cubicles in this place are Lucite. God forbid anyone has to scratch his or her ass at work. Everyone would see you doing it. There's absolutely no privacy. Fuck, I wonder if the bathroom stalls are clear?

We sit down at the, you guessed it, clear table. I'm already sick of Lucite. I decide to just get right to it. We've been here well over an hour already, and we've just gotten started. "We're here for William Gibbons's pay stubs and retirement information. You know, the ones ordered by a judge?"

"Oh, that's right. I forgot about that. Hang on, let me check on that for you," she says, getting up from the table. She exits the room and walks to the far end of the large room.

Luckily, we can see everything she's doing.

"Jesus, how long is this fucking meeting going to last?" asks Kent angrily. "They're fucking with us. Just watch, she'll come back with some excuse why we can't have the paperwork."

I know he's right. I watch as she looks through filing cabinets, then looks on her desk a little, picks up her phone, and speaks. She's just wasting more time.

"Let's go," I say, rising from my chair. I open the door and walk toward MacClenny's office.

As we pass a desk outside of her office, a young woman, probably her assistant, tries to stop us. "Sirs, excuse me. Can I—"

I put my hand in the air to stop the admin assistant as Kent flashes his badge this time. She sits back down. When we reach MacClenny's office, she looks up at us. She's still on the phone and holds up one finger to stop us from talking. God, I hate this woman, and I hate this fucking office.

"Right. Yes. I understand," she says into the phone. She hangs up and sighs. "Well, it seems there's been a mix-up."

"A mix-up?" I ask loudly.

"Yes, unfortunately, we don't have those documents for you yet. There was a glitch in our system, and we weren't able to get those printed."

"Can we speak to CFO Chris Collins?" I ask, attempting to sound friendly.

"You mean Christopher?" she corrects me. "Oh, I'm so sorry," she coos. "He's out of the country right now."

Sure he is.

"When will you have those printed?" Kent asks through clenched teeth.

I have no doubt that all she has to do is access his accounts and press print. They're stalling. All this does is prolong the investigation, but it also makes me even more convinced that his murder has something to do with the pay stubs and his retirement accounts. I just don't know what it is.

My thoughts are interrupted by Kent. "If we don't have those fucking documents by the end of the week, I'm getting the DA to charge you with obstruction. You get me?" he growls.

Janet MacClenny flutters her eyelashes, attempting to show fear. It doesn't work. "Oh, dear. Yes, of course. I'll make sure it's done by the end of the week." Then she smiles, and it gives me a shiver.

This woman. There's something about her that makes the hair on the back of my neck stand on end. Yes, she's unattractive, but that's not the issue. It's the fact we know she's playing us. No matter. I can deal with that; I can play the game too. That is until she impedes my murder investigation. Then she's on my shit list. And just now, Janet MacClenny made it to the tippy top of that list.

We walk out of the building and to Kent's car in silence. He uses his key to unlock his door and then reaches over to unlock mine. His power door locks quit working in '09. Jesus, he needs new wheels. I'm surprised it made it out of the city, to be honest. Thank fuck the A/C still works, or he'd have to squeeze his portly ass into my ride.

Finally, Kent speaks. "There's definitely something going on with his money. They're working overtime to delay us. I can't believe MacClenny is doing this alone, though. That fucking CFO Collins is involved. I know it."

"Maybe. We won't know until we get the documents, unless the techs find something. Jesus. This is taking forever," I growl.

Nothing else is said as we ride back to the city, and my mind turns to Sophie again. I can't seem to help myself. Damn, she's beautiful. I remember the feel of her as I plunged inside. So fucking tight. Sex has never felt that good before. Sure, it could have been because I was bareback. That feeling was intense, but she was so unrestrained, like she wanted me as much as I wanted her. Just thinking about her is making my dick hard. That's the last thing I need when I'm in the car with Kent. He'd never let me forget.

Fuck. I should have put on a damn condom. What is wrong with me? I've never gone bareback before. Ever. Even in a drunken stupor, I always remember to wrap it up. Jesus, I wish I hadn't been such a tool. If I'd been nice, she'd be waiting for me at my place tonight. Instead, I'm going home to an empty house, and she's at hers—and she's probably in danger. Fuck!

22

SOPHIE

A week after the end of my *sort of* relationship with Henry, I'm summoned to the office of one Philip H. Gustofson, attorney at law. I know it has something to do with the will, but I don't know why I'd need to be there. Even though I'd known Willy for ten years, we weren't close. We were pleasant to one another, sure. He had a soft spot for my gran and she for him. They played cards together on Saturday nights, and she looked forward to that each week. I think Willy missed her almost as much as I did. But I had been too caught up in my own mourning and struggles to pay attention to Willy's loss. Thinking about that makes me feel regret and sadness, even more so now. Poor Willy.

When I enter the office, I see Julia Gibbons. She's sitting on a plush chair next to the receptionist, dressed to the nines. I think her pink suit may be Chanel—or a great knockoff. Her long hair is styled in a sophisticated chignon at the nape of her neck. Her makeup looks as though it was applied by a professional makeup artist. It's a sharp contrast to her appearance when she visited a couple of weeks ago wearing jeans and an inexpensive blouse. She wasn't overly friendly then, but I'm getting an angry vibe from her today. She's tense, and by her expression, she's not happy to see me.

"What are you doing here?" she spits.

"I don't know. I got a call from Mr. Gustofson. He told me I needed to be here."

"I can't imagine why. You were nothing to him."

"He was my friend."

"Yeah, right," she scoffs.

I ignore her until we're called into Philip's office fifteen minutes later.

"Welcome, Julia and Sophia. Thank you for coming. Let me say how sorry I am for your loss, Julia. William was a kind man. I always enjoyed working with him." He takes a deep breath. "Now, as you can surmise, we are here today for the reading of William Gibbons's last will and testament. You are both here because he has named each of you in this document. If, as I am reading, you have questions, please wait until I've finished with the entire document to ask questions. Sound good?" he asks, nodding to us both.

I nod and smile in response.

Julia mutters, "Whatever."

"Right. Let's begin." Philip reads every single word from the legal document in front of him.

"Last will and testament of William James Gibbons Jr. I, William James Gibbons Jr., a legal adult with the address of 1511 1/2 West Highland Avenue, Chicago, Illinois, 60660, being of competent and sound mind, do hereby declare this to be my last will and testament (hereinafter, "last will and testament") and do hereby revoke any and all wills and codicils heretofore made jointly or severally by me. I further declare that this last will and testament reflects my personal wishes without any undue influence whatsoever.

"At the time of this last will and testament, I am unmarried and without children. I hereby nominate and appoint Philip Gustofson as executor/personal representative of this last will and testament. Should the aforementioned individual be unavailable, unable, or unwilling to serve as executor/personal representative when needed, then I nominate and appoint Julia May Gibbons as the alternate executor/personal representative of this last will and testament. Immediately following my death, the executor/personal representative will be authorized to exercise all provisions of this last will and testament and to use the assets from my estate to make necessary arrangements, without any unnecessary delay, for the payment of personal debts, obligations, and funeral expenses.

"After payment of all personal debts, expenses, and liabilities, I request and direct that my property be bequeathed as follows: To K. Sophia Kincaid, I give, devise, and bequeath $10,000 to assist with expenses while she searches for another tenant for my residence at 1511 1/2 West Highland Avenue, Chicago, Illinois 60660. In addition, I give, devise, and bequeath the entire contents of 1511 1/2 West Highland Avenue, Chicago, Illinois 60660 with the following note."

I can feel Janet's eyes on me suddenly. I shift in my seat, uncomfortable with all of this. What was Willy thinking, giving me money and the contents of his house? I do my best to sit still so I can concentrate on the attorney as he reads Willy's note.

"Sophia, I know you work very hard and may not have the time, but I am leaving you the contents of my apartment. Besides, my sister won't want to deal with it. It will take you a while to go through my belongings to see what you would like to keep, but I suspect you'll like my finds because, like me, you do not judge a book by its cover. Anything you choose to discard you may sell, donate, or dispose of as you see fit. Best wishes to you, sweet Sophia. Sincerely, Willy."

I start to speak, but Mr. Gustofson continues.

"Should K. Sophia Kincaid not be living, then I give, devise, and bequeath all of the remaining and residual property I have ownership in at the time of my death, whether real property, personal property, or both, of whatever kind and wherever situated, to Julia May Gibbons.

"To my only living relative, my sister Julia May Gibbons, I give, devise, and bequeath all of the remaining and residual property I have ownership in at the time of my death, whether real property, personal property, or both, of whatever kind and wherever situated, absolutely and entirely. Should Julia May Gibbons not be living, then I give, devise, and bequeath all of the remaining and residual property I have ownership in at the time of my death to K. Sophia Kincaid. Upon my death, I direct my remains to be cremated and released into Lake Michigan, Chicago, Illinois.

"In witness whereof, I hereby subscribe my name to this last will and testament, as of the date set forth below, at the address set forth below, in front of the attesting witnesses, who also subscribed their names to this last will and testament below on the same date, at my request, and in my company. Signed, William Gibbons Jr. Witness 1, Gladys Johnson, assistant to Philip Gustofson."

As soon as Philip finishes reading the will, Julia says, "So, how much am I getting? I hope there's enough left over after he gives such a big chunk to Sonia," she snipes, pointing at me.

"Sophia," corrects Philip.

"Whatever. How much do I get?"

"As of close of business yesterday, you will inherit approximately $175,483.53"

"What? You're kidding! How? Well, I'll be damned. That little nerd really knew what he was doing." She adds callously, "When do I get it?"

My God, this woman is terrible. I can't believe Willy left her anything. He should have donated to an animal shelter or something—anything but to her. But it's not my business. I feel so touched and relieved that Willy left me anything at all. He has made it possible for me to take the time I need to get the place ready for another tenant.

"Sophia, I have your money here." Philip leans forward, holding a check-sized piece of paper. "You can cash it at any time. Julia, you will need to wait longer. We need to make sure his funeral is taken care of, and then there is probate. Plan on waiting six months to a year for your final settlement amount to be available. Also, plan for the amount I mentioned above to be reduced once all of his outstanding accounts have been settled."

"Well, why does Sonia get her money? That's not fair."

"Because *Sophia's* money was set aside in a different manner than your much more significant amount. William wished for Sophia to continue to live in her grandmother's house."

"What's it to him? Why would he care about these people? I'm his sister!" she exclaims.

"It was William's wish," responds Philip calmly.

"I should fight this. I should get a check today!"

"If you choose to fight, you may lose your entire inheritance to legal fees, and it will prolong any disbursement of funds even further, but that is your choice," Philip deadpans.

"Whatever," Julia mutters. "I'll be in touch." She gets up, turns, and marches out the door.

"Do you have any questions, Sophia?"

"No. I don't. That was very nice of William. He didn't have to do that."

"He cared about your grandmother and for you, and he wanted to be sure you were taken care of just in case. Heed his note to you, Sophia. There's more to that than just words. I'll forward a copy of the will and his note to you in the next week or so."

"Um, okay. Thank you, Mr. Gustofson."

"You're welcome, Sophia. Please, call me Phil."

"All right. Thanks, Phil. Goodbye."

"One more thing, Sophia. The funeral is scheduled for this Friday. I'll email you with the details. I'm sure he would want you to be there."

"Yes, I want to pay my respects. Thank you, Phil."

"Goodbye, Sophia."

When I exit the office, I notice two things: one, Julia is standing in the lobby with her hands on her hips, leg jutting forward, foot tapping. Two, Henry is next to her, leaning his back against the wall with his arms crossed over his chest. He has an angry expression on his face too.

What the heck?

I walk toward the door, doing my best to ignore both of them.

"Sonia. Stop!" shouts Julia.

I stop and turn to her. "Yes?" She's intentionally calling me the wrong name. It's her way of showing me that I'm not worth remembering. People have been doing that to me for years, so it doesn't really sting anymore.

"Remember what I told you. If you find *anything* in his place worth anything, it's mine!"

I blink a few times and then turn to leave. I'm not agreeing to anything. I take a step and feel a big hand on my upper arm. "Sophie, wait," says Henry, quietly.

"I've got nothing to say to you." I attempt to walk away again.

"Please, Soph."

I turn back to face Henry. "You know what? I'm done. I'm done being pressured and harassed, and I'm over being treated like shit." I face Julia. "Willy left the contents of his place to me." I point to my chest. "I highly doubt he had anything of value, since his computers are gone, but whatever is in there belongs to *me*. If you wish to fight this, I'll hire Phil back there and see where you get. Got it?"

Julia just blinks and then glares. "Whatever. Have at it. Bitch. It's nothin' but junk in there anyway. I hope you choke on it."

Wow, what a pleasant woman.

"As for you...." I point at Henry. "I am tired of your mood swings. One minute, I'm *yours*; the next, I'm a gold digger. One minute you want to be my hero; the next, I'm a burden to you. Well, you know what? I do *not* need you. I was fine on my own before you waltzed into my life. And I'll be just fine after you're gone."

Henry nods and runs his fingers through his hair. It's getting long, and his beard is getting thick. He looks like a sexy mountain man.

God, forget about him and his sexiness. He's not for you, Sophie Kincaid. He's not for you!

As I leave, I hear Henry talking to Julia. He's asked her to wait as he speaks to the attorney. I'm guessing she's become a suspect now that she's inherited, but she was as surprised as I was about the money. She's a terrible person but doesn't seem like the type of person who would kill her brother for money. I hope I'm right. Poor Willy.

23

HENRY

Julia agrees to meet me at the station. When Kent met with her at William's place, she was courteous and eager to help. He was confident she wasn't involved. But now that she's inherited, he and I both agree we need to learn more about Ms. Julia Gibbons. While I'm here getting the low-down on the will, Kent is already at the station, preparing for the interrogation. Neither of us have Julia as our killer, but she needs a reality check. Acting like her shit doesn't stink, especially as it relates to Sophie, is not gonna fly with me.

When I walk into the station, Kent is at his old desk. The department bought us all new desks a few months ago, but he refused to switch. His was probably manufactured in the 1970s, and it's solid wood. Our new ones are made of metal and particleboard. They are a hell of a lot easier to move than his thousand-pound monstrosity, but the guy's been with the force for a long while. He should get to use the desk he likes—my opinion. Yeah, the guy's a dick, but he's a good cop.

I step up to Kent's desk. "She on her way?" Kent asks.

"She's behind me. Should be here in a few. Got the room ready?"

Kent loves to use the interrogation room. He messes with the temperature in there, making it hotter than necessary to make our guests uncomfortable. It's miserable for us too, but it works because they always want to get the hell out of the sauna he's created. Kent has read a lot about the psychology of questioning witnesses. Whether or not it works, I can't say for sure, but more often than not, Kent is successful.

He looks past me at the sound of heels clicking across the floor. "She's here," he says anxiously.

This is the shit Kent loves.

"Ms. Gibbons?" Kent asks with a smile, standing up from his desk. "How are you today? You look pretty. Can I get you something to drink?"

"No. I wanna get this over with. I've got a lot to do to get ready for William's funeral."

Kent was hoping she'd refuse the water. The thirstier they are, the better. He's trying to make her feel at ease before he gets to the good stuff.

Kent gives her his signature salesman grin and leads the few steps across the room to an open door as he says, "All right, let's go into our conference room. It's quiet, and we can get through this faster if we can just concentrate on you." He raises his arm to invite her into the room. "After you."

He's such a gentleman. Yeah, right. That thought makes me laugh.

She smiles back at him and obliges. We all walk into the conference room. The temperature is normal now, but one of our guys will change the setting to make it progressively warmer as we talk.

Twenty-five minutes in, and Julia has removed her jacket and unbuttoned the top two buttons on her blouse. She's fanning her face and asking for water.

"We're nearly done. Then we can grab you a water," I say.

She gives me a dirty look. She doesn't like me, and the feeling is mutual.

"Okay, we know you were in Seattle at the time of the murder, but when was the last time you were in Chicago?"

"I've never been here. William and I weren't close. Our parents weren't very loving. I don't think they wanted children. I think they had us because it was expected of them. Look. I'm sweating like crazy. Can you turn the air conditioning up or something?"

"Er. It's broken," I mutter.

She talks about her dysfunctional family life and how William kept to himself growing up and how, especially after he got his first computer, he spent all of his time in his room. She fans her face as she talks, sweat dripping down into her top.

"But he was your only living relative?" Kent asks her again.

"You aren't—weren't—close and yet he left you almost two hundred grand?" I say.

"I'm as surprised as you are. I had no idea he had that kind of money."

"We checked out your bank records. You're having a hard time making ends meet. This money will come in handy," Kent snarls.

"You poked your nose into my finances? That's... that's none of your business."

"In a murder investigation, everything is our business," I reply.

"But...but...."

After an hour in the sweltering heat, I'm at my wit's end. She's got nothing for us. My overall impression of her, though, is that she's defensive but too broke to afford a professional killer. Since we can't find any suspicious bank activity, we rule her out as a suspect. It sucks because we're back to square one. I'm confident she didn't know she would inherit. By the time we let her go, she's sweated through her blouse and the back of her skirt is damp.

"You need to get that air conditioning checked. That was pure torture in there."

"We'll get right on that," I deadpan.

After Julia leaves, Kent and I meet back up in the main room. I drink a bottle of water and pull off my T-shirt—too fucking hot. "So, what's next, oh great one?"

"Don't be a smart-ass. I got a message from the techs today. They've found some financial stuff on one of those flash drives. They're printing it all out and sending it over. I've got a call in to one of our forensic accountants to see if she can meet up with us to look it over. I know *you*," he says pointing at me, "won't understand any of it." Kent laughs like the idiot he is.

At Kent's dig at me, I just shrug. He has no idea I have money. He thinks I rent my house from my dad, which allows me enough money to lease my *"fancy* car." I've done nothing to clarify that. I don't want anyone at the precinct to know about my investments. One, it's none of their business, and two, it would make things awkward around here.

I toss my damp tee over the back of a vacant chair and plop my ass in mine. Leaning forward, I pull my cell from my pocket to turn the ringer back on. We always silence our cell phones when we're interrogating a suspect. It's distracting, and a distraction is prelude to a failed questioning. That's Intro to Cop Class 101.

Scrolling through my texts, I see I missed one from Keith, one from my dad, Declan, and my mom sent one reminding me about Sunday dinner. Damn, I need to hit a Sunday dinner. Maybe Sophie... *ah, fuck.* What is wrong with me? She'll never agree to that, not now.

Interrupting my depressing thoughts, Kent says, "Let's meet

up here tomorrow morning to see what they've got. Sound good?"

"Sounds good."

ON TUESDAY, we meet with the tech who found the financial information along with the forensic accountant at the station. We also get a stack of pay stubs from Luciph Corp, finally! But they only sent stubs from his first three years of employment.

"Swear to God, Kent. I'm holding my gun in my hand the next time I talk to that HR director bitch."

"Calm down. Let's see what we've got. Then we can go into Luciph with guns drawn," Kent says, sounding calm.

He's never calm. What the fuck?

Tanya James, the tech with the flash drives, shows up early to bring up the digital file. She's got stacks of papers with her but wants to show us the points of interest all at once.

The forensic accountant, Gretchen Wright, arrives, and we all sit down and let Tanya lead the meeting.

"Here's what we found. It seems our vic was an accomplished hacker because he got into Luciph's retirement fund database and copied everything from the last seven years."

"Okay, I'm not the smartest tool in the shed, but there's something going on here. The company sent me his pay stubs from the first three years of employment. He's got the last seven years of their retirement data here. Three plus seven equals the ten years he actually worked there. Something began there within the last seven years."

"There's something fishy in Denmark," adds Kent.

I crack up at that. "It's not *fishy* in Denmark, asswipe. It's 'there's something *rotten* in Denmark.'"

"Whatever. There's something about that retirement fund

that had ole Willy suspicious. Suspicious enough to risk hacking into their database," grumbles Kent.

"Agreed," says Tanya.

I turn to Gretchen. "Can you look all of this information over and see if you can figure out what William was looking for?"

"I'll do my best. I have some ideas, but I'll let the numbers tell the story. I'll need a few days. I'll call you as soon as I have something for you."

Standing up, I grab my copies of everything and turn to my partner. "Great. Thanks. In the meantime, we need to pay one very naughty Ms. MacClenny a visit. Got your gun, Kent?"

"Sure do. Let's head out."

When we get to Luciph, the same receptionist is sitting at her see-through desk, wearing another short skirt and blouse that's open at the top. I get a glimpse of a black bra. She looks at Kent and then smiles at me seductively. "How can I help you, gentlemen?"

"We need to speak with Janet MacClenny," I ask, smiling. Might as well play along.

"Oh, I'm sorry. She's out for the week."

"Then we'd like to speak to the person in charge this week," growls Kent.

"Well, let's see..." She pretends to look at her phone list, picks up the phone, and says, "Denise? It's Monica. There are two gentlemen here to speak with Ms. MacClenny." Monica listens into the phone for a moment. "I know. I told them.... Mm-hmm.... Okay, thank you." She turns back and says, "She'll be right out."

"Do you mean right out or forty-fucking-five minutes from now like last time?" Kent bitches.

She attempts to look shocked. "I assume she'll be right out. That's what she told me."

I hope they pay her well. She's great at that lying shit. So we wait. And wait. And wait. Thirty-five minutes later, an average-looking woman with blonde hair walks out. She looks to be in her mid-fifties. She's wearing a long, navy-blue skirt and a red, cable-knit sweater. A sweater in August? She must be cold-blooded.

When she approaches, a fake smile peels across her face. She looks rather ashen. "Hello, I'm Denise Thomas. What can I do for you today?"

Kent jumps right in. "We're here, *again*, about William Gibbons's retirement records. This is your last warning before we get the DA involved."

"Oh, dear. We don't need that. I apologize. I'm unfamiliar with this situation. Let's go back to my office, and I'll see what I can do."

I get the feeling she's telling the truth. And if that's the case, then MacClenny is full of shit. Thomas leads us back to the Human Resources department, points to a conference room on the other side, and says she'll be right with us.

I hope to fuck we don't have to wait again. We sit down at yet another clear table and wait. Luckily, it's only a few minutes.

Denise brings in a laptop and a notebook. "Now, what is going on with Willy's case?"

Willy? She must have known him. "You knew Willy?"

"Yes. I hired him. He was a nice man."

"We've heard the same. We've been asking for his pay stubs and his retirement records, but we've been getting the runaround from your boss."

"Okay. Let me see what I can do for you." She types away at her laptop and then frowns. She types more and frowns again. "Um, this is strange."

I groan. "What is?"

"His accounts are locked up. I can't access them. That's

against company policy. Even if he's deceased, I should be able to get into his files."

"Who has the authority to lock up someone's accounts like that?" asks Kent.

Good question.

"Not me, that's for sure. I'd have to say probably Janet and definitely Chris Collins." She looks up and adds, "He's our CFO."

"We know," Kent and I say simultaneously.

"Is he here today?" I ask.

She shakes her head. "No, he's out of the country, I guess."

Kent groans an expletive I couldn't quite decipher so I ask, "How long has Janet MacClenny worked here?"

"Well, let's see. I've been here twenty years—not always in HR, though." She looks up like she's calculating something. "She came at the same time as Christopher Collins. You know what? I think they used to work together at his last job." She clicks on her computer. "They both started here a little over seven years ago. In April of that year."

"Interesting. Very interesting." Kent nods.

"It certainly is."

"Why?" she asks, looking surprised.

"No reason," Kent adds.

"If I were you, Denise, I wouldn't mention this conversation to your boss."

"Why not?"

"It could be hazardous to your health." Kent snorts.

Denise's eyes get huge. "I won't say a word. I'll tell them you were here for the records, but I told you to come back and speak with Janet. I'll email her and tell her that. Is that okay with you?" She looks worried.

"That sounds fine. We'll back you up on that."

Kent and I both nod as we rise from the table. We now know

whatever William figured out started right around the time Collins and MacClenny began working at Luciph.

I turn to Denise. "Do you know where they worked before Luciph?"

She looks up from her computer and says, "I think it was Tyrex."

"Thanks, Denise," I say, smiling at her.

She still looks worried.

"Yeah, thanks," adds Kent.

As we walk to the elevator, Kent asks, "Isn't that a computer software company?"

Searching on my phone, I reply, "Something like that. I know it has something to do with computers. According to the web, it's a tech company. They specialize in mobile devices, semiconductors, and software."

"Great. Now we need to add Tyrex to our list of shit to check out. The list keeps growing, but we aren't any closer to the answer," Kent whines.

"We're getting closer. I now have two suspects I'm feeling pretty fucking good about. The trick is to figure out a way to catch 'em."

Back in his car, we sit in silence again. I'm sure he's thinking about the case, just like me. What are those two assholes up to? That's the tough question right now. And how far will they go? If they're willing to murder over this, it's got to be over something huge.

ON FRIDAY, Gretchen calls my cell to let us know she has something. Since I'm attending William's funeral this morning, we make arrangements to meet in the afternoon.

When I walk into the funeral home, I see about ten people

in attendance. It's sad, really. The guy kept to himself, didn't have friends, no girlfriend, and no kids. He died alone. Shit, he was only seven years older than me. It sucks to think about dying alone.

As I look around, I see a familiar face. Denise Thomas from Luciph. At least she came to his service. That's cool. It's then I spot Sophie near the back of the church. My guess is she wants to stay as far away from Julia as possible. I walk toward her and watch her attempt to ignore me. It's not working. She's fidgeting in her seat.

She wants to make a run for it, but I move in on the open side of the pew and slide in next to her. "Sophie, how are you?"

"Fine."

"Just fine? Had any other 'accidents' that I should know about?" I look at her injured hand and see a change. "Get your stitches out?"

"Yes. This morning. And everything is fine. I'm fine. Work is fine. I'm fine."

"That's a lot of 'fines' in there, sweetheart."

She turns her head to glare at me. "Stop. Calling. Me. Sweetheart," she says through gritted teeth.

I've never seen such fire in her. It's sexy as hell. "I can't help it, babe. You *are* sweet."

She huffs out a breath and then attempts to stand up. "All I wanted to do was pay my respects to Willy. Can you let me do that, please?"

I stay put. She can pay her respects with me by her side. Or not....

She slides out the long way, asking the few people in her path to excuse her. I jump out of the pew and follow. She makes her way out the front door to the sidewalk. It's hotter than usual today, even for August in Chicago.

"Sophie, wait!"

"I can't, Hank. Just... just leave me alone. Okay?"

"I wanted to let you know my brother will be over tonight to replace your window. Okay?"

She sighs. "Yeah, that's fine. Tell him there's a key under the planter by the front door if he gets there before I do. Tell him thanks and to leave the bill on the table," she mutters as she walks away from me.

I sigh. She's got a fucking key to her house under the planter? That's idiocy. Any thief or rapist would know to check there first. *Jesus.* After the window is in, I'll take the key for safe-keeping. For now, I guess I'll let her have her space.

24

SOPHIE

"Sophie, before you leave tonight, restock all the order forms for bridal and for the tux area." Brooke is extra bossy these days, which means she's extra lazy. She sits in her office all day searching the internet for gossipy stories about celebrities instead of working in the store. "Also, the printers all need paper and check the ink cartridges. I don't want to have to do that on Sunday when I come in to work. You're off tomorrow, so it's the least you can do since I'll be working *alone*."

I work alone all the time, but whatever. "No problem, Brooke. I'll take care of it. You go have fun."

She's going out on the town with some old college friends of hers, so she's leaving work early to have her hair, nails, and makeup done. Apparently, there's competition between her classmates to look the best for their age. Brooke spends so much time and money on herself, she's bound to win.

With Ashley only working a half day today, it leaves me to close up shop. See? Alone. At five, I lock the front door and finish up with closing. I clean all the mirrors and windows, straighten the gowns in the front window, and double-check the dresses are ready for Brooke's appointments tomorrow. I make my way back to the storage room at the back of the store. It's one of those rooms you dread going into because it's dark, with only a dim bulb hanging from the tall ceiling. Plus, it's cold as hell. The one and only vent sits high on the ceiling, close to the heating and cooling system on the roof, so it blows out powerful gusts of air all day long. I've tried to adjust the vent with a broomstick, but the room's got to have twelve-foot ceilings. I wrap my sweater around me and dash in to grab the printer papers and forms. I find the printer paper and tuxedo rental forms right away but can't seem to find the bridal-purchase forms.

"Damn it. I know they were here the last time I looked for them," I grumble. As I pull boxes and other bridal extras around, I hear the door slam shut. "What the heck?"

I quickly turn this way and that weaving through everything we've got crammed in this small space to get to the door. When I attempt to turn the nob, it's locked. "Shit!" As I try to turn the nob again, I hear someone giggling. "Hello?" I slap the door with my hand. "Let me out. This isn't funny."

"Oh, yes, it is, Miss Piggy. It's fucking hilarious."

"Ari? What are you doing here? Let me out."

"No can do, chubs."

I bang on the door louder. "Goddamn it, Ari. Let me out!"

"Have fun in there, fatty. I hope you die."

"Ari!" I scream. "Let me out of here. It's cold."

"Not for long," she cackles.

What did she mean by that? It's then I feel a shift in the air. The harsh cold air is no longer blowing on my neck. It's warming up, which feels good. I sit on a box and think about my options. There's no phone in the closet, and I left my phone in my purse, which is out on the counter. I look around at the tiny space. There's nothing in here that I can climb up onto to get up to that vent. If I could, I may have been able to climb through the vent.

I snort at the thought. "Yeah, if I were a size two." *I'd never fit into that ductwork.*

As I consider my options, I feel noticeably warmer. The vent has started blowing air again, but it's not cold air; it's warm. No, not just warm, it's hot and getting hotter. Did she turn up the heat on me in here? That changes things. I know Brooke will be here in the morning, so I'll have to do what I can to stay cool. The longer I sit, the warmer the room is getting.

If I were MacGyver, I could figure a way out of here. But I'm no MacGyver. The closet walls are all concrete. The good news is those generally stay cool. I get up and pull off my lightweight cardigan sweater and move to the back of the room, farthest from the vent, and rearrange the boxes filled with old stock, papers, and other stuff that should be tossed. Once the floor is clear, I sit with my back against the wall. I worked up a sweat moving that junk. Now I wish I had something to drink.

I stand up and dig around in the boxes and look on the shelves lining the sidewalls. Behind a small plastic tub is a twelve-ounce bottle of water with only about an inch of water remaining. It'll have to do. I'll sip it. If I'm lucky, Brooke will stop back before she heads out, and I can get out of this sauna. And it is becoming a sauna. She must have turned the furnace on to the highest temperature and turned it to ON so it will run continuously.

After a while, maybe an hour, I can't tell—I took my watch off earlier and put it in my purse—after however long it's been, I remove my blouse. I don't care if anyone sees me in my bra at this point. I delay removing my leggings, but after another ten minutes, I give in. Sitting in my bra and panties, I lie down and try to get as close to the concrete in the back corner as I can.

As I lie there, for what seems like hours, I realize that I'm no longer sweating and I no longer feel the need to urinate. I know that means I'm getting dehydrated. I take a small sip of my water. I'm down to about a half inch of water now. I'd love to pour it over my head. It's so damn hot. I can't breathe very well either. I feel like it's a struggle to get air into my lungs. I crawl to a new, cool spot.

Please, Brooke. Get here soon. Those words replay in my head over and over. My mind wanders to other things—things like Henry Flynn. Why did he have to be such an idiot? I actually thought he liked me. He seemed to like having sex with me, but maybe he's like that with all of his sex partners. The thing is, it felt special. It felt right. But I think I was alone in that feeling. Henry made it perfectly clear what he thought of me.

I slide my hand over my belly. What if I'm pregnant? Maybe I should have taken that stupid pill. If I am, I'd have to sell the house, for sure. I could make enough money from the sale to make a new start. I could move to Iowa. My best friend, Tracy, has tried to talk me into moving to Iowa City so we could be in the same city. I could go back to school. The University of Iowa has great English and literature programs. The Writer's Workshop is there. See? Things aren't that bad. Right?

And what about Henry? Will he want to be in the child's life? I scoff, but it turns into a wheezing cough. If he wanted a child in his life, he wouldn't have run out first thing in the morning for that pill.

God, I'm such an idiot.

It's surprising how tired you can get in a space this hot. I just want to sleep. Maybe if I get some sleep, it will be morning before I know it, and Brooke will open the door, and I can get the hell out of here. I feel my eyes get heavy. I clutch the little bit of water I have to my chest and let sleep take me.

25

———

HENRY

My phone rings at eight thirty in the morning. I was up till five this morning going back over all the financial stuff in William's case. I reach over to my bedside table and grab my cell. "Flynn. This better be fucking important."

"Hank, this is Joel Peters—Detective from the Fifth. We worked a couple cases together."

Jesus, is this a social call? "Yeah, I remember," I say, groggily.

"I'm down at a scene at a place called Bridal Belles. Ever heard of it?"

Suddenly panicked, I throw my blanket off and spring out of bed before I can think. "Yeah, what's going on?"

"One of the uniforms told me you knew this girl. He helped out with a murder investigation you've got now."

"What the fuck is going on? Is Sophie...?" *God, I can't say it.*

"No, she's not dead, but she's not doing good. You need to get down here."

"I'll be there in ten," I say as I pull on yesterday's jeans and tee. I grab my keys and wallet off my dresser and run out the door. I'm sure I look like hell, but who the fuck cares. "Shit, I should have asked him what I'm walking into."

I run out to my garage, hit the door opener as I'm starting up the car, and back out as fast as I can. There's no traffic this time of the morning in my neighborhood. When I get to the store, there are police cars, a fire truck, an ambulance, and a bunch of first responders working in and around the shop.

I double-park near a squad car, flash my badge to the uniform, and race to the ambulance. The back doors are open, and I peer inside. Sophie is lying on the gurney. Her skin is flushed a deep red. They've got oxygen on her face, but her eyes are closed.

I turn to the EMT next to her. "How is she?"

"Not good. She's still unresponsive. Hopefully, getting fluids into her will help."

I want to stay with her but need to find out what the fuck happened. I jog into the front door of the store, and the first thing I notice is how fucking hot it is in there. "Was there a fire?" I ask the first person I see.

"No. Digital thermostat was up to a hundred and twenty degrees," he replies. "And it was set to stay on."

I still don't understand what's going on. Joel Peters is talking to a paramedic with a concerned look on his face. I lift my chin at him as he walks over at a brisk pace.

"Hank, glad you made it so fast."

"What's going on? Why is it hot as hell in here, and why was the thermostat so high, and what does this have to do with Sophie?"

"Damn, give me a second, man. This is what I learned from the store owner, Brooke Bellamy. Sophie worked Saturday and closed on her own. Brooke was scheduled to work on Sunday but decided not to."

I snorted at that. She's one lazy bitch.

"When she came in this morning, she noticed how hot it

was. She also noticed a chair was jammed up against the door-knob to that closet over there."

"Yeah," I say, nervously.

"When she opened the door, she felt an intense flash of heat coming from inside the closet, then saw Sophie lying prone in the corner of the room. She was unresponsive."

I run my fingers through my hair and pull. "Fuck!" I shout. "Where is that bitch of a boss?"

"Hank, come on. Calm down. You need a level head right now."

"Where. Is. Her. Fucking. Boss?" I glare at Peters.

"In her office."

"Of course she is. Jesus." I rush toward the back of the shop. *This is all her fault.* When I walk into her office, she's surfing the web. *She's fucking surfing the fucking web.* "What the fuck are you doing?"

"Huh?" she asks, looking confused.

I lean over her desk and peer at her screen. "Sophie could be dead, and you're reading celebrity gossip?"

"Well, what else am I supposed to do? I can't leave my store. I'm here alone."

"Why is that? Why are you here alone? Where are the other bitches that work here? Aron or Ari, whatever, and the other two?"

"That's none of your business."

I flash her my badge. "It *is* my fucking business, so unless you want me to cuff you and take you down to the station, *talk.*"

"Ari and Brit no longer work here."

"Why not?"

"Why not, what?"

"You're wasting time here. Why don't they work here?"

"I fired them."

"Why?"

"I can't say."

"You've got five seconds to tell me why?"

"Fine! Jeez. They were stealing dresses."

"How did you figure that out?" She doesn't seem bright enough to change a light bulb.

"We caught them?"

"*We?*"

"Well, Sophie... Sophie caught them and videotaped them."

Fuck, fuck, fuck! Why didn't she tell me about this? About them? It has to be one or both of them hurting her. "Did you change your alarm code after you fired them?"

She hesitates but then says, "Well, no. It's complicated. I wasn't sure how to—"

"So, you're telling me after you fired two thieves, you did *not* change your security codes to the store?"

"I couldn't remember how to do it."

"You pay a security company to monitor your shop, yeah?"

"Yeah. And?"

"Did you know they'll come out and change your code if you're too stupid to do it yourself?"

She huffs and puffs at my insult, but I don't care.

"I need their addresses."

"Addresses?"

I stare at her. I want to pull out my gun and blow her fucking head off. I swear I do. "Ari's and Brit's. Addresses. Now!"

"I can't give you that. It's confidential."

"They no longer work for you, correct?"

"Correct."

"It's no longer confidential. Besides, unless you want to be named as an accessory to this situation with Sophie, you'll get those addresses for me. Now!" I shout, leaning down over her desk.

She's pulled herself as far back as she can go. "Okay. I'll get them," she mutters.

As I'm waiting, Officer Billings knocks. He's the uniform who helped Sophie when her window was broken. "Hank, you need to get to the hospital. EMT said she came to—she was saying your name, man. St. Michael's North."

"Fuck. Can you get those addresses and text me? You still got my number?"

"Sure do. I'll send it right away."

I pat him on the back and run out the door. I've wasted time talking to that simpering bitch, but I needed to know what was going on. Racing to my car, I hop in and gun it. *Sophie needs me.*

———

26

HENRY

I run into the emergency room of St. Michael's hospital, reaching a reception desk right inside the doorway. There's someone talking to the receptionist, but I'm not afraid to interrupt. I wait to make sure they aren't in panic mode like me before doing so.

"Excuse me. I need to find someone."

The people he's talking to move on to the waiting area.

"Well, me too, honey. I think I've just found him," the receptionist coos.

Is he flirting with me? Yeah, the receptionist is a guy. I want to expedite this, so I whip out my badge and stare at him as coldly as I can. "Katherine Sophia Kincaid. Where is she?"

"Ooh, a p*oh*leese man!" He clicks away at his keyboard and then says, "I have a Sophie Kincaid. Is that her?"

"Yeah, where the hell is she?"

"My, my, you sure are tetchy." He looks up and, as soon as he sees my expression, quickly adds, "She's still in the ER. Go that way." He points to his left. "They'll take you to her."

"Thanks," I say as I move away.

"Anytime, sweetie," he coos.

When I get to the doors, I flash my badge to get through to the emergency room without stopping and then grab the first person in scrubs I see. "Sophie Kincaid. Where is she?"

"Sir, only family members are allowed back here."

"I'm her fiancé; she was asking for me. Where the hell is she?" I decide not to flash my badge this time. This is personal. The police part of this will come after I know she's okay.

"I'll take you," the nurse says.

Thank fuck. Maybe she can tell I'm about to lose it.

I *am* about to lose it. At least that's how I feel when I get my first glimpse of Sophie. She looks so tiny in the hospital bed— tiny and very ill. She looks unconscious with tubes running from each arm up to machines, some of which hold liquids while other just beep, quietly monitoring her vital statistics. *She's alive. She's alive.* I need to remind myself about that before I lose my shit.

She's still flushed a bright pink all over her body. They've placed small bags of ice around her, near her wrists, between her legs, under her arms, and behind her neck.

I move closer to her until I've got my hand on the cold metal railing that's keeping her secure. Her breathing is fast—faster than normal. Why is that? I reach out to touch her hand. It's chilled from the ice pack near her wrist, but I can tell she's warm. I rub my thumb on her hand gently, wanting her to know I'm here, if it's possible. As I stand looking at her, someone clears his throat. I turn and see an older man in a white coat. The doctor, I presume.

"Only family is allowed in here. Are you family?"

"Fiancé," I say, reaching out to shake his hand. "Henry Flynn."

"Ah, right. I'm Dr. Jenkins. She's one lucky young woman. We almost lost her. She's still not out of the woods yet, I'm afraid."

"I know. When will she wake up again? EMT said she asked for me."

"It's difficult to tell, but it's not necessarily a bad thing. It's her body's way of coping with the stress. When she wakes, be prepared. Exposure to extreme heat for that long can cause many symptoms."

"Like what?"

"Seizures, confusion, irrational behavior, dizziness, nausea and vomiting, and there may be heart issues. We'll have to wait and see. Her heart seems to function properly, but we'll get a cardiologist in here to make sure."

I look back down at my girl. Jesus, she's got a long road ahead of her.

"The nurse will be in periodically to check her vitals. We'll move her to the intensive care unit in about an hour. She'll get round-the-clock attention until she wakes up," he says, patting my back. "Sit tight."

"I will." I pull up the chair from the corner and sit on her right side, farthest from all the machines. *I'll just sit here and touch her hand, so she knows I'm—well, that someone is here.*

As I wait for something, anything, I watch the nurses move in and out of the room, caring for Sophie. They are gentle with her, which I like. After about an hour, a group moves in with a rolling bed.

"What are you doing?"

"We're moving her up to intensive care," says an orderly. "She'll be in room 310A if you'd like to make your way up there. Third floor."

I stand and watch them lift her limp body and slide her onto the other bed. Goddamn, this isn't good. When the gurney rolls out, I follow it until they reach the Hospital Staff Only elevator. That's not me, so I walk out into the large reception area and sit on a chair near the window. I'm not quite ready to go up to the intensive care unit. I'm dazed. This is all so strange, so surreal. What if she dies? The doctor said she's not out of the woods yet. I lay my head back against the window. Should I call someone? She's got no family, so no calls needed there. My poor Sophie. I lean forward and rest my face in my palms. *My* Sophie. "I'm sorry, baby. I should have been there," I whisper to myself. It's true. I should have known she wasn't home on Saturday night or even on Sunday night. I should have known.

When I've finally gathered myself, I take the elevator to three. Her room in intensive care is large and cool. She's still surrounded by machines whirring and beeping constantly, but she's in a larger bed that looks slightly more comfortable than the small padded table in the ER.

I rest my head on the side of the bed and close my eyes. It's ten o'clock at night, so that means I've been running on pure adrenaline since eight thirty this morning. I'm crashing now. Still touching her, I doze for a while.

Movement awakens me. Feeling Sophie's fingers move against my hand, I jerk my head up and see her eyelashes fluttering as her eyes slowly open. The room is fairly dark but for small lights on the perimeter of the room. She opens her mouth like she's trying to speak, but her lips are dry.

I quickly grab the cup of water they've had at the ready for a while. There's a bendable straw in the lid. "Thirsty?" I ask. "Are you thirsty, baby?"

Her head turns toward my voice. She blinks a few times, but her face holds an expression of confusion. "Henry?" she says in a raspy, dry voice.

"Yeah, angel. It's Henry. I'm here."

"Why?"

"Why what?" I lean over with the cup and place the straw over her lips. "Tiny sips. Just take a tiny sip for now."

She wraps her lips around the straw and sucks, then licks

her lips and rests her head back on the pillow. Taking a breath, she says, "Where am I?" Her voice sounds like she's been smoking a pack a day her entire life.

"At St. Michael's ICU. You were locked in a closet. It was hot...." I don't get the rest out because her facial expression tells me that she's remembering.

"Ari. Ari locked me in the closet."

"Are you sure it was Ari?"

"Yeah, I talked to her through the door after she locked me in. She's insane." Sophie takes several deep breaths. She's getting herself upset.

"Calm down, angel. It'll be okay."

Our conversation is interrupted when two nurses walk into the room. One moves directly to the monitors while the other says, "You're awake? That's great, Sophia! How are you feeling? Can we get you anything?"

"Thirsty," Sophie rasps again.

"I'll get you fresh ice water, but you'll need to take it easy on that. Small sips."

"Okay." She nods.

"The doctor will be in first thing in the morning, hon. Buzz us if you need anything," she says, looking at me. "We're right outside the door. Okay?"

I answer for Sophie. "Got it. Thanks."

For the rest of the night, Sophie dozes on and off, waking to drink water. We change her ice packs until she shivers. Her temperature is close to normal by morning, so they remove the cold packs from around her body.

At seven o'clock, a short, balding man in doctor whites steps into the room. "Sophia! I heard you were awake. I'm so glad. I'm Dr. Montell, and you're one lucky young lady," he says reaching out to tap her hand. He looks at me and asks, "And you are?"

"Fiancé."

I can see Sophie's expression from my peripheral vision. Her mouth is hanging open, and her eyes are huge.

The doctor looks from me to her and then at me. "Are you sure?"

"I'm positive."

He turns to Sophie and asks, "This your fiancé, Sophia? Is it all right for him to be in here while we talk?"

She slowly nods and mumbles, "Yes."

"Okay then," he continues. "I must ask you some questions. If it gets to be too much, I'll come back later. Does that sound good, Sophia?"

She nods.

"Do you know what happened to you?"

"I was locked in a closet. It was hot."

"Boiling. Like I said, you're very lucky. Any longer in that extreme heat and we would have lost you."

She winces at that. I wish he'd stop scaring her. I can tell from the look on her face she's nervous and afraid. I wrap my hand around hers.

"The recovery for this type of injury, extreme heatstroke, will take time. There are symptoms that result from it that could last days or even weeks."

"Like what?" she asks.

"Heatstroke can temporarily or permanently damage vital organs, such as the heart, lungs, kidneys, liver, and brain. Our cardiologist on staff will visit you later today, and we'll check out all of those areas to be sure you're all right."

"Is there a chance you could be pregnant, Sophia?"

As soon as the question is out of his mouth, I respond, "No."

At the same moment, Sophie says, "Yes."

I look at her in shock. She's not looking at me yet, but she will. "I thought you took the morning-after pill?"

"I didn't have time," she whispers.

"You didn't have *time?*" I attempt to whisper, but it comes out as more of an angry hiss.

"There were side effects. I couldn't miss work."

"Jesus, you and that fucking job. What if we're stuck with a kid? You'd miss work *a lot.*"

Sophie looks like she's just been slapped.

Dr. Montell interrupts. "She doesn't need this stress right now." He's pissed. I can tell. He should be. I'm being a dick. "Sophie, would you like me to call someone else or would you like to be alone?"

"There's no one else to call. He should listen to this, and then he can go," she says resignedly.

The doctor looks at me like he'd like to kill me, but he continues. "I need to tell you, Sophie, that if you are pregnant, the baby is at risk. Being exposed to that temperature for that long may cause miscarriage or permanent damage to the fetus, resulting in birth defects. You may want to consider *all* of your options if you are, in fact, pregnant. Have you taken a pregnancy test?"

"No, it's too soon." Tears are running down her cheeks.

I try to soothe her even though I know she won't listen to me. "Soph, it will be okay." I attempt to hold her hand, but she pulls away and looks at me like she hates me. I don't blame her.

"We'll take blood while you're here. We should know for sure before you leave if you're pregnant or not. If you are, there are tests we can perform to see how the fetus is doing. Does that sound good to you?"

"Yeah." She nods.

"Henry, can I speak with you outside for a moment?"

Fuck. I'm in trouble.

Once we step out the door, he turns on me. "Sophia doesn't need the added stress. She's been through enough. She needs calm so she can recover. Maybe you should let Sophia be for a while, give her some space."

"Yeah, you're right." *I'll give her space.*

With a final stern look, the doc moves on to the rest of his rounds. Before I leave, I walk back into the room. Sophie is pretending to be asleep, but I can see a fresh tear rolling down her cheek.

"I'm sorry, Sophie," I whisper.

She just nods as I walk out the door.

The thing she doesn't know is that the news she might be pregnant isn't the part that scares me. It's the part where she may lose our baby, or he may have birth defects that terrifies the fuck out of me. I walk out of her room and down the long hospital corridor, skip the elevator, and take the stairs down three flights to the main level. As I walk out the door, I pull my phone from my pocket and hit a contact. I run my hand through my hair as it rings.

"Yo, big bro. What's up?" Keith chirps.

"Keith?" I choke. I'm barely holding it together.

"Hank, what's wrong?"

"It's Sophie." I clear my throat. "It's Sophie... she's...." I let out a sob. Yep. A sob.

"Jesus, what's wrong? Is she okay? Are you okay?"

"No, she's not okay. She's in the ICU of St. Michael's. Someone tried to kill her."

"Fuck! What do you need, Hank? Tell me."

"I need to talk to you. To Mom and Dad. I'm barely holding it together."

"You don't need to hold it together, man. It's okay if you let your emotions out."

"There's more."

"Shit. What is it?"

"It's too hard to explain over the phone. I'd rather talk to you all at the same time. Can you meet me over at Mom and Dad's place?"

"Dad and I are both off today, so I'll meet you over there in twenty."

"Thanks, Keith." I hang up my phone.

I'm so lucky I have Keith and my folks—my entire family. Sophie has no one. Goddamn, more fucking tears. I'm such a pussy. I can't help what this is doing to me. This week has been fucking awful, and it's only Tuesday. Wetness slides down my cheeks again. Unfamiliar with crying, I was raised to be a tough guy, but I'm figuring out I'm not so tough after all.

27

SOPHIE

I'm on day three in this hospital bed. In that time, I've been poked, prodded, and rolled around this place for every test known to man. I feel a bit abused. I'm sore and exhausted. If anyone tells you it's restful at the hospital, don't believe it. Nurses wake me up every hour to take my vitals, give me meds, and make sure I'm drinking my clear liquids. I'm sick of clear liquids. *I want some French fries!*

I've also been questioned by Detective Peters, who is in charge of my case. The interesting part of all of this is what I learned from him. Since I don't remember much after my first couple of hours in the closet, he told me how I saved my own life. Apparently, I built myself a cave of sorts, out of boxes and a damaged wedding dress. It kept the hot air from blowing directly on me and kept the coolness from the concrete wall and floors encased in the area. It was still way too hot, but if I hadn't been so resourceful—his words, not mine—I'd probably be dead. I can remember thinking I needed to keep that hot air from hitting my back. I guess I did something about it, and I vaguely remember moving things around to get more comfortable.

At noon, I hear a light tap on my door. I don't acknowledge

it because I assume it's just the nurse or orderly letting me know they're entering my room. Maybe it's lunch—a real lunch. I'm starving. *No more clear liquids, please!*

"Hello?" says a voice from my doorway.

I look up and see a tiny woman, about my height but older than me. I'd guess she's in her late fifties. Her hair is silver and shoulder-length. She's wearing dark jeans and a pretty, floral tunic. I smile at her.

When she smiles back, I feel like I've met her before. Maybe she was in the emergency room when I came in; I can't remember.

"Sophie?" she asks, sounding unsure.

"Yes."

She steps into the room until she's a few feet from my bed. "Sweetheart, you don't know me but... well, I'm Henry's mother, Sarah."

What? "Henry's mother?"

"Yes, dear. Henry came to see me yesterday. He was very upset. He'd been crying."

"Crying?"

"Oh, shoot. Please don't tell him I told you. He'd have to give up his man badge."

"You mean his man *card*?" I giggle.

She lets out a hearty laugh. "Yes. Man card. That's it."

I swallow, waiting for her to speak again. Why is she here?

"You're probably wondering why I'm here. We've never met. Heck, I only found out about you yesterday. Henry talked to us for over an hour. He told us everything. And I mean *everything*," she says, rolling her eyes but smiling.

"I don't understand. Why would Henry talk about me—to you?"

"Because he loves you, honey."

"No. No, he doesn't love me. I only met him a month ago.

Besides, he's... he just feels sorry for me. I annoy him. I.... He told me he—"

"Well, *he* didn't say the *L* word, but I know my son. He loves you. He's just afraid to take the plunge again. His first wife, Angela, was something else," Sarah says, rolling her eyes. "I never liked that girl. Now *she* was a gold digger."

I fidget uncomfortably in my bed. "He... um... he told you about that?"

"He told me everything. I mentioned that, didn't I?"

"Yes."

"He feels terrible about that whole thing. I made sure he knew what a jackass he was, and his brother Keith told him as well. My husband, Declan, also gave him a piece of his mind. Between the three of us, he's good and sorry."

"Okay." *What does she want?*

"The reason I stopped by was because I wanted to see how you were feeling. I also wanted to get a look at the girl who has my oldest child so smitten," she says, laughing. "I've got to say I'm not disappointed, Sophie. You're a beautiful woman."

I blink, speechless. How could she say that? I'm not beautiful. I'm plain old Sophie. "Thank you. I'm feeling fine. Better. The tests have all come back okay."

She's moved over to the side of the bed. "Would you mind if I sit?"

"No, go right ahead."

She scoots the chair closer to my right side. Next, she reaches up and takes hold of my hand. "Now, sweetheart, tell me honestly how you're feeling. I'm a mom. I know when I'm hearing a load of malarkey."

I laugh at that. "Okay," I say, resigned. "I'm sore and exhausted. They wake me up every hour to poke and prod me. The police have been here to question me three times, and there are countless doctors who find me a curiosity. I guess I'm one of the few people who have survived such extreme conditions for such a long time or something."

"You're a brave little one, aren't you?"

"I don't know about brave." *Or little.* "It's sort of forced bravery."

"You're brave, nonetheless."

At that moment, Dr. Montell steps in. "Sophia. How are you today?"

"Good. How are you?"

He chuckles. "Fine. Thank you for asking. I came with news from your blood test," he says, looking at Sarah.

"Honey, let me step out of the room," she says, trying to give me privacy.

"No. Please stay. I'd like someone with me right now."

"If you're sure."

I nod to the doctor.

"It was negative, Sophia. You're not pregnant."

"Oh," I squeak.

"I know this is upsetting for you, but under the circumstances—"

"I know. It's for the best," I finish for him. But why does it hurt so much to hear that news?

"I'll be back in a little while to examine you. In the meantime, buzz the nurses' station if you need anything. All right?"

"Thank you, Dr. Montell."

He walks out the door, and I look away from Sarah. I let my tears fall, happy I don't have to worry about an unwanted pregnancy but sad I don't have a life inside of me. Happy the baby won't have to suffer some terrible defect and sad I won't be able to nurture a tiny life.

I feel arms wrap around me then. They're small but strong. She doesn't say a word. She holds me while I cry.

"I'm sorry, Sarah. I don't know why I'm crying. It's a relief, really." I sniffle.

"I have six children. I had two miscarriages that only Declan, and now you, know about. One was before Henry, and another happened between Michael and Emily. There is nothing quite as painful as losing a child."

"I wasn't even pregnant. I shouldn't be sad. Henry, he didn't...."

"Oh, Sophie. Even though you weren't pregnant, it was still a loss. The idea of a child can be just as real. As for Henry, he was torn apart about the idea you could lose the baby or that the baby could have something wrong with him."

"He didn't want a baby, at least not with me."

"Let me tell you something about Henry. He's as stubborn as a mule—and thickheaded. But he is fiercely loyal and protective. The thought of you here, hurting, is hard on him. The fact that you could be pregnant and sitting here alone is tearing him apart. I know he's sorry for saying those asinine things. I'm sure he'll find a way to show you how sorry he is, and when he does, I hope you'll listen."

"It's too late. It's too late for us, Sarah. Too much has happened."

"Oh, dear. I guess Henry's not the only stubborn one here."

I laugh at that. "My dad used to call me 'Stalwart Sophie.'"

"Well, between the two of you, I suspect you'll work things out by the time I'm eighty. I hope you figure it out before then."

I sigh and then smile. "I'll think about it. But would you not tell him the results of the pregnancy test? I would like to be the one."

"Of course. That's information for his ears only. Just know I'm here for you if you need me. Now, you need to get some rest. You can't get overly tired, or you'll never get to go home."

"It was nice meeting you, Sarah."

"I'll be back tomorrow. I'll bring one or both of my daughters along. You'll like them. They're stubborn too." She snickers. "They'll like you back, sweetie."

"You don't have to visit. I'm fine."

"You're not fine. You need visitors to keep your spirits up. Don't argue."

I laugh and agree to her terms. She drives a hard bargain. Something tells me she's the one in charge in the Flynn household.

The rest of the day drags along. Nurses and doctors intermittently interrupt the boredom to examine me, draw blood, take vital statistics, and other fun things. I've been up and walking several times today. I feel pretty good, but it shocks me how tired I get from just walking from one end of the hallway and back to my room. Plus, I'm sore from the dehydration and still tired and weak.

The doctors are happy I seem to be doing well. Mentally, I'm not confused. I've had no seizures, and I've stopped feeling like I want to vomit. See? All good.

The problem is I'm wishing that Henry were here with me. I know. I know. I told him to leave me alone forever. But if what his mom said is true, he really cares about me. By the time visiting hours are over at eight, I have accepted that he will not visit me today. The only word I can use to describe how I feel about it is *disappointed*.

28

HENRY

On Wednesday morning, I decide my focus should be on the investigation. Even though I know I'll upset her, I need to check on Soph right after I see how Joel Peters's case is coming along. I pull my phone out of my back pocket.

"Peters? This is Hank Flynn. What've you got on Sophie Kincaid's case? I'd like to help."

"Hank, this is my investigation. You need to stay out of it. You're too close to the vic."

"I'm good. Let me help. I know the players. What have you found out about Ari Templeton?"

Peters sighs heavily but relents. "Arianna Porsche Templeton, age twenty-two."

"Porsche?" I snort. "Jesus, she's a pretentious little bitch, isn't she?"

"Yeah. I haven't met her yet, but I can't wait," he says sarcastically. "All right, here's what I know..."

He lists off a fairly substantial amount of evidence from the scene along with observations and conclusions he's drawn. I pay special attention when he talks about the surveillance cameras that the other businesses around Bridal Belles have that are targeting that back alley. He's got the feeds from three out of four, but the three are enough to identify a woman using the keypad to enter the shop at approximately 5:10 p.m. on the night of the incident.

"Brooke Bellamy has identified that woman as Arianna Templeton."

"Don't trust Brooke Bellamy," I warn.

"Way ahead of you. I already advised her not to contact Arianna or Brittany Smith or I'll arrest her for impeding an investigation along with a few other charges I pulled out of my ass. Besides, do you wanna know the kicker?"

"What?"

"Arianna was caught on video leaving the place at 5:22 p.m. with a huge white dress in her arms. She stole another dress from Bellamy after she imprisoned Sophie in that tiny room."

"What a murderous, thieving bitch! I suspect Bellamy was pretty pissed about another stolen dress. Bet she wished she would have pressed charges in the first place."

"She was unhappy, to say the least."

"What else?"

"Did you know your girl MacGyver'd herself in that closet?"

"Huh?"

Laughing he says, "That's what she called it when I told her about it."

He's been talking to Sophie? Calm the fuck down, Hank. He had to question her.

"She only vaguely remembered doing it, but she made herself a tent with cardboard boxes and an old wedding dress that protected her from the direct heat flowing into the room. She was tight against the concrete wall and floor in the coolest part of the room—if you can call it cool—and probably saved her own life by doing that."

I smile with pride. My girl is smart, resourceful, and beautiful. "It's not a surprise. She's smart as a whip. What's next? How can I help?"

"What's next is you can stay the fuck out of my investigation. Don't you have a murder to solve or something?"

I do. I've put off my work on Willy's murder because of all of this with Sophie. "I do, but I want to be a part of this in some way."

He sighs. "I'm on my way to Arianna and Brittany's place. I also plan to question one Ashley Morgan. She works at the shop."

"Wait! Ashley lives with them too?"

"Arianna and Brittany are roommates. Ashley doesn't seem to be part of any of this, but she may know something."

I got the impression that Ashley was okay. It seemed as though she and Sophie were friends. Well, work friends. Back to the task at hand. "I'll meet you at their place. I've got the address."

"Hank," he warns.

"I'm just going to observe. I won't say a fucking word."

"You'd better not. I'll kick your ass."

I snort at that. Like that guy could touch me. "See you there."

"ARIANNA TEMPLETON? I'd like to ask you a few questions," commands Joel Peters as he enters Ari and Brit's apartment.

Their apartment is swanky—too nice for a couple of woman who work at a bridal shop. I should say *used* to work at a bridal shop.

"Nice place," I quip.

Peters looks at me like he wants to kill me.

"Thank you," says Ari sweetly.

God, she's a piece of work.

Peters says, "Is Brittany Smith available?"

"No, she's working."

"Where?" I ask.

She giggles. "Donut Hut, just down the street."

"Are you working?" I ask.

"No, not yet. I'm waiting for *just* the right opportunity," she says, cheerily.

Yeah, like stealing more shit from Bridal Belles.

"We'd like to ask you a few questions about an incident that occurred on Saturday, August sixth."

"Oh dear, what incident?" she feigns concern.

"An employee of Bridal Belles was locked in a small room for a long period. She nearly died."

The gleam in that sick bitch's eyes makes my skin crawl. Sociopath. She's got the look of a sociopath.

"That's terrible, Officer, but I don't know what I can do to help you."

Peters jumps right in. "Where were you between the hours of 4:00 p.m. and 6:00 p.m. on Saturday evening?"

"Me? Why would you be asking me that?"

"Just answer the question, ma'am," I add.

"Well, I was out with friends. We shopped all day, then had dinner together. Then we went to a club."

"Who are these friends? We'll need names and phone numbers," Peters says.

"What? Why? Am I a suspect? I'd never hurt Sophie. She was a good, good friend when I worked at the store."

"I don't think we mentioned the name of the victim. How did you know we were referring to Sophia Kincaid?"

Damn, Peters is smart. Got her!

"Well, Brooke must have told me."

"When did you speak with Brooke Bellamy?" Peters continues.

"Sunday. She called on Sunday. We're still friends."

"Sophie wasn't found until Monday morning," says Peters.

Just then, huge tears run down Arianna's face. She's practically wailing. We've been here five minutes, and she's already lost it.

"It was Brittany. She *made* me do it. She's so mean. She *hates* Sophie."

I highly doubt that. "We're going to speak to Brittany as soon as we get her to the station." Which will be any minute since we had her picked up by a couple of beat cops half an hour ago.

She looks shocked and a little nervous. "You are?"

"Arianna Porsche Templeton, you are under arrest for the attempted murder of Katherine Sophia Kincaid. You have the right to remain silent...."

"Wait, I'm under arrest? Attempted murder?" She's screeching like an owl. "I told you: it was all Brittany's idea."

Peters continues reading her Miranda rights. "Anything you say can and will be used against you in a court of law." He cuffs her wrists together at her lower back and pulls her out the door.

"No! This isn't fair! It's always about that fat pig, Sophie. I'm so sick of her," she screams.

"You have the right to an attorney. If you cannot afford an attorney, one will be provided for you" Peters doesn't stop.

It's making me chuckle.

"Do you understand the rights I have just read to you? With these rights in mind, do you wish to speak to me?" Peters asks.

Arianna pulls herself together. Tears and snot flowing down

her face, but she gathers herself enough to stand tall like all good sociopaths. "No! Of course not! My uncle is an attorney. A good one! I'll be out before dinnertime," she scoffs.

I doubt that, but I keep my mouth shut.

29

———

SOPHIE

Thursday morning dawns, and I want to get out of this dang hospital. I'm tired of this bed and the IVs and the needles. The staff here has been wonderful. I've had amazing nurses and docs, but enough is enough. When the morning nurse assigned to me walks in at seven, the first thing out of my mouth is, "When do I get to go home?"

"I don't know, darlin'. You need to ask the doctor when he stops by today." I watch her as she writes her name on the whiteboard in my room: Delores.

"Okay," I say, defeated. "How 'bout real food? When do I get that? Oh, and a shower? I'm gross. I haven't showered since...." I shiver, thinking how long it's been.

She chuckles. "Sick of the hospital's food?"

"Yes, I want real meat. And something fried to a crisp." *God, I'm so hungry.*

"I'll see if I can drum you up something good for breakfast. How does that sound, sweetie? As for the shower, let me check."

Why can't I shower? I only have one IV going right now. But best not be grouchy now. "Okay." *Jeez, I sound like a whiner.*

"No problem. I'll be back shortly. Do you need anything else for now?"

"No. Thank you, Delores."

I turn on my television, and all that's on are the morning talk shows. I can't bring myself to watch them. While I'm flipping through the channels in search of an old movie, my breakfast is delivered. "Yuck," I grumble. "Scrambled eggs and bacon."

I like eggs and bacon, but these are a strange color. The pancakes are the only things on my plate that look edible. I pour the pack of syrup over the top and take a bite. Meh, they're okay. After only one small pancake, I'm full as a tick.

Once my breakfast tray is removed, I doze for a while. Delores awakens me as she works to remove my last tube. Yay! She helps me walk to my bathroom and strips me out of my hospital gown so I can shower. She sets a shower seat in the middle of the stall, and I sit underneath a warm spray of water. It's the most blissful shower ever. Maybe it's not as good as Henry's shower, but it rivals it. As I scrub my body and hair, I do my best to keep the memories of Henry from my mind.

Now that I'm squeaky clean, Delores is my new best friend. She's brought a fresh hospital gown and socks. I hate walking around with my butt showing in the back, but I've got nothing else to wear. As I exit the bathroom, I stop in my tracks. Sitting next to my bed is the most gorgeous man I've ever seen. He gives me the most beautiful smile too. It disappears as soon as I ask, "Henry? What are you doing here?"

Instead of answering, he stands like he wants to help me to my bed, but Delores has got it. I walk gingerly back to the hardest mattress ever created and sit. "Do I need to get reconnected to that machine?" I ask, pointing to the monitor.

Delores chuckles. "No, honey, you're all done with the tubes and machines."

"Thank God. Now if I only had a pair of my own pajamas," I grumble.

"It won't be long now. You may get to go home tomorrow."

"Really?" I say excitedly.

"Maybe. You need to ask the doctor for sure, but that's what I heard at the nurses' station."

I clap my hands together like it's Christmas morning and I'm five. Getting out of here would be a dream come true.

I raise my feet up so I can rest them on the bed. The process of walking to the bathroom, showering, and then walking back to my bed has thoroughly exhausted me. I rotate around until I'm sitting up. Delores throws my thin, rough sheet up over my legs, and I take a deep breath. That was a lot of work to shower and walk ten feet. I hope it won't be long until I get my strength back.

I turn and look at Henry. "What are you doing here?" I sound like such a bitch, but I'm not happy he didn't visit me yesterday. I know, I told him to go, and he went, but still.

"Sophie, how are you feeling today?" he asks, sounding rather stiff.

"Better. You heard Delores? I may get to go home tomorrow. I'm pretty excited about that."

"I bet. Long hospital stays are not for sissies," he says with a small smile.

I giggle at that. "No, they aren't."

Enough small talk, I guess. Henry jumps right in. "The reason I'm here is to update you on your case."

Of course that's why he's here. He's not here to see *me*. "My case?"

"Attempted murder."

"Attempted murder?"

"Well, what did you think Ari was trying to do? Keep you locked in a sauna so you could lose weight?"

I wince at that comment. I know I'm fat, but that doesn't mean words like that, from him, don't hurt.

"I-I didn't mean that the way it sounded. I think you're perfect, Sophie," he says, attempting a retraction.

"It's fine. Attempted murder. What happened with Ari?"

"She's in custody, as is Brittany Smith."

"Brit too? I guess it's not a complete surprise. The two of them are inseparable."

"We've got a good case against Ari. Brit has agreed to testify against Arianna, but Ari is trying to pin the entire thing on Brittany."

I snort at that. "No way. Arianna was the queen bee with those three at work. Heck, even Brooke did her bidding. No, Ari's the ringleader for sure."

"We know. Plus, there's video footage of her exiting Bridal Belles alone about the time she locked you in the closet."

"Video? Did Brooke install cameras? I didn't know that."

"No. But the surrounding businesses have, and they captured the images. She also stole another dress on her way out."

I gasp at that. "That's *four* dresses," I mutter. "Well, she may have stolen more since she could still use the code. Brooke is an idiot."

"Yep. She sure is. Well, that's all I wanted to say. I'll get out of your hair. Glad to hear you're getting kicked out of this place, Soph. I'll see ya." He stands and walks toward the door.

"That's it? You're leaving?"

"Yeah, I've gotta go. Still a lot to do with William's case."

"Oh, right, of course," I whisper.

"Goodbye, Sophie."

Shit, why did that sound so final? "Bye, Henry." After I see his beautiful, firm, round, ass leave my room, I feel sadder and more alone than I have in a long time—and that's saying something. I wish things could work out with him, but it's just too late.

AFTER A LUNCH COMPRISING OF PUDDING, two rock-hard chicken strips, and an apple, I take a short nap. A tap at my door wakes me from a restless dream. I croak, "Come in."

It's Sarah Flynn at my door. "Sophie? Are you awake, dear?"

"Um, yeah," I say, groggily.

"Oh, we woke you up. I'm so sorry. Should we come back?"

We? "No, I'm fine. I'm just mind-numbingly bored, so I sleep."

Sarah giggles at that. I look up and see two gorgeous women standing behind Sarah. They must be Henry's sisters. Holy moly, they are stunning—and tall. From what I've seen so far, the Flynn children take after their father. Both of the young women have strawberry-blonde hair, heart-shaped faces, and big blue eyes.

"Wow, you're both beautiful," I say with awe.

They both laugh at me. "Oh, stop," says the older one.

Or I think she's older. Sandy? "Are you Sandy?"

"That's me, and this is little Emily," Sandy says, pointing a thumb back to her sister.

Emily isn't little. She's at least five foot ten and slim.

"I know what you're thinking, Sophie," says Sarah. "They look nothing like me, do they?" She laughs.

"You're beautiful too, Sarah. But the children I've seen so far all look like Mr. Flynn."

"I know, thank goodness!" Sarah exclaims.

Both of her girls try to make her feel better. "Mom, stop it. We all love you. A lot of us have your personality," says Emily, sweetly.

"So we've got that going for us," adds Sandy. Smiling, she walks toward my bed with her hand raised. She's got a strong handshake. I feel like my hand will be bruised. "It's nice to meet you, Sophie. I'm sorry it's under these circumstances."

"Me too," adds Emily, smiling. "Glad to meet you. I had to see the woman that has my big brother all insecure and pathetic." She giggles.

"Henry is not pathetic, Em," Sarah snaps.

I can see, just from that comment, Sarah is protective of her children.

"He's a mess, Mom. I talked to him yesterday, and I've never heard him so lost. I feel sorry for the guy. You should take pity on him and take him back, Sophie," Sandy explains.

"We aren't.... We weren't ever together."

Sandy nods. "I'm sure he did his part to confuse the situation. He was fucked over by—"

"Language!" shouts Sarah.

"Sorry, Mom. Anyway, he was screwed over by Angela."

"But that was like ten years ago. He needs to get over that," interjects Emily.

"Says the woman who was ten at the time," snipes Sandy.

"Twelve," reminds Emily.

"Whatever, we kept you out of that drama. You were too little. And you *loved* Angela."

My head ping-pongs back and forth as I watch the exchange between Sandy and Emily. Sarah is not paying any attention to their verbal battle. She's watching me instead.

"She had great fashion sense, what can I say?" explains Emily.

"You could say she was a money-grubbing bitch." Sandy turns and says to me, "Now *she* was a gold digger."

Horrified, I ask, "You know about that too?"

"Oh, we *all* know. Nothing is a secret for long in the Flynn family. Word to the wise, if you don't want all of us to know something, keep it to yourself." Emily snorts.

"True dat," adds Sandy as they high-five each other.

"That's enough, girls. Can't you see you're overwhelming Sophie?"

"No, it's fine. It's fun watching them talk to each other. They're very animated."

All three women laugh at that.

Sandy adds, "If you think we're animated, you should see us all together."

"You should!" exclaims Emily. "Sunday. Come over on Sunday! I'll bet you'll be out of this place by then. It'll be epic! You *have* to come."

"Oh, I don't know. I'll have to see... maybe."

"Don't fret, Sophie. You're always welcome. When you feel up to it, we'd love to have you," Sarah says, putting an end to that conversation.

The Flynn women only stay for about half an hour—long enough for me to get worn out again. I doze most of the day away. The doctor stops by at four o'clock. He's happy with my progress and agrees that I can probably leave tomorrow. I'll need to arrange a ride home. I should call Henry, but I don't want to. Maybe Detective Peters could give me a lift. I have his card right here.

At six o'clock, knocking pulls me out of my most recent nap. I've never slept this much in my entire life, I swear. "Come in."

The door opens slowly, revealing Henry holding bags.

I must look surprised because he asks shyly, "Did I catch you at a bad time? I can leave."

"No!" I say, way too excitedly. "Come in, please."

"I've come bearing gifts." Henry holds up the bags. One is white plastic with the Macy's logo on it, and the other is brown paper.

"What is it?"

"In this bag," he says, holding up the brown sack, "is the world's best cheeseburger and French fries from Sammy's."

Ooh, I love Sammy's burgers. "It smells amazing!" I'm so hungry I could eat the sack the food comes in.

Setting down the brown sack, Henry says, "In the other hand is...." He pulls out the contents.

"Pajamas?"

"Well, loungewear is what the clerk called them. I heard you say this morning you wished you had real clothes, so I picked you up some. I hope you like them. I couldn't find any with pictures of pizza or cupcakes on them, but these reminded me of you."

They are adorable. It's a T-shirt and a pair of cropped leggings. The tee is white with dainty little flowers of every color on them, and the leggings are black. "They're cute. Thank you so much!"

"I'm not done. While I couldn't find any pants with food on them, I found these." He whips out a pair of panties, placing them in my hands.

I giggle. "They're covered in donuts."

"Not just any donuts, the best kind: *sprinkle* donuts."

I laugh. "I love them. Thank you so much, Henry." I smile from ear to ear. It feels like I haven't laughed or smiled for so long. My cheeks hurt from the new sensation.

"Do you want me to help you change?"

I expected to see him making some pervy facial expression, but he looks sincere. "Sure. Thanks." He's already seen me naked. I won't get self-conscious now. Besides, being in the hospital, you learn fast that modesty is not possible.

I slide to the side of the bed closest to him and turn my upper body so he can untie the back of my gown. I slip the top down and reach for the tee.

"Damn, Sophie. You've lost so much weight." He doesn't sound happy about it.

I slip the tee on and then lean forward to stand. "Don't worry. I'll gain it back with the help of cheeseburgers and fries from Sammy's."

He nods, looking serious. "Hold on. Let me slide these over your feet first, then you can stand." He slides the donut undies over my feet first and then the leggings. "Put your hands on my shoulders. Keep them there." I do as he suggests holding tight as I stand up. Bending over, Henry pulls up the panties first and then returns to the floor to grab the pants. I'm glad I've got my hands on his shoulders. I'm woozy right now.

"There! You look good as new," Henry says, smiling.

"I feel good as new. I've missed real clothes. Thank you so much, Henry. Now, let's eat!"

Running around the room, it only takes him minutes to set up my dinner on the rolling tray. He has food for himself too, so we eat in companionable silence until he asks, "Want to watch television?"

"Sure. Maybe there's a movie on or something." I take a bite of my cheeseburger and moan, "Oh my God. It's so good."

"Jesus, Soph. Please don't moan like that."

"Like what?"

He looks at me with one arched eyebrow.

"Oh." I giggle. "Well, this burger is better than sex."

"Excuse me?"

I refuse to get into this argument. I can't win it. "Let's watch the Cubs."

It worked. I've distracted him. "The Cubs? It's their year again, you know?"

"Yeah, right," I grumble. "That's what they say every year."

"It is! Just you wait and see."

I change the subject yet again. "Your mom came to visit."

"Yeah, I thought she might."

"I also met your sisters."

"Great," he deadpans. "When did you meet the gossip girls?"

I laugh at that. They did like to gossip.

"Today. Your mom came alone yesterday and brought your sisters with her today. I liked them. They were funny, but I especially liked your mom."

"Mom's great. She's strong and loyal. You remind me of her a little."

"I noticed that we're both short and our hair's a similar style."

"Oh, yeah. I guess you're right. I hadn't thought of that. I'm glad you liked them. I'm sure they'll tell me how much they like you when I see them next."

"How do you know they like me?"

"Everyone likes you, Soph."

"Not everyone," I say, looking around my room. *Some people hate me.*

We watch the Cubbies as we eat and don't say much else. It's okay. I sort of like sitting around with Henry, not talking. It's much better than sitting alone. He's good company even like this.

"Sophie, what are you going to do when you get home?"

"What do you mean?"

"I mean, who will take care of you?"

"No one. Me. I'll take care of myself." His question makes me feel somewhat defensive. I don't need round-the-clock care.

"Soph, you'll have a hard time at first."

"At first, yeah, but after that, I'll be fine. I need to get better so I can go back to work."

"What? Where are you going to work?"

"What do you mean? I'll work at the bridal store."

His face turns a vivid shade of red. "The fuck you will!" he shouts.

"I will. And you can't do anything about it!" I've balled up my napkin so tightly the Cubs could use it.

"Sophia Kincaid, you will *not* go back to Bridal Belles. And that's an order!" His voice is so loud I'm sure the nurses will be in soon.

"You're not my father. Jeez, Hank. You don't get to tell me what to do."

"You can't go back to work for Brooke Bellamy!"

"Why not? *She* didn't lock me in a closet!" We're both shouting now. Any minute and a nurse or security guard will run in here.

"She may as well have been the one that locked you in there!"

"What do you mean? She was nowhere near the store when it happened."

"Precisely!" he says, pointing his first finger at me and shaking it in front of my face. "Let me tell you something about Brooke Bellamy—she was negligent in at least four ways."

He holds up four fingers, ticking them off as he makes each point. "One, she did *not* press charges against Arianna and Brittany when she first discovered they were stealing. If she had, they would have been charged with a felony—grand theft—and Brit and Ari would have been in custody and, therefore, would not have been able to harass and hurt you. Two, she did not change the security code on the back door of the store. That enabled Arianna Templeton access to the store and, therefore, access to you. Three, she did not show up for work on Sunday. No doubt, you were expecting her to be there so you could be... so you could be freed."

He sounds a bit choked up as he says that. It's true. I was

holding on to hope that Brooke would let me out on Sunday morning, but she chose to take the day off instead.

"Four, while the police were swarming her store after you were found, she was in her office surfing the web, looking at celebrity news sites. She wasn't rushing to the emergency room to sit at your side. She didn't even ask anyone if you were alive. She doesn't give two shits about you."

I gasp at the last comment. I know deep down she doesn't. "But that's not why I work there. I do it for my brides." *Yeah, I can keep telling myself that forever.*

"Sophie, you need to get a lawyer as soon as you get out of here. Then you need to sue her for those points I've just made. She should pay your hospital bills, lost wages, and an additional settlement that will enable you the time you need to heal and find other employment. If you don't do that, then Brooke Bellamy will just go on with her self-centered, self-serving existence just waiting to hurt someone else and treat them like shit."

"I don't want to talk about this with you, Hank. It's not your problem," I say as I cross my arms angrily.

"It's not my problem? Not my problem!" He jumps to his feet and begins pacing as he runs his hands through his hair.

"You've been my problem since... God, never mind. I'm out of here," he shouts as he stomps to the door, throws it open, and exits.

As soon as he's out the door, I cry. I'm a *problem* to him? I swear I've never cried so much in my life, and it started the day I met Henry Flynn. God, I'm a mess.

30

HENRY

As soon as I step out of Sophie's room, I lean on the wall next to her door. People are staring at me, but I don't give a fuck. I wasn't yelling at Sophie to be an asshole. I was yelling because she needs to listen. What is she thinking? Does she want to go back to work at that place? Is it not *my problem?* The cheeseburger is better than sex? Better than sex with me? There's nothing better than sex with Sophie. Goddamn, I'm losing my freaking mind. I need a beer.

Good thing my favorite drinking buddy is only a few minutes away. I grab my phone and give him a call. "Keith? It's Hank. You free tonight? I need a beer or ten."

"No can do, bud. Got something going on with Beth."

Beth is Keith's girl. They've been together for two years, living together for one. She's cool. Normal. She has her moments, especially when there are too many Flynns around their place for too long. I get that.

"All right. Talk to ya."

"Yep." Click.

Man of few words. I can appreciate that.

So, that leaves me with two options. Well, three options. I

could call another brother or sister to meet me for a few beers. I could drink alone. Or I could call Kent and see if there's anything I can do on the Gibbons case. Work will help take my mind off Sophie.

Besides, Kent's taken up a lot of slack this week since Sophie was hospitalized. It's what partners do, but it's time for me to get back to it. I find Kent's name in my contacts and press Send.

"Jesus, Hank. It's about damn time."

"Sorry, Kent. I'm back to it. What do you need from me?"

"Be here bright and early for a briefing. I think we figured something out. But not *your* early, *my* early. I'm talkin' 8:00 a.m. Got it?"

"Got it. See you then." I wonder what he's got. I guess I can forget about getting drunk and get a good night's sleep instead. If I can stop worrying about Sophie long enough to sleep, that is.

On my ride home, I dial Mom. Maybe she can talk sense into Sophie. "Mom?"

"Hello, Henry. How are you tonight?"

"Fine. Not fine. Listen, I need your help."

"I'm listening, honey."

"Sophie wants to go back to work right away. I don't think she should."

"Where's she going to work? I bet Dec and Keith could use a hand in the office."

"Mom, she wants to go back to work at the Bridal Belles."

"Oh, no! What is she thinking?"

"I know, right? She won't listen. She's so damn stubborn."

"Like someone else I know," Mom says under her breath.

"I heard that."

"Why don't I pop over there tomorrow and have a chat with her. Does she get to go home tomorrow?"

"Yeah."

"Well, I'll go over first thing in the morning. She won't be released until later in the day. I can give her a ride home if she doesn't have one yet."

Damn it, I didn't think about that. I bet she's got no one. Fuck. "Thanks, Mom. Love you."

"Love you too, honey."

JESUS, eight in the morning is like the ass crack of dawn for me. I think the earliest I've been to work in recent months was nine. I sit in the squad room waiting for Kent to show. There's a file on my desk relating to Gibbons's death. I leaf through the papers, seeing copies of pay stubs from the last year or more. *Those assholes finally sent them.*

Another half hour passes, and I find my way into the break room to pour a cup of the world's worst coffee. Whoever made this pot is particularly evil. It's as thick as tar. Ugh. At least it will wake me up. Where the fuck is Kent?

I make my way over to my desk again. "Well, hallelujah, the asshat showed."

"Shut it, Hank. I was *investigating*. Remember how to do that?"

"Yeah. Sorry, man. Thanks for picking up my slack. Tell me what you've got?"

"Come on, we're all meeting up in the conference room in five. Let's go."

I follow Kent over to the elevator. I usually take the stairs to get a little cardio in, but I think three flights of stairs would kill Kent. Once in the room, I grab a seat near the front.

Captain Cooke is ready to start as soon as we enter. "Gentlemen and lady"—he smiles at Vickie Smart, the lone female detective in our precinct—"we have a break in this fucking case. Thanks to Hank for figuring out this had something to do with

Gibbons's pay stubs and retirement account and for Kent and Hank's diligence in tracking down those pay stubs from the last seven years and to our techs and the forensic accountant for putting this all together so it makes sense to us mere mortals." Cap chuckles at his own joke and then takes a deep breath.

"Here's what we have. Mind you, we've still got work to do, but we have a solid lead. We think William Gibbons discovered money was being taken from his retirement account systematically. It was tiny sums of money, but over time, it added up. He appears to have been a tad OCD about tracking his money and other accounts. His flash drives and even the old disks were full of financial crap from the last couple of decades."

Kent jumps into the conversation. "Someone has been taking a little over $1.50 every month from every employee for about seven years. The amounts vary from month to month and year to year. Our forensic accountant spoke to a financial planner who specializes in corporate retirement funds. He said there's a strange charge on William's retirement paperwork. There's a fee for 'Trading and Maintenance.'"

The captain says, "Our retirement expert says it's a bogus charge. When we did the math on Gibbons's papers, the exact amount listed under 'Trading and Maintenance' was the same amount his retirement fund was reduced each pay period."

"Long story short—"

"Too late," some ass yells from the back.

"Fuck off, Kimball," Kent mumbles. "Long story short, there's a shit ton of money going somewhere, and William Gibbons figured it out."

"Do you think whoever killed him knew he was on to them?" asks an idiot rookie in the front row.

"Well, Sherlock, yes, we do. He hacked into the Luciph database to get that information. Our techs say companies like Luciph have ways of tracking unwanted visitors into their system. Unless Gibbons used a proxy of some type to hide his footprint, they could have and probably did figure out it was him."

"Who are we looking at for this?" Peppers asks.

"My guess is MacClenny did it, or it was that fucking tool Christopher Collins," snipes Kent.

"We found out they worked together at Tyrex in Human Resources," I add. "I did some cyberstalking on LinkedIn and found out they both went to Rutgers. They graduated in the same year with the same major. Odds are they've known each other for a long time."

"Damn good work, Hank," says the captain, smiling.

"When did you have time to do that with all the shit that went down with your girl?" asks Kent.

"I did it while she slept. Smartphones are man's best friend," I say with a chuckle.

"Okay," interrupts Cap. "It's time to get a judge to sign off on getting both of their bank records. Let's see if we can follow the money. They're our best bet. If this is as big as I think it is—and I think this is fucking huge—I suspect there will be a ton of money that's gone bye-bye, and I guess it's now offshore. So you know what that means?"

"Fucking feds!" yells Matt Hampton.

"Fucking feds," I grumble. "If they get wind of this, we're off the case."

"Yep," replied Captain Cooke. "You don't have much time. I'll have to call them if this in fact went offshore. So get out there and find that money. Get the techs on this one, would ya? Everyone else, dismissed."

After the meeting, Kent and I head out for coffee and a chat. "I wish we could get in there and arrest Collins and MacClenny. I know they did this. My gut tells me they've done this before."

"Murder?" he says with his mouth full of sub sandwich.

"No. Embezzling money. I'm gonna check that out with Tyrex. You wanna chase down their bank account information?"

"Yeah. I'll get on it."

"Great. We can talk tomorrow." I finish up my coffee and Danish, throw my trash away, and head out. Time to call Tyrex Inc.

31
─────

SOPHIE

The sun streams in through my hospital window and my first thought as I blink awake is, *I get to go home today!* I've never been so excited about anything in my life. I can't wait to see my run-down old house because I miss my bed, my kitchen, my coffee maker, and most of all, I miss my books.

My love affair with books has been lifelong. My dad and I would go to the library every single Saturday even before I could read. He'd let me pick out three books. It was like getting presents every visit. I still love the library, but I use my e-reader most of the time now. I can still check books out of the library through the device, but sometimes I miss a real book. That's when I head to my office and scan my bookshelves to pick up an old friend. I also buy books at secondhand stores, thrift shops, and sometimes at the library if they are selling off old editions of books. Because of that, I have several bookshelves full of classics and personal favorites.

It was my love of books that lead me to my major and dissertation: "The Origin and Meaning of Literary Names from Fiction." I love discovering the author's secrets by analyzing the character's names and places referenced in each tomb. Some authors are better at that than others, like F. Scott Fitzgerald, Shakespeare, and Ernest Hemingway, just to name a few.

As I lie in my hard hospital bed, daydreaming about my books, gentle tapping draws my attention to the present. "Come in," I say sleepily.

"Hi there, Sophie. It's just me again. I hope I didn't wake you. I feel a little like a pest."

"Hi, Sarah. No. I've really enjoyed your visits. Thank you for keeping me company the last few days. I get to go home today! I can't wait," I say with a squeak.

"I bet. Hospital stays are the worst," she says with a look of pity on her face. "Listen, Sophie, I need to talk to you about something."

"Uh-oh. Am I in trouble?"

Sarah chuckles. "No, honey, of course not. But since you mentioned it, Henry called me last night with a few concerns."

"Uh-huh," I say tentatively. *This ought to be good.*

"Now, I know we just met and it's none of my business, but as a mom, I need to tell you it's not a great idea to go back to that job at the wedding store."

"Uh-huh," I say, attempting to calm myself. *I want to kill Henry.*

"Just hear me out." She's almost pleading.

"Okay." I sigh.

"It's not safe for you there, sweetheart. We don't know how long Ari what's-her-name will be locked up. She could be out on the street right now. It's just not safe."

"Well, I won't be going back to work for a couple of weeks, doctor's orders." I was surprised that Dr. Montell had given me so many restrictions, one of which was not returning to work for at least two weeks. Even then he wants to see me before he releases me. So it could be even longer.

"That's a relief! Are you going to hire an attorney?"

"I don't know."

She opens her purse and rifles through the pockets. "Wait, I know I have a card. Oh, here it is."

Sarah hands me a small card that reads Sharon Thompson, Attorney at Law. "She's a terrific lawyer and a good friend of mine. We went to school together. Call her. Talk to her. Tell her everything and see what she advises. It won't cost you a cent to call her. Will you do that? Please?"

"Okay," I say, reluctantly. "I will. It won't hurt to talk to someone." I look at Sarah warningly. "I'm not guaranteeing I'll do anything, though. But I will call her."

"Wonderful. Terrific! That's all I ask." She smiles wide. "Now, do you need a ride home today because I'd be—"

"No. Thanks. I've got a ride home. I don't know when I'll be released on my own recognizance." I giggle at my joke. "But I've got it covered. Thank you for offering, Sarah. That was very kind."

"My pleasure. I hope to see you soon. Dinner on any Sunday—it's an open invitation."

"I remember. Thanks."

She leans in and gives me a peck on the cheek. "You're a wonderful young woman, Sophie. I'm glad you're in my life."

That makes my eyes and nose burn. That was a nice thing to say. She's glad I'm in her life? "Me too," I say, smiling.

Three o'clock. That's the time I get out of this place. I have a call in to my ride. I'll be packed and ready to go at three on the dot. I can't wait!

"HERE, SOPHIE, HOLD MY HAND," Detective Peters says as he reaches for my hand to help me out of my wheelchair. His car is parked near the hospital entrance, but I have to step down a curb to get into his passenger door. I'm still weak but getting stronger every day. I know I'll have things to do at home. I hope I still have food at my place. I don't have it in me to make a trip to the grocery store.

He wraps his arm around my waist to make sure I'm stable, and I grab the door up by the window for extra support and turn to sit in the seat. I'm out of breath and tired. After packing up my things, along with the adrenaline involved with getting released, just walking two steps has taken it out of me. I slide my legs in, and he shuts the car door.

"Thank you, Detective Peters."

"Call me Joel. Okay?"

"Okay."

Running around to his side, he opens his door and slides in. His car is basic—not the sports car Henry owns. "I've got your address in my GPS, but you'll want to pay attention and let me know if I've made a wrong turn. Do you want me to stop anywhere? Do you need anything?"

"No. I'm good. I'm sure everything I need is at home." Not. I don't want him to have to stop for me, so I'll figure it out. I could have groceries delivered if I'm desperate.

Time flies, and before I know it, Joel has pulled up in front of my house. I look out my window and smile. I love this old house. I hope I don't have to sell it.

I reach to open my door, but Joel stops me. "Let me help you, Sophie. You're still weak."

I nod reluctantly. I hate depending on others, but what choice do I have? Joel comes around to my side. Once I have both feet on the concrete, he wraps his arms around my waist and walks me up the curb.

"Not far until we get to your front steps. Are you up to the climb?" he asks.

"I think so." I bring my arms around him for a friendly hug. "Thank you so—"

"What. The. Ever. Loving. Fuck?" shouts Henry.

"Great," mutters Joel. "You didn't tell him I was taking you home?"

"No. It's none of his business."

"Jesus," he grumbles. "Sophie, Hank is—"

"Hank is what, asshole?" Henry asks.

"I would say selfish, egotistical, and fucking jealous," Joel says, laughing.

Why is he laughing? Henry looks like he wants to kill him.

"All true," Henry admits. "Get your fucking hands off her, Peters. Before I tear your arms off."

"Hank!" I yell. "Knock it off. Joel was just doing me a favor."

"Joel? You're calling him Joel? What's going on here? Are you dating him?" he says, pointing at Detective Peters.

"God, no," Joel quickly answers.

"Gee, thanks!" That hurt, even though I wouldn't date Joel either. It's just the point. "God, you're *both* assholes." I attempt to walk on my own, but that doesn't work. I take my first step toward my stoop and wobble. My legs are like Jell-O. Before I can lose my balance, big arms wrap around me, securing me to a solid chest. *Henry.*

"Let me go, Hank. I can do it. I need to do this on my own. Just let go!" As I rant, I hit him on the chest with both hands. It's not hard enough to hurt a fly since I've got no strength. It's kind of pathetic, actually.

Henry wraps his hands around mine to stop my punching. "Baby, calm down," he whispers.

I immediately stop. He hasn't called me baby for a long time. I can't remember the last time. "You called me baby."

"Yeah. Because you *are* my baby."

"I'm not anyone's baby. I'm just me," I recite weakly.

Our little tussle is interrupted when Joel asks, "You got this, Hank?" I know he's hoping he can leave without getting beat up by Henry.

"Yeah. Leave. Please," Henry spouts.

"Henry. Stop it. He was just helping me. He's a friend."

"I don't know how I feel about you having a guy as a friend, babe."

"Get over it. You don't have a say in the matter." I look over and see that Joel is already behind the wheel of his car. In a matter of seconds, he's gone. "Now what?" I ask Henry.

"Now I help you to your house and see what kind of state the place is in. I want to check your fridge."

"Oh, right." He's going to be sorely disappointed. There's not much there. "I haven't shopped in a long while. Plus, there could be expired things. Fuzzy things. Scary stuff."

"Never fear, Henry is here," he says, puffing his chest out slightly. He laughs, which makes me laugh.

"Henry, you're a dork."

He leans down and gives me a soft kiss. I'm glad it was a soft kiss. Anything more and I would have passed out. Before I can think, Henry has me lifted in his arms as he's walking up my front steps.

"Key?"

"In my purse."

"I'm gonna need a set of keys, Soph."

"Why?" Part of me likes the idea of Henry with a set of my keys, while the other part is terrified at the notion he'd have twenty-four-hour access to my home. Instead of answering, he just gives me a look. Since I know I need help for a day or two, I relent. "I have a spare set in the kitchen drawer closest to the coffee maker."

Pulling the key from my purse, I unlock my door, and push

it wide. The heat from inside engulfs me, and I stiffen in his arms. God, the heat is freaking me out. I wrap my arms around him tightly. "It's too hot, Henry! It's too hot," I cry out.

"Shh, it's okay. You're okay." He stands me up close to the front door, his hand on my stomach to keep me upright. "Okay, let me think for a second." He spots my window air conditioner. "Stay right there while I go turn on the A/C units. Give me five minutes." I lean against the house as he disappears inside. When he comes back, he asks, "You got any air conditioners upstairs?"

"Yeah, in my bedroom and in the spare bedroom."

I wait, holding onto the edge of the door. It's so damn hot, and it's too much. It feels like that terrible closet. It's not long before Henry is back and I'm in his arms again.

"Give it a few minutes to cool the place down, and I'll get you comfortable," he advises.

He helps me into the living room and settles me on the sofa closest to the cool air.

"I may never be able to turn off the A/C. That will cost me a fortune," I confess.

"I'm sure you will. You've just got to give it more time, Soph." Henry hands me a glass of water and a cool washcloth. "Your fridge isn't bad, but that's because there's nothing in there. I tossed the milk and bologna."

"I just bought the bologna. It didn't need to get tossed."

"Babe, bologna is disgusting. It needed to go. I'll get you comfortable. Then I'm gonna run to the store. Sound good?"

"Hank—"

"Henry," he says, warningly.

"*Henry*, I appreciate your help, but you can go home. Live your life. I'll call and get a few things delivered. It'll be fine."

With his hands on his narrow hips, he stares me down. He

takes a deep breath, in and out, then another one. "I guess it's time we had the talk."

"The talk?"

"The come-to-Jesus talk you obviously need."

"*Come-to-Jesus* talk?"

"Yeah, because you're clueless, Soph."

"I'm clueless? You're clu—"

He lifts his hand up to stop me from continuing and then kneels down in front of me, running his hands up from my knees to my upper thighs. His face is close enough to kiss. "Sophia Kincaid, you are clueless. You haven't caught on to what's going on here."

"What's going on here?"

"Us. You. Me. *Us*," he says, pointing first to me and then to himself.

"Us?" I sound like a parrot.

Taking yet another deep breath, Henry moves up onto the sofa next to me and wraps his hands around my waist, lifting me so I'm on his lap. He seems to like that position. "I need you to listen please."

Ooh, he said please. "Okay."

His hand rubbing my lower back feels amazing. His other hand rests on my upper thigh. "The minute we met, I felt something. I saw your beautiful face, and it hit me here." He pats his chest. "I can't explain it, but looking into your big brown eyes and at your freckled nose and perfect lips, it affected me."

I can't think of anything to say, so I don't.

"Then you wrapped your little arms around me when you tried to measure me, and it took my breath away. Leaving the store, I thought I'd never see you again. But fate had another plan for us, Sophie. I'm sorry it took William getting killed to make that happen, but we can't control fate."

"Fate? Really, Hen—"

"Shh." He places a finger over my lips. "I'm not done."

I remain quiet.

"Fate is real, Sophie. We are living proof of that. Anyway, the minute I stepped into your back door to interview you, I felt an amazing sense of calm come over me. I also felt protective of you... and turned on." He winks. "You're a sexy little thing, baby. Especially in those tight yoga pant things with the pizzas all over them."

I blush at that, but I also roll my eyes. I'm not sexy. "Jeez, Henry. I—"

"I'm still not done. So there I sat in your kitchen, feeling horny and protective. You were upset about Willy and so sweet I started falling right then and there."

"Falling?"

"Yeah. Falling. That happened right there in *that* chair." He points toward my kitchen. "And I'm still falling for you."

I let out a gasp that shocks even me. "But you said—"

"I know I fucked it up with you, multiple times. I'm sorry about that. Angela messed with my head, and I was fighting this thing with you and acting like a douche. I wish I could go back and get a do-over, but I can't."

"No. You can't."

"Oh, shit. Sophie, are you telling me you don't want this? You don't want to explore what we have? You can't deny it. I know you feel something for me."

"I do. Henry, I do. I'm just scared. I told you. I can't take the ups and downs with you. It's an emotional roller coaster."

"I know. I won't lie and say I won't overreact about things or I won't fuck up. I will. It's inevitable because I act before I think sometimes."

"That's for sure," I mutter.

Laughing, he keeps right on going. "I know, but please give us a chance. I've known you were mine since that first day at the tux shop. I feel as though I was put on this earth to take care of you, Sophie."

"But I don't need you to take care of me. Things are fine for me."

"*Fine for you?* What do you call all of this shit that's been happening to you? I worry about you. It's a two-way street, you know. I need someone to take care of me too. I guess I'll have to wait and see if you're up to that challenge."

I smile at him. That was a good choice of words for sure. Without saying a word, I lean in and kiss him. I don't have the energy for anything else but a kiss. I deepen the kiss by using my tongue to encourage him to open his mouth.

He opens right away and runs his tongue over mine. I can feel him get hard beneath me. I guess I do turn him on. I run my fingers through his hair. It's getting long, but I like it. His beard is scruffy, and I like that too. I love all of his textures. *Love? Did I say* love?

His hands pull me closer to him so we are chest to chest. Breaking the kiss, I whisper, "I'm falling for you too, Henry."

His smile is so big and beautiful, it makes me weak. Leaning in, he kisses me all over again. Henry doesn't take it any further, though. Instead, he kisses my face and my neck before lifting my hand to his mouth and kissing my fingers. "I'll get you settled here, and then I'm running to get groceries. I'm starving, woman."

Laughing, I agree to his plan.

"I won't let anything else happen to you. I won't let anyone hurt you again, sweetheart." He says the last part as he leans down and gently kisses my lips. "And if you're pregnant, I won't let anything happen to our child." His palm settles on my stomach.

"Henry?"

He looks at me expectantly.

"I forgot to tell you. So much was happening, and you got mad at me and..."

"And?"

"I'm not pregnant. I wasn't pregnant."

He looks almost defeated—sad and defeated. "Oh."

"It's okay to be relieved. I won't be upset. It's probably for the best anyway."

"I guess," he says, distantly.

"Henry?"

"Yeah?"

"It wasn't meant to be."

"I... yeah. You're right. It wasn't the right time." He still sounds like he's lost in thought. "Well"—he pats my leg—"let's get you comfortable on this couch, and I'll run to the market."

"Yep." I try to sound upbeat. "Can you get me a book from my bookshelf in the office? *Great Expectations* if you can find it. They're in order by author, so Dickens."

"Sure thing. Anything else you need?"

"I've got water, and I'll have a book. I'll be fine until you get back."

After bringing me my book, he kisses my forehead. "I'll be back as soon as I can. Call my cell if you need anything. Oh, and I grabbed your spare set of keys," Henry says as he heads out the front door.

Wow. So much has happened in the last month that my head is spinning. But nothing, even the murder of William, surprised me more than hearing Henry Flynn tell me he's falling for me. Henry Flynn wants me. That just doesn't seem possible.

I lie back on my old sofa and open my book. As I prepare to read the first paragraph, my front door opens again.

Henry steps in and sets down a large black duffel bag. He winks and says, "Be back before you know it, babe." Then he shuts the door and locks it with the key.

I blink at the door and then stare at the black bag. *What the hell? He packed a bag? He isn't staying here, is he?*

32

——————

HENRY

Damn it, I wish I had asked her what she likes to eat. I couldn't tell from the little she had in her refrigerator. She had even less in her cupboards. There was a bunch of those cheap ramen noodle packs, soup, and bologna. There wasn't even any bread. Crackers. She had several boxes of soda crackers. It makes me wonder how she even survived.

I will not panic. I've picked up enough food and supplies for my mom over the years; I can make educated choices. Tea. My mom loves tea. She also loves those fancy cookies with her tea. I'll get a bunch of different teas and cookies.

I circle every aisle looking for things I've seen Mom use. I wish I could tell you that my short marriage could help me with this, but Angela didn't eat. She drank, smoked, and chewed gum. Her biggest fear in life was gaining a pound. I still can't figure out what I saw in her.

Focus, Hank! You need food for your woman! She needs healthy food with extra calories, so she can gain that weight back. She's skin and bones. Instead of overthinking, I grab things from each section of the store like meat and cheese, bread, milk, butter, eggs, yogurt, and cereal. I also buy napkins, paper towels, dish soap, laundry soap, soft cleaning soap for sinks, tampons, maxi pads—yeah, don't even ask how humiliating that is. I buy beer for me and wine for Sophie along with soda pop, bottled water, sparkling water, snack chips, vitamins, shampoo, toothpaste, and more beer.

When I've got everything, I check out and load my car to the brim with plastic bags. The last time I shopped like this was for my Super Bowl party last year. Even though my beloved Bears didn't make it even to the playoffs, I had a party. I *always* have a Super Bowl party. It's a Flynn family tradition. I wonder if Sophie likes football.

My ride home is quiet as I think about the events at home. *Home?* I remember thinking we were home when I took Sophie back to my place. Maybe home is just where she is or where we are together. Yeah, that feels right.

I get lucky and get the spot directly in front of her house. I'd love to make an area to park my car in the back off the alley sometime. Maybe I'll talk to her about that. Hopping out, I pop my trunk and grab as many bags as I can carry and still unlock her door. I ease it open and peek inside. She's asleep. As quietly as possible, I push the door open and walk to the kitchen. I set the first load down and head back out for my second run.

"Henry? What are you doing?"

"Grabbing the groceries, babe. Back in a sec." Now that she's awake, I can do this faster and noisier. It takes four trips to bring in everything from the car. On my last trip in, Sophie is sitting at her kitchen table, her mouth hanging open.

"Henry, what the hell? I'll never eat all of this food."

"It's not just for you."

"Am I having a party or something?"

"It's for both of us."

"Still. You could never eat all of this in one night. Or can you?" She looks at me with worry.

I chuckle at her cute little nose all scrunched up. "Babe, I'll be here for a while." *Hopefully forever.*

"What does 'a while' mean?"

"Until I think I should go."

"Until *you* think you should go? Do I get a say in any of this?"

"You don't want me here?" I'm slightly hurt by this. "Because I thought you liked me, at least a little."

"I do like you, Henry. I just didn't sign up for this. It's like you're moving into my house."

I chuckle again. *Yeah, I am.* "No, Soph, I'm just here until you get back on your feet." *Yeah, right.*

"Oh. Okay. I guess that's fine. I appreciate that you've helped me so much. How much do I owe you for all of this?" She looks flushed at that question.

"Since I'll eat 75 percent of this stuff, I'll just pay for it. You can get the next round." *Over my dead body.*

"Next round? I thought you said—"

"It's just a figure of speech, Sophie. You know what I mean, right?"

"I guess."

My baby is so nervous about all of this. It's cute as hell. Do you know how many women would love to have me staying with them? I know I sound like a braggart, but it's the damned truth. I'm a catch. I chuckle.

"Why are you laughing, Henry? You're acting weird tonight."

"I think you're adorable, baby." I lean over and kiss her cute pixie nose. She blushes. It's so beautiful. "Let me put these things away. Do you want a cup of tea and a cookie while you watch me work?"

She giggles at that. "Sure. That sounds great."

"I picked up frozen pizza and a salad mix for dinner. Is that okay with you? I'm not much of a cook, so you'll have to put up with that until you're up to cooking."

"Sure. Pizza sounds good. Thank you."

"You're welcome. Why don't you go in the living room and relax? Pick something out for us to watch. Can we eat in front of the television?"

"Yeah. I'll see what's on the tube."

After she goes into the living room again, I bring her a cup of tea and a paper towel with several cookies. "How's that?"

"Great! I could get used to having you around. You'd better watch out." She giggles again.

I'm counting on it.

After putting away all the food, I slide the pizza into the hot oven and toss the little salad kit that I bought. I love these things; everything is inside the bag. It's just bam, and you've got salad. Eleven minutes and our pizza's all done. I load up our plates with pizza and salad then set them in front of her before heading back into the kitchen to grab a beer for me and a glass of milk for Sophie. She needs her protein.

"How's that? Can I get you anything else before I sit?"

"No. But, um, I don't like milk very much."

"Sophie, you need the protein. Try to drink it. I can put chocolate syrup in there if you'd prefer." In case you aren't aware, chocolate milk is a great recovery drink after workouts. So, if she wants it, it would be a good thing.

"Do you mind? I'd love chocolate milk," she asks shyly.

"No problem." I grab her glass and head back to the kitchen. I return with a chocolaty concoction for my girl.

"Mmm, thanks."

We watch a weekly game show that's always on around

dinnertime. After dinner, I put our dishes in the sink to clean up later then curl up with her on the couch to watch the Cubs game. She leans her head on my shoulder, and before the second inning is over, she's asleep. It feels... it feels right.

Before I fall asleep too, I turn off the television, stand up, and lift Sophie off the couch. She wakes before I have her against my chest.

"Henry?"

"Shh, I've got you. Let's go upstairs."

"I can walk."

"Tomorrow. You can walk up the stairs tomorrow." I carry her up to her room and set her on the bed. "Do you need to use the restroom?"

"I want to shower. I feel gross. I'll sleep better," she says, standing.

I take her hand and walk her into the bathroom. It's one of those old bathrooms with the claw-foot tub. There's no shower, only a handheld shower device. No wonder she wanted to shower at my place. Looking around, I notice that there's plenty of room in here to add a large walk-in shower.

"Strip, babe."

"What?" she asks, surprised at my demand.

"Strip. I'll help you get into the tub. I'll come back and wash your hair for you. I promise, no funny stuff. Tonight." I wink. She takes off her clothes, and I can tell she's nervous about it. "I've seen you before, remember?"

She's blushing, the pink traveling down her neck to her chest. "Stop embarrassing me, Henry."

"I didn't mean to embarrass you, angel. Just trying to help you into the tub."

She nods and pulls off her yoga pants.

I reach over and turn on the water in the tub. It takes four years for the water to even get warm. Yeah, I exaggerated there, but damn, what's wrong with her water heater?

She notices my impatience. "The boiler is super old. It takes a while to get warm water up here."

After quite a few minutes, the water finally warms up enough to put the plug in the drain. I reach over and hold her hand and arm as she steps in. As she settles in the tub, I hear her sigh. It must feel good to her sore body. "I'll go change and come back to wash your hair. Okay? Don't get out of the tub without me here. Got it?"

"Got it, bossy." She salutes.

"Smart-ass."

She giggles and grabs the spray nozzle to wet her hair. I jog down the steps to grab my duffel, double-check the lock on the front door, and swing by the kitchen to grab two bottles of water and to make sure I turned off the oven, old habit. I switch off all but one light downstairs and jog back upstairs. I peek into the bathroom in time to watch Sophie wash her body with a cloth and soap. It's the sexiest fucking thing in the world, and I have to will my dick to stay down as I turn to change.

I need a shower too, but I'll wait until morning. I'm out of my clothes and into the pajama pants my mom bought me last Christmas. I've never worn the things. I usually sleep in the buff, but that might make Soph feel uncomfortable. I'll just have to deal.

I step into the bathroom and grab the shampoo, pour a quarter-size dollop in my palm, and rub the two of them together. I lean over and run my hands through her hair, remembering how much she liked it the last time.

"Mmm, that feels so good, Henry."

I can hardly hold my dick together. When she moans like that, I lose it. "I'm glad, babe."

I work as fast as I can to soap up her hair and then rinse.

Standing back, I hold the towel out with one hand and use my other to hold her hand as she steps out of the tub. I wrap her up in the towel and lean in for a kiss. "You're so beautiful, Sophie."

She smiles sweetly at me. "Now that I'm clean, right?" She giggles. "Four days in a hospital makes a person gross."

"You were never gross."

She rolls her eyes as I use the towel to dry off her hair. "Let's go back to the bedroom to dress so you can sit on the bed."

Sophie doesn't argue. She sits on her bed to let me dress her. Looking down at her, I ask, "Where are your pajamas?"

"Bottom drawer of my dresser," she says, pointing to the corner of her room. She's got a girly room. Light-blue wallpaper with tiny cornflowers covers the walls. It's the largest of the three bedrooms on this floor. I checked them out quickly when I turned on the air conditioners earlier. There's a small closet near the entrance that can't hold more than a few things. She has a large wardrobe in one corner and a dresser in another. All of her furniture is white and feminine. It suits her.

I open the bottom drawer and pull out a pink nightgown. It's the least sexy thing I've ever seen, but I bet Sophie will make it look good. "This okay?" I ask as I hold up the gown.

"Yes. That's good. It'll be cool to wear tonight."

I walk over and hold up the bottom of the gown. Sophie raises her arms up, and I slide it down over her body. She stands up briefly and pulls it down over her hips and sits back down. Yep, she makes that gown hot as hell.

I clear my throat, attempting to take my mind off sex. "Which side of the bed is yours?"

"Left," she says, pointing to her spot.

I reach over her and pull back her sheet and light summer blanket. Once she's comfortably tucked in, I walk to the other side and slide to the center of the bed before wrapping my arms around her little body and pulling her toward me so that her back is to my front. She sighs. We're spooning. I've never spooned anyone in my entire life, but with Sophie, it feels right. It feels perfect.

"Good night, baby," I whisper.

"Good night, Henry."

33

SOPHIE

I wake up in a daze, confused about where I am. When I blink my eyes open, I realize I'm home in my comfy bed, but I'm not alone. Henry is in my bed, and I have to figure out how this all happened. Not only is he in my bed, but I'm practically on top of him. My face is in the spot between his chin and his chest, my arm is wrapped around his shoulder, and my leg is straddling his center.

I breathe in through my nose and get a whiff of Henry's scent. It's musky and woodsy. I wonder what cologne he wears. I should snoop in his stuff to find out. Then, when he's gone, I can buy a bottle of it, so I can remember what it was like to have him in my bed.

Henry is in my bed. Henry Flynn is in *my* bed.

He brought a duffel bag with him. He wants to stay for a while. It's all so freaking strange. He's falling for me? I'd love to think this through, but then I'll ruin it. I overthink everything, and I refuse to overthink this. I need to enjoy this time I have with him because it's fleeting. Willy's death and my near death should convince me of that.

With the courage I never had before, I kiss his neck—twice. His whiskers are rough against my lips, but it feels good. I run my fingers over one of his nipples. I wonder if it feels as good to him as it is when he does it to me? I trail kisses up his neck below his ear. He's still sleeping, but I feel him stir. Without thinking, I take his earlobe into my mouth and first bite and then suck on it. I've read about that in romance books. Those characters seem to like it. An arm wraps around my waist and another run over my bottom. As I bite his ear again, that hand on my butt squeezes. Damn, it feels good. His hands are amazing, even just with a little squeeze.

In a deep, husky morning voice, he asks, "Soph, what are you doing?"

I let out a small giggle. "Kissing you."

"Sophie, you're recovering—"

"Shh, I say. Let me enjoy this." I kiss down his neck again, heading for his chest. I run my tongue over his erect nipple.

He flinches. "Seriously, babe...."

I ignore his protests and move to his other nipple. It hasn't escaped my notice that he's hard against my belly. I slide my hand down so I can rub up and down his shaft from the outside of his pajama bottoms.

"God, Sophie," he gasps. "That feels so fucking good."

I move back up his body and put my lips on his, using my tongue to urge his mouth open. I'm so turned on, I'm almost frantic. I slide my hand into his pants and realize that he's gone commando.

"Fuck. Baby, you've got to stop."

"Why? You feel so good, Henry," I practically purr.

"Because if you don't stop, then *I* won't be able to stop."

"Good. I don't want to stop."

"Goddamn it," he says as he rolls me onto my back. He devours my mouth with his. His hands run up from my bottom to the inside of my nightgown. "Nightie off. Show me those tits, baby."

God, he's so dirty. I know I should think he's crass, but I can't. Not right now in the heat of the moment. Maybe later. I lift my arms up over my head, so he can slide off my nightgown. The feel of his fingers on my skin as they move up my body makes me feel hot and chilled at the same time. My skin is alive. He has my right nipple in his mouth in seconds. His left hand squeezes and pulls on my other one. I arch into him because I never want him to stop.

He trails kisses down my stomach and past my belly button. I slept without panties, so now he's face-to-face with my, well, my center. His nose nuzzles my pubic hair, and I'm frantic. I want him to do it. I want to feel his mouth on me down there.

"You smell so good, Soph."

I highly doubt that, but I'm not about to argue as he runs his tongue over my mound.

"Open your legs for me, babe."

Fearless this morning, I open my legs so it's all right there in front of him. He runs his nose down the crease of me, and then I feel his tongue slide all the way from the back to the front. My hips jerk up from the bed when his tongue hits my clit. It feels so good.

"God, Henry, don't stop," I plead.

He doesn't. He licks and sucks on all of me. It's like a kiss but more frantic. He runs his left hand up to my breast, playing with my nipple. Two fingers on his other hand move in and out of me while he licks and sucks.

"Henry," I squeak. "I'm gonna... I'm—ahhhh, fuck!" I shout. I come so hard I fear passing out.

Henry rises up and scoots his body so we are face-to-face again. "Did you like that, angel?"

"Yeah." I sigh. "So good," I pant. "So good." I can barely get the words out. I blink my eyes and see he's above me. I reach an arm up and pull him toward me to kiss him hard. He tastes like me, and it's not terrible. It's not great either, but I don't care. "I want you."

"It's too soon."

I push my bottom lip out in a pout. Where the hell did that come from? I'm not a pouter? "Please, Henry. I need you."

"Soph."

I can tell he wants to give in, so I help him. I wrap my legs around his waist and use my heels to push him toward me. "Fuck me, Hank. I need to feel you inside of me. I *need* it."

"You need me?"

"Yes. I need you. Inside." I'm playing a dangerous game, I know, but I do need it. Him, I mean.

He kisses me passionately as he slowly slides into me. Jesus, he's huge. "Don't stop."

"Fuck. It feels so good." He pushes himself all the way in, and we look at each other. He smiles sweetly at me as he leans down and kisses my nose. "So beautiful, Sophia."

I smile up at him. "So you gonna fuck me or what?" I say with a giggle.

"Oh, baby. You have no idea." He pulls out and thrusts back in so hard I nearly hit my head on my wooden headboard. "You okay?" he asks, looking concerned.

"I'm great. Don't stop."

He pumps into me over and over. At one point, he stops and pulls out completely. I whimper, thinking he's done with me; instead, he uses my hips to roll me over gently. He then lifts my hips until I'm on my knees.

"Put your hands on the headboard," he commands.

He's sexy when he's bossy in bed. I place my hands on the edge of the headboard, and he covers my hands with his own.

He nudges my legs farther apart and then thrusts into me. I feel him deeper and in new places. It feels so, so good.

"God, baby. You feel amazing. I never want to stop fucking you. Ever!"

I never want him to stop either since he's hitting a place inside of me that makes me want to ignite. "Don't stop Please. Oh my God. Harder!"

He only grunts in response as he uses his beautiful pelvis to make me scream out the single most powerful orgasm of my life. My insides flutter around his shaft—I feel myself pulsating. It's so good I could come again.

"One more time, babe. Come around my cock one more time."

"I c-can't." I'm so tired.

"You can. Do it." He pushes into me at a slightly new angle.

He's right. I can do it. I come again. It's not as powerful as the last one, but it feels just as good. It's then I hear him moan out his release.

"So good, babe. The *best*," he pants.

Letting go of the headboard, I place my face and hands on the bed. My hips are still up, and he's still inside of me. As he slides out, I feel wetness run down my legs. Ah, damn it. No condom. I'm the dumbest woman who ever walked the earth. I swear. Should I say something? I'm afraid to, to be honest. I like having him here, and as soon as he realizes what we've done, he'll bolt.

I move down the rest of the way to the bed, sliding over to my side so I can cover myself.

"Where are you going?" he asks, pulling me into him.

We're spooning again, and he runs his fingers over my shoulder, then to my breasts, and on to my hip. His fingers feel good against my skin. My body is completely relaxed, and before I know it, I'm asleep.

When I wake up, I notice the time. It's noon. I don't remember the last time I've slept until noon. The only problem is, I'm alone. I was right. He's gone.

remember the last time I've slept until noon. The only problem is, I'm alone. I was right. He's gone.

34

———

HENRY

Yeah, I did it again. I neglected to wear a condom. But unlike last time, I don't regret it.

I'm not sure when it changed for me. Maybe it was the night she walked out on me after I was an asshole. Or it could have been when the doctor told her our baby could be in danger after she was nearly killed. Then, when she told me she wasn't pregnant, I was sincerely disappointed. I guess I'd been experimenting with different scenarios in my head—about Sophie and our lives together, raising our child together. I liked the idea more and more. I'm thirty-five. I'm older, wiser, and in a good place personally and professionally. I think I'd make a good father. I learned from the best, after all.

I know Sophie would be an amazing mother. So, what's wrong with taking a risk? Well, nothing except I know Sophie, and she's probably freaking out upstairs. If she's awake, she's already wondering if I left. I'd better get back up there.

When I walk into her room, it's just as I feared. She's curled up into a ball, and I see red, puffy eyes. "Babe? What's wrong?"

She looks up at me, startled. She didn't expect to see me.

"Henry? Wha-what are you still doing here?"

"What do you mean?" I know what she means.

"I tho—I thought you left."

"Why would I leave? You need me, right?"

"Please don't stay because you think I need you."

What the fuck does that even mean? "I'm not. I'm staying because I want to be here with you, to help you."

"I don't need pity, Jesus, Henry. Just go home."

I don't understand where this is coming from. I expected her to leap into my arms once she realized I didn't bail. "I don't pity you, Sophie. I *want* to be here."

She cuts right to the chase. "We didn't... again. What if I'm... pregnant? Why didn't you wear a condom, Hank?"

"Henry. I know. I should have, but I didn't have one on me, and you said you *needed* me."

She growls. She literally growled. "Do not make this my fault again!" She throws her covers off her nude body and stomps to the bathroom.

I make a mental note—she's getting around well today. "Sophie, what's wrong?"

"Where do I start?" she yells from behind the bathroom door.

Hmm, where to start? "I don't know. Where do you want to start?"

She opens the door to the bathroom, sadly, no longer nude. The ugliest robe I've ever seen now covers her body. There are pathetic yellow ducks all around the bottom, but they've seen better days. The thing must be fifty years old. "Nice robe."

She pouts. "Shut up. It was my gran's."

Yep, fifty years old. I've offended her too. *Great job, Henry.*

"Look, Hank, you don't need to be here anymore. I'm fine. I feel better today than I have in a long time. I slept like twenty hours. I'm good. You can leave," she says with hands on hips, stressing each of the final words.

"I'm not leaving." *Ever*.

She harrumphs. "I don't need you here. All you do is stress me out and frustrate me and make me cr—just go."

I make her cry? I stress her out and frustrate her? That's not the impression I want to leave on her. I want her to lo—like me, a lot. I want her to.... I just want her. "Sophie. Please calm down. Let's talk about this."

"No. We talked the last time, and look how that turned out. Please, Henry. Go. Don't you have work to do anyway?"

"I took a few days off. I want to help you get started on William's place."

She sighs. "Oh, I forgot all about that."

"Understandable considering what you've been through. I figured the five of us could get through this fast."

"Five of us?"

"Yeah. You, me, Mom, Emily, and Sandy."

"You asked your mom and sisters over here? Today?"

"Um, yeah. Is that okay?"

"Hank! No! You don't invite other women over to a person's house without telling her. Now I have to clean this house first!"

"No, you don't. It looks fine."

"No!" She lets out a panicked sob. "No, it's not fine. It's dirty," she says with more sobs. "It's a mess. Your mom can't see my place like this."

"Sophie, my mom will not care. You've been in the hospital for Christ's sake."

"It. Doesn't. Matter. It's dirty, and I don't want her seeing it like this. God, I'm so sick of you."

Me? She's sick of me? "You're sick of me?"

"Yes! Fuck!" she screams. "Just go home!" She runs back into the bathroom and slams the door.

I hear the sound of the lock click then. She's sick of me? Nah, she's just mad at me. That's totally different and understandable. I grab my phone off the dresser and text Mom.

Me: Change of plans. Not gonna need help today. Sophie isn't up to it.

Mom: Ok. Poor thing. Give her my love.

Me: Will do. Love ya, Ma.

Mom: I love you too, Henry.

I knock on the bathroom door. "Sophie?"

No answer.

"Sophie, I cancelled my mom. Okay?"

I hear her sniffle. "Okay."

She doesn't come out of the bathroom for another half hour. When she does, I'm sitting on her side of the bed, waiting for her.

"Hank, I can't do this."

"Do what?"

"This thing with you. I can't deal with you and all of your mood swings and changes of heart. You aren't being fair. You expect me to go along with whatever you want, and I don't work like that. I need to think about things. I need time to work things out for myself. I don't need you running my life for me. I don't *want* you running my life."

I sigh. I know what she's saying. I'm bulldozing my way into her life. I'm erratic and unpredictable. "I know. I'm sorry. I have no idea what I'm doing when it comes to you, Sophie." I take her hands in mine. "I told you how I felt about you."

"Not really."

"Not really?"

"You said you were falling for me. That doesn't tell me anything."

"You haven't been forthcoming about this thing with us either," I say, a bit too defensively.

"Can you blame me?"

"No. I guess I can't." I look into her beautiful brown eyes when I say, "I'm not ready to say the word *love* yet, Sophie. But I can tell you I feel very strongly about you. When I'm with you, no matter where it is, it feels like home—like it's where I'm meant to be." I pull her closer so I can rest my hands on her hips. "I know you may not feel the same about me. If you don't, I'll accept that and go home. But I want to be with you, babe. I want to stay here with you and see if it's real."

She still has tears clinging to her lashes from her angry cry. Her lashes flutter, and the wetness hits her cheeks. God, she's beautiful.

"Henry?"

"Yeah?"

"I don't know what I feel yet either. I do know I like having you here with me, though, and that I'm more comfortable with you than I have been with anyone else. I feel at home with you too, but like I said, you're unpredictable. You may feel this way today, but who knows what you'll say tomorrow morning?"

"I know. I'm sorry." I pulling her even closer, running my hands along her back. "All I can say is I mean what I'm saying to you. Yes, I'm also a hothead and a jackass. I'll do my utter best to show you I'm sincere."

"What if I'm pregnant?" She cuts right to the chase again.

"Then *we're* pregnant. I won't lie and tell you I'm sorry about this morning. I'm not. When you told me you weren't pregnant, I was disappointed. Since the hospital, I've thought about what it would be like for us to have a baby, and I like the idea. I see you as the mother of my children."

She looks like she wants to throttle me.

"Yeah, I know. I'm bulldozing again." I sigh. "I'll wear a condom from now on until you're ready to talk about a kid."

"Hank, you're so frustrating."

"Henry."

She laughs. "*Henry*. You're so frustrating!"

"I know, babe. I know."

SOPHIE

I spend the rest of the afternoon on my couch. I've finished *Great Expectations*, and now I'm reading *Pride and Prejudice* by Jane Austen. I can't help but think about Henry when I read about Fitzwilliam Darcy. Both men are stubborn, serious, and loyal. I hope my story ends like Elizabeth Bennett's—happily.

I should get started on Willy's place instead of just lying around on my butt. Henry was called into the station for a meeting about Willy's case. Even though he took a few days off, he's still on call whenever there are updates on his open cases. I hope it's good news. I want them to arrest Willy's killer. No matter what happened, he didn't deserve to die, especially like that.

I drag myself off the couch to make myself a snack. Henry has my kitchen so stocked with food, I'm not sure what to eat. My usual fare comprises of soup and crackers or a bologna sandwich. It's cheap and easy to make. I open the fridge and pull out grapes, cheese, and turkey and place a few small slices of cheese on a plate next to the grapes along with two slices of turkey. I rarely have real meat like this in the house. Deli meat is expensive. Sheesh, Henry is a snob about his luncheon meat. I chuckle about his reaction to my bologna.

I put the unwanted portions back in the refrigerator. As I glance out my kitchen window into my backyard, I see Willy's apartment. I know I'm not supposed to leave the house—Henry locked me up in here like it's Fort Knox—but that doesn't mean I can't go out to his place and see if I can get started on the cleanup. I'll only be out there for a little while. It'd be good for me to move my body a little.

I unlock the back door, place my foot on the doorjamb, and pull. I've got a system for opening this sticky door that works most of the time. Once the door wrenches open, I step out and down my cracked steps. When I get to Willie's, his door is locked. Grandma hid a spare key in a fake stone near the door. Spotting it, I pick it up, slide open the bottom portion, and retrieve the key. I'm in.

His place is eerie. I feel like I'm intruding on him, but he said he wanted me to have his things. So I step in and flip on the light. Thankfully, his electricity is still on. I need to remember to call about switching his utilities over to my name. Another bill for me, but it has to be done. It's hot in the room, but I'm not panicked about it. I walk over and turn on his window air conditioner.

This carriage house is only about 550 square feet. One small A/C unit cools the room quickly. I switch on the rest of the overhead lights and several table lamps and take a visual inventory of the place. Willy's bed is gone. Thank goodness. I don't think I could stand to see it. The spot where the bed used to be is empty. It's the perfect spot to place the boxes for sorting his things. One for items getting donated, one for things I'd like to keep, and another for trash.

I know I have boxes in the basement, but I can get those later. I can just make piles for now. I look around for paper and a pen and spot his printer over in the corner. Grabbing three sheets of printer paper and a pencil, I write the names of each pile and set them on the open floor.

"Where should I even start?" I ask aloud. That's when I spot a small bookshelf against the wall between the kitchen and the television area. "Aha, books! I really shouldn't talk to myself. It makes me look crazy."

I pull over his one and only kitchen stool and plop down. The bookshelf only stands about four feet tall and four feet wide, so this won't take long. As I peruse his titles, I notice that the majority are about computer programming languages, gaming, and gaming shortcuts. I begin moving those books to the donate section, and before I know it the top and middle shelf are empty. I grab two huge books on COBOL and FORTRAN.

I snort out a laugh. "They sound like books about alien planets." *Stop talking to yourself, Sophie,* I think as I lug the books over to the donate pile. It's the only one growing.

As I'm bent down to grab another stack, I see a small blue book next to another computer-nerd book. It's out of place with all of these large tombs. It's the size of a hardbound novel. I pick it up and open the front cover to see that it's *The Great Gatsby* by F. Scott Fitzgerald.

"Oh my gosh, it's one of my all-time favorite books!" I squeal a little. I have several copies.

I pull the old, blue book jacket away from the cover to see that this one is pristine. It looks brand new. I hug the book to my chest and thank Willy for the gift. A major portion of my dissertation would have been about this book if I'd had the chance to finish up my degree. I sit in one of Willy's chairs and read. I'm not sure how much time has passed, but I soon realize that I should work, not read. I place the book in my keep pile and force myself to continue working.

Just as I'm bending down to grab the last large textbook off the shelf, I hear, "Goddamn it! What the ever-loving fuck are you doing, Sophie?"

Surprised, my body jerks upward, and the book flies out of my hands, landing in the middle of the floor. "Hank. Stop scaring me! Jesus, you almost gave me a heart attack!" I yell back at him.

"You shouldn't be out here. I told you to stay in the house."

I give him the dirtiest look I've got in my arsenal. "Do not tell me what to do, Hank. I'm not doing anything wrong. I was bored, so I thought I'd get started out here. I've only been out here—" I look at the clock over his kitchen sink. "—um, two hours?"

"Two hours? What the hell? You should be resting. I told you I'd help you with all of this."

"And you will. I just wanted to get started."

He walks over to take a look at the labels on the floor: donate, toss, and keep piles. "You've got a good start for donations." He turns and then looks down at the book that flew out of my hands. It fell open, and there's something inside the book.

"Holy shit," he mumbles. Henry walks back to the door to grab two rubber gloves. The CSI people must have left the box here. He returns to the book and picks it up. "I'll be damned."

"What? What is it?"

"I think our Willy was either a genius or paranoid, and since he was murdered, it was probably good to be paranoid. He just wasn't paranoid enough."

"Hank? What is it?" I wait but hear nothing. "Henry? Henry! What is it?"

He holds the book open toward me, and I see the chapter title on the left side of the page: *Retirement Planning*. On the right page, there's a small rectangle cut out of the book about half an inch by two inches. Inside is a small black bar.

"What is that?"

"It's a flash drive or a thumb drive. People use these to store information on like the old floppy disks."

"Do you think it has something to do with his murder?"

"I'd bet my job on it, Sophie. You found a clue that, I suspect, will break this case wide open. Hang on. Let me call Kent." Henry pulls his phone out and hits a button. "Kent. Yeah, shut up for a second. I've got something here that you're gonna want to see."

He pauses, listening to Kent.

"Yeah. Get over to Willy's place. Hurry." He hangs up his phone and gives me his megawatt smile.

The man is breathtaking. I smile back at him like it's natural for me when it's not.

"You're beautiful when you smile, Sophie."

"You are too, Henry."

He sets the book down and walks over, pulling the blue gloves off as he moves. His hands slide into my hair, and he pulls my face upward, bringing his down to mine, giving me a soft, sexy kiss. "Next time I tell you to stay in the house, please do it. I worry about you enough without you giving me a heart attack the minute I walk in the door. I couldn't find you, baby," he whispers.

"I'm sorry. I didn't mean to worry you. I'll text you next time."

He groans.

I don't think that's the answer he wanted, but that's the one he got.

"Fine," he growls.

As soon as Kent enters the carriage house, I make my way back to my home. It's getting late, and I'm hungry again. I never ate that snack. I left my bottle of water untouched too. I need to drink my water at the very least. I peer into the refrigerator, the freezer, and my cupboards. There's so much to eat, I'm not sure what to cook, if that makes any sense. I see everything I need to make my homemade mac and cheese: pasta, butter, milk, and several different cheeses. This is going to be delicious. I usually make the kind that comes in the blue box, but thanks to Henry, I've got everything handy to make my own.

I set a pot on the stove to boil the noodles and place a small pan next to it in which to make my cheese sauce. I would normally bake this, but I'd rather not heat the place up using the oven. When the noodles are ready, I pour the melted cheese sauce over the steaming pasta. Yum. My stomach growls from the smell alone. I hope Henry likes it. Something tells me he'll eat anything.

Walking out the back door, I stride back to Willy's place to let Henry know I cooked. As I approach the door, I hear Kent's voice. "Are you sure you know what you're doing, Hank?"

"Yeah, of course."

"She's not your type. I've seen your type, and that's not it, man."

"No. She's not my type. I guess. I don't know. I'm just experimenting."

Experimenting? What the fuck? I knew it! I'm such a frigging idiot. I can't deal with all of this tonight. It's been emotional enough. I'll keep this to myself for now and figure everything out later.

I pretend that I've just arrived at Willy's place. "Hank? Kent? I made dinner if you're hungry." I try to sound chipper and oblivious, but my voice is shaky. I peek in the door, smiling. "You guys hungry?"

"Always," Henry says back.

"I could eat," adds Kent.

I bet you could, asshole. "Well, come on before it gets cold." Jesus, I sound like a sitcom mother. *Come on before it gets cold.* I mock myself. When did I become so pathetic? Oh, I know. It all started the day I met Hank Flynn. That's the day my life went down the toilet.

The guys follow me into the house. As we walk, Henry tries to grab my hand, but I pretend to wipe them on my jeans and speed up so I can get into the kitchen first. Once inside, I pull down two bowls and two glasses.

"There you go. Help yourselves," I say cheerily.

"Aren't you going to eat, babe?"

"I had some before I came to get you. I was hungry," I lie. The last thing I want is to eat dinner with the asshole that's *experimenting* with our relationship and his dickweed of a part-ner. Hell. My language is atrocious. "Besides, you two probably need to talk. I'll just head upstairs. I'm pretty beat. Night!" I say with my perkiest voice.

I stomp up the steps and get ready for bed. I take a quick shower, throw on a T-shirt and shorts, slide into bed, and turn off my light. My stomach growls, but I don't care. I'm not going back downstairs. I'll eat tomorrow. Since I overdid it today, I fall asleep quickly. The bed dips sometime later, and I feel arms wrap around me to pull me to the center so he can spoon me. I fall back to sleep right away, doing my best to forget about Henry for a while. I need to do everything I can to get healthy and strong again. Then, I can get on with my life. Alone.

36

———

HENRY

When I wake up in the morning, Sophie is already out of bed. I slide my ass out and walk into her bathroom. I already hate showering in her tiny claw-foot tub. I should talk to her about a bathroom renovation. I could pay for that myself since it's only important to me. She'll be happy for the help, I'm sure.

Downstairs, I see no sign of her. The coffee pot is full of fresh coffee, so I grab a mug and pour myself a cup. She must be at Willy's. I wrench the back door open and walk down the sidewalk. I'm freshly showered but still wearing my sweats and no shirt. She'll like that too. She digs me without a shirt.

I push Willy's door open and see her bent over, pulling things out of a drawer. Jesus, she's got the sweetest tush. I walk up behind her and bump into her with my front. Already a little hard from just seeing her like that, I say, "Hey, babe. You're up early." I take a drink of my coffee while wrapping my left hand around her middle. "Find anything good?"

She slowly stands up and turns.

Her smile is forced. I can tell. I've seen the real thing, and this one is fake as fuck. What did I do now? "Soph? You okay?"

"I'm fine. I woke up early and thought I'd get a jump on things. You know how it is?"

"I guess. I was just hoping you'd want to come back to bed."

"No can do. I'm going to work on this for an hour, and then I've got to get ready."

"Ready for what?" She'd better not tell me she's going to work.

"I'm meeting with an attorney. You know, the one your mom recommended?"

"Great! I'll drive you."

"Nope. Not needed. I've got a ride. Thanks, though."

It better not be Joel fucking Peters. Nah, she wouldn't.

"Well, all right. Then I guess I'll get dressed and head in to work."

"Good plan!" she says, a little too happily.

Is she trying to get rid of me? This woman is so confusing. The doc said she could be confused after the ordeal in the closet. I need to cut her some slack.

"Okay. I'll see you tonight? Right?"

"Of course!" She leans up and gives me a quick kiss on the cheek. "Have a good day, dear," she says, laughing.

I chuckle back. "Yeah, you too."

I walk back to the house, dress in my work clothes, and head to the office. Kent will be thrilled to see me before noon.

When I walk into the precinct, several of the guys are all standing around Kent's desk, including Peters, Hampton, and Captain Cooke. "What've we got? Any news on the flash drive I found yesterday?" I know, technically Sophie found it.

"Yep. William Gibbons had it all figured out. He's even got account numbers here. The banks are in the Cayman Islands. Not a surprise there. This thing also had a letter on it, outlining his theories along with the proof we need. It was the CFO Collins. William had been in contact with an agent with the feds already. Her name's Collette Miller. So that means we need to be in touch with her. Today," says the cap.

"The question I have is why didn't the feds flag this before now? If William had been in touch with her, shouldn't she have sought *us* out?" I ask the guys.

"You'd think. He mentions in his notes that she put little stock in his theories, so she probably just blew it off. It doesn't mean we can leave her out of the loop, though," adds Captain Cooke.

Kent hands me a printout of Willy's notes, saying, "I've typed out the main points from his letter here. I think he had it spot-on but got too close. Because of that, he went dead."

- Check with Christopher Collins's former employers. Did he add surcharges there? If so, it could be several million more.
- When he spoke with Luciph's HR department about the fee on his statement, his notes said she was told to add the fee by the (then) new CFO, Christopher Collins, and that it was common for the company facilitating retirement funds to add such a fee.
- After his research, he found her statements to be false.
- Collins flirts with HR department head, Janet MacClenny. She's single. He's divorced. Could there be a romance there or something more sinister?

"DAMN, I love that guy's notes. He should've been a spy," I say, chuckling. "*Sinister?*"

Kent continues, "It *is* sinister. You have to admit. Oh, another interesting tidbit for you to chew on since we asked for retirement records, that little surcharge has been removed. When I asked Janet MacClenny about it, she told me she was asked to remove it. She wouldn't tell me who requested the change, but I'm thinking a little time in our sauna, it'll come out." He looks at me sheepishly and says, "Sorry, Hank."

"I know. It's okay." Talk of hot rooms is not something I want to deal with right now.

After our meeting, I head back home. Well, to Sophie's place. She may still be at the attorney's office, so I can whip us something up for dinner. I hope she's home, though. After trying her mac and cheese, I want her to cook everything. That shit was the fucking bomb. Kent wants to move in too. I told him no fucking way.

I walk directly to the kitchen. There's nothing on the stove or in the oven. That must mean she's not home yet. I jog up the stairs to change out of my work clothes and into something I can work out in when I hear something. I look to the bathroom door. It's closed. "Sophie?"

"Go away!" she moans.

"Sophie? What's wrong?" I try the door, and it's locked. I hear a sound like she's getting sick. "Sophie. Let me in. Do you have the flu?"

"Leave me alone, Hank."

Henry, I say to myself. I see the door lock is one of those you open with an old skeleton key. I peek through the tiny hole and see her on the floor, leaning over the toilet. Yep, she's sick. "Let me in, Soph. Now!"

"Jesus." I watch her crawl over to the door and flip the lock. When I walk in, I'm terrified by the sight in front of me. She's not only physically ill, but she's also bleeding. Her shorts are covered in blood.

"Sophie? What happened?"

She lays her head on the cool tile, and her eyes flutter closed.

"Sophie? Can you hear me?"

She moans. I swear she told me to fuck off in her haze. What did I do now?

A serious amount of blood is on the floor below her. I could call an ambulance, but I pick her up in my arms and run down the stairs instead. I can get her there faster if I turn my cherry on in the car. I hold her as I reach into my pocket for my key fob and hit the button to open the car doors. By the time I'm at the passenger side, the door is open. I place her in the seat, latch her seat buckle, and then race to my side. As my door shuts, I grab the police cherry light from my center console, place it on top, and flip the switch. Bright light illuminates us. I tear out of my parking spot and make it to the St. Michael's emergency unit in minutes. I could have taken her to an urgent care place closer, but these guys all know her and her case.

I run around the car, pick her up, and carry her into the ER. A nurse recognizes us from the last time, sees the blood, and points my way through.

"In here," she says. "Lay her down. I'll get the doc on duty." The nurse runs out of the room, and before I know it, Dr. Jenkins is at the door.

"What happened?" he asks, remaining calm.

"I don't know. I came home from work and heard her getting sick in the bathroom. She wouldn't let me in, but I finally talked her into unlocking the door. As soon as I walked in, I saw all the blood. She passed out right after that. I picked her up and raced here."

"Do you know when she began feeling ill?"

"No. I got home at about three. So, before that."

"It's three thirty now. You worked quickly. That's good."

As we talk, Sophie moans. "I'm gonna puke. I feel sick."

Dr. Jenkins grabs a small green bowl and pulls her over to her side, resting the bowl next to her mouth. "Go ahead, Sophie. If you need to get sick, there's a bowl here."

He turns back. "Did she take anything that you know of?"

"No. She was fine when I left this morning. She was going to see an attorney today. I had a long meeting, so I hadn't talked to her yet to find out about any of that." *Damn it. Somehow, I know this is my fault.*

"We'll get fluids going. We can't let her get dehydrated again. I'll also start her on some anti-nausea medication. We'll clean her up, and I'll check on the issue of the bleeding. Once she's more lucid, we can ask her if she knows what happened."

"Okay," I say with a deep breath. "Sophie? It'll be okay, babe."

She grunts at me.

Can she be pissed at me while she's throwing up? I guess so.

"Perhaps you should wait in the—"

"No way! I'm not leaving her," I say urgently. *I'm not leaving her.*

"Fine. Sit back over there and please let us work."

"I will."

I watch as they cut her out of her clothing. She's bleeding vaginally, but the doctor is fairly certain that the worst of that is over. Sophie's been nodding and answering the nurse's questions with one-word answers so far, and she's no longer vomiting.

When Dr. Jenkins returns, he sees she's more lucid. "Sophie, do you know what happened? Did you eat something that upset your stomach? Did you take anything?"

With a raspy voice, she says, "Yes. I took the morning-after pill."

"What?" I say, shocked. "Why?"

She looks at me with a pained expression. "I'm an experiment to you."

"A *what?*"

She rolls her damn eyes at me. "I heard you. You told Kent that you were just experimenting with me."

"You heard?"

She nods.

Fuckity, fuck, fuck, fuck. "It's not what you think, Sophie. Kent is... he's a tool. I wanted him to leave it alone. What we have is between us."

She rolls her eyes again. She took that fucking morning-after pill to be sure she wasn't carrying my kid. "Was that the pill I gave you?"

"Yes."

Dr. Jenkins interrupts our heart-to-heart. "Sophie. Those pills have side effects. Those include nausea, cramping, bleeding, dizziness, and a few others. You seemed to have experienced most of those. I want to keep you here overnight for observation."

She groans.

"I know you don't want to stay, but I want to be sure you've gotten fluids, and I want to watch to make sure you have no more issues. I think it's also safe to say you should probably stay away from that type of medication."

Sophie nods.

"If you'd like to talk to someone about birth control, you should schedule a visit with your gynecologist. I don't think you should take birth control for a few weeks, however. Let's give your body time to heal from your previous trauma and from this new issue. Sound good?"

"Yeah. Thank you, Doctor."

Sophie won't look at me. Her eyes are on the doctor or the nurses but never on me. She hates me, I guess. I don't blame her.

I keep fucking up in ways that baffle even me. My mom will kill me. I chuckle.

"You think this is funny?" she finally speaks.

"No. None of this is fucking funny, Sophie. I'm sick about this."

"You're sick? That's rich," she mutters under her breath.

"I refuse to fight with you right now. You need to get better so I can get you home and we can—"

"I want you gone from *my* house, Hank!" she says angrily. "By the time I'm out, you need to have gotten your clothes, your food, and whatever shit you have at my place and take it to your fancy house. I'm done here."

She rolls over, giving me her back.

She can ignore me, but Sophie's met her match. When it comes to stubborn, I'm the king. I'm not going anywhere.

37

SOPHIE

When I blink awake, I'm disoriented. Where am I? I look around the room, and it's like déjà vu all over again—I'm back in the hospital. I concentrate on the events from the last two days, and it hits me. I took the morning-after pill, and it kicked my ass. I groan.

It's then that I hear rustling and movement. I look to my left and see the bathroom door and, to my right, a disheveled Henry Flynn. "Henry? What are you doing here?" It's all coming back to me now. The word *experiment* comes to mind. My eyes squeeze shut and pinch my face into an angry scowl.

"How're you feeling, babe?" he asks sweetly.

"Fine. What are you still doing here?" I remember asking him to leave and to move out of my house. But he's *still* here. The guy can't take a hint or a direct order.

He ignores me. "Can I get you anything? Thirsty? Are you hungry? You haven't eaten in a long time, Soph."

"Why are you still here?" If he doesn't answer the question this time, I may lose my mind.

"I'm still here because we need to talk. That and I wasn't going to leave you here alone."

"I'm not alone. Look around; the place is crawling with other people."

"Ha, hysterical, Sophia."

Oh, he's calling me *Sophia* now? That's just great.

"Mom was here to see you last night, but you were out of it. She sends her love."

Her love? Wow, that *is* nice. Sarah is something special.

"She'll check in on you today. I'll let her know what time we get to go home."

Damn it, Henry Flynn! I growl, "Henry—"

My nurse for the day walks in and jots her name on my whiteboard: Nancy. "Hey there, sugarplum. Glad to see you awake. You sure did scare your young man here, hon. He's been pacing and pulling his hair out; it's a wonder he has any left." She cackles.

I look over at Henry and see his hair is a mess. "Did you sleep at all?"

"Some. Enough."

I doubt that. I sigh. "Henry?"

"Yeah, baby?" He walks over to the side of the bed and takes my hand in his big, warm one, looking down at me. "Can I get you anything?"

"Just water."

"You're not hungry?"

The thought of eating makes me feel nauseated again. "No food. Not yet. Maybe not ever."

Henry chuckles. "You'll feel better soon. I promise."

How can he promise that?

After Nancy leaves, Hank pulls a chair up to the side of my bed. "Can we talk now?"

I nod.

"I know you were upset about what you heard me say to Kent."

I wince, remembering.

"Let me say that I didn't mean what I said. At. All. But Kent is a pain in my ass, Sophie. If he got wind of how I felt about you, he'd never let it go. He busts my balls at the station for everything I do. He loves to patronize me in front of the guys. It's hell when he's got something personal about me to spread."

I remain quiet. I understand what he's saying. I'd never confide in anyone at work about my personal life.

"The only people I trust with personal shit are Keith, my dad, Mom occasionally, and now you. If I had told Kent that I was in love with you, he'd be a fucking nightmare."

I must have heard that wrong. Love with me? He's in love with me? I blink frantically. "Love?" I croak.

He smiles at me. "Yes. I love you, Sophie. I was fucking terrified to tell you. I'm still terrified to tell you. What if you never love me back?"

I know I'm going to cry, but I try to hold it back. "Henry? You love me? Are you sure you just don't feel protective of me like my *knight-in-shining-armor* kind of feelings?"

He chuckles again. "I'm sure. I do feel protective of you. I can't help that. I feel protective of all the people I love, babe. But, well, I guess the thought of losing you, of not coming home to you at night, not waking up with you in the morning, hurts here," he says, pounding on his chest. "It hurts like a fucking bitch, Sophie. These last few days living with you have been the best days of my life."

I can't hold back my emotions anymore. I sniffle as a couple of rogue tears make their way down my cheek. "I feel the same about you, Henry. I hate thinking of my life without you."

He has to have noticed that I didn't say the word *love*. I will—just not right this second.

He smiles at me in that breathtaking grin of his. "Now, let's talk about you taking that pill."

I groan. "Let's not."

"I understand why you took it. I may have done the same thing."

"Huh?" I squeak.

"After my reaction that terrible night, I thought a lot about a kid—a kid with you, Soph. I liked the idea but thought you'd already taken the pill. Then at the hospital when I found out you could still be pregnant and that our baby was in danger, it broke my fucking heart."

"I know. Your mom told me."

He rolls his eyes. "Never trust the Flynn women to keep a secret. Remember that."

I laugh at that. They'd told me that nothing is secret in their family. "Duly noted."

"So *then* when you told me you were never pregnant, I was bummed, babe. In my head, I had plans for all three of us. I'd move into your place. We'd fix it up together and raise our child there. Can you picture that?"

I nod. I can.

"When you weren't pregnant, I decided to do my fucking best to change that outcome. I wanted to knock you up."

I gasp. "Henry, having a baby needs to be a decision we both make. What if you change your mind tomorrow? I've seen you do it, so don't act surprised by my question."

"I won't change my mind. I want us to be a family, Soph. I want kids with you. I never wanted kids before you. I love you so fucking much, Sophie."

"Oh, Henry...." I reach my arms out in the hopes he'll get the hint and hug me. I need for him to hold me right now. He stands up, leans over the bed, and wraps his big arms around me. I'm still hooked up to one machine, so his access is restricted, but that doesn't stop him from climbing into my bed to hold me in his arms.

"I love you, Sophie," he whispers in my ear.

"I love you too, Henry." And I do.

I'M FINALLY RELEASED from my latest hospital stay at noon on Sunday. I hope I never see the inside of a hospital ever again. Henry helps me into his sleek car, and off we go to my—I mean, our house.

"Are you hungry?" he asks.

"A little. But I want nothing greasy. Ooh, is there any mac and cheese left?"

He looks at me with a guilty expression. "Uh, no. That was gone that first night. It was fucking delicious."

I smile at him. He likes my cooking. "That's okay. I can make more when I get home."

"Oh, hell no. You're not doing anything for the rest of the day. I'll make it. You can just sit on your sweet little ass and tell me what to do."

I giggle. "Are you going to take orders from me then?"

"Of course. I'm your whipping boy now, honey."

I giggle again. "This ought to be good."

Once home, I settle in a comfortable chair in my kitchen. Henry carried in a cushioned chair and ottoman for me, so I can sit there like a queen bee and order him around. On the table sits the copy of *The Great Gatsby* that I found at Willy's place. I pick it up and touch the blue paper cover.

Henry looks over at me as I fondle the book. "So, of all the things he had in that apartment, the only thing you want to keep is that book with the crappy cover?" He chuckles.

I look down at the book. It does have a crappy cover. "Yep. This cover may be crappy, but what's beneath it is perfect."

He smiles at me, and that's when it hits me. My face must

have morphed into something horrible because Henry reaches me fast. "What's wrong? You feel okay? Do you want to lie down?"

"I'm fine. It's just... Willy's letter. Let me grab it." I stand up too quickly and feel dizzy, but I get myself together. My copy of the will and his letter are on my desk. I walk back to the office, grab the letter, and return to the kitchen.

I tear open the envelope and pull out his note. "Here, listen to this," I say, peering at Henry. I scan through the first part of his note quickly. *Sophia, I know you work very hard...* "Yadda, yadda, yadda..." *It will take you a while to go through my belongings to see what you would like to keep but...* "Here, Henry! Here's the part! 'I suspect you'll like my finds because, like me, you do not judge a book by its cover.' That's it! That's the part. Do you think he was talking about this?" I ask, holding up the blue book.

"Is that book rare or something?"

"Not necessarily." I pull open the front jacket and read the copyright information. "New York, Charles Scribner's Sons, 1925," I read aloud. "Henry, this may be a first edition."

"Is that good?"

"Well, yeah. I'm not sure how valuable the book could be, but it's good. Here, can I use your phone?"

"You gonna call someone who knows about books?"

"No, I'm searching Google for something."

Henry hands me his smartphone, and I click on his browser. I type in "Rare Great Gatsby edition." I click on the second article and read. "Oh my gosh."

"What? What are you reading?" Henry sounds excited.

"Just hang on." I flip the book. "Oh my God, Henry!" I squeal.

"What? Tell me!" Henry shouts. He's now right in front of me.

"Let me read this to you if I can. It's an article from *Time* magazine. They interviewed a book expert named Jones. I'll try to summarize what he said. With the first edition Gatsby, one of the most important things is a typo on the back of the dust jacket."

I turn the book over and show Henry. "See? 'Jay Gatsby' is spelled with a lowercase *j*. Typo," I squeak. I continue to read. "It says that condition is very important. Fine-to-very good is what you want."

I read further. "Henry? It says if the book is in fine condition, which is the best, I could get whatever I wanted out of this. Oh my God! A book in very good condition sold for $345,840 at a recent auction. Do you know what that means, Henry?"

"It means if this book is what you think it is, you'll be fucking loaded, babe. I've found myself a sugar mama." He laughs.

I laugh at that too. "Now who's the gold digger?"

We both laugh as I wrap my arms around his neck to kiss his beautiful face. He lifts me off the ground and sits down in my chair with me on his lap. He loves this position.

"Henry, I'd say this book is definitely in fine condition. It looks brand new—no foxing, no tears, no fading, and no yellowing. That article was written in 2013. So, if this is one of those, it could be worth even more now, or it could be less, if there are others out there."

"It also means you need to keep it somewhere safe, and you need to keep quiet about it. It's dangerous for anyone to know about it until you get a definite answer at least."

"I agree. I wonder if there's a way to contact this book expert to ask him about this?"

"Here, let me look him up on my phone." Henry takes his phone and clicks away. "Here. They have a website. They're based in London."

"Oh, no."

"What? Is that bad?"

"I can't go to London. It's too expensive."

"Babe, if this is what we think it is, something tells me ole Jones will fly here to see the book."

"Maybe. Should we email him?"

"Yeah, we should. First, let's take pictures of this to send him and then find a secure place to hide this thing. It makes me nervous to have it around, and I'm a damn cop." He laughs.

I wrap my arms around Henry. "This may be the meaning behind Willy's message. He left me an awesome gift even if it's worthless. If it's real and I can sell it, it could be enough to fix up my house. There may even be enough for me to go back to school, Henry."

"Don't put the cart before the horse, babe. Let's see what you have first. Sound good?"

"You're right. I need to remain calm. It's probably a forgery or a fake. Things like this don't happen to me."

"If it's meant to be, it will be."

"Henry, you're such a dork." I lean in and kiss his full lips.

He kisses me back, and I can tell he's holding back. He swipes his tongue over my bottom lip and then inside my mouth. Our kiss becomes frantic, but he pulls back right before I tear off his clothes.

"Let me finish cooking. I need to feed my woman." He chuckles.

"Dork. Definitely a dork."

38

HENRY

With Sophie's step-by-step directions, I have made mac and cheese for the first time in my life. I am not counting the kind that comes in the blue box. Any idiot can make that stuff. This wasn't difficult, but there were quite a few steps in the process.

I plate up our dinner and take it to the living room where Sophie has the television on the local news. I fucking hate the news. It's so depressing, and I get to see a lot of it firsthand. But she mentioned that she's behind on her local and national news, so we're watching the news.

"Here you go, Soph. I hope you like it. It's now one of the three things I can make from scratch."

"Mmm," she moans as she takes a bite. "So good, Henry. What are the other two things?"

"Pancakes and anything on the grill."

"Grilling? Sounds manly." She winks.

I laugh. "Oh, it is. I can grill the fuck out of stuff."

Sophie breaks out into a contagious giggle that makes me laugh again.

"Sometimes, you can be so funny, Henry," she says, attempting to catch her breath after her laughter subsides.

Damn, I've laughed more around Sophie than I have any other woman. I've also cried, and that's never happened over a woman, so there's that. I don't count my sisters and brothers in that mix because they're always cracking me up with their fucked-up lives. One of them is always in some mess. It's best to laugh it off, or I'd go insane with worry.

I lean over and kiss her nose. "You're joyous, Soph." She blushes at that. I guess she liked it. But it's true. She is joyous. And she's beautiful. I hate to bring this up, but I need to know. "Did you hear from Mom's attorney friend?"

"She left me a message."

"Good. What did she say?"

"Well, it wasn't long, but she said Brooke Bellamy wasn't happy with me. I'm supposed to call her back tomorrow."

"Did she say anything else?" I'm getting the distinct impression she's keeping something from me.

"Mm-hmm. She said something about a countersuit."

"A what! A fucking countersuit? That fucking bitch!"

"Henry! Stop!"

"If the shoe fits, babe. Brooke Bellamy is a bitch!" As I'm finishing up my cheesy goodness, my phone rings. "Flynn."

"Uh-huh," I say, listening to Kent tell me what he knows. "No shit?" I stand up and pace the room. "Fuck! I knew it."

Sophie stops eating to listen. She mouths a silent, "What is it?"

I shake my head and put up one finger. I'll tell her in a minute.

"All right. Yeah. Let me know if I need to come down." I hang up and run my fingers through my hair. It's a habit I've had since my teen years. It's a wonder I still have hair after a month like this one.

"What is it, Henry? Was it something to do with William?"

"Yeah. I can't say much to you, but the feds have been on this since the beginning. They were running an investigation parallel to ours."

"Why didn't they tell you?"

"I will assume they didn't want to spook the suspects."

"The suspects? Who is it? Who killed poor Willy?"

"Some bigwig at Luciph. I'd bet my badge on it. The feds are taking him in for questioning in William's murder and on embezzlement charges. I doubt they'll be able to get him on murder for hire, but maybe they know something we don't."

"Why would someone kill Willy for a little money?"

"Millions, babe. We're talking millions. That's reason enough for some people."

"Oh. But still...."

My sweet girl can't see it. People suck. They're evil and sick. She's seen it firsthand with that bitch Arianna, but she still wants to see good in everyone. It's one more reason to love her.

"I still say it's not a good reason. But I know greed is a very ugly thing," she explains.

"It can be. Kent may need me to go in tonight, but I hope not. I'm afraid if I leave you alone again, you'll go for a jog or something."

Sophie snorts out a laugh. "Henry, I guarantee that you'll *never* have to worry about me going out on a jog. I'm more of the yoga kind of girl."

"Ooh, flexible," I say as I lean in for a kiss. "I like flexible."

"You're terrible."

Our mouths meet up as soon as she's finished speaking, and I lose myself in the kiss. She's gotten so assertive in the short time I've known her. I hope that means she's getting used to me and getting comfortable with us.

"Wanna go up to bed?" I ask, raising my eyebrows up and down suggestively.

Soph giggles again. "It's only seven." She kisses me again and then says, "Sure, stud. Let's go to bed."

We walk up the stairs hand in hand. I lead the way to the bedroom and help her with her clothes. She helps me with mine. We won't do anything tonight. She's still healing. But I kiss and hold her until I hear her breathing even out.

"I love you, Sophie," I whisper. I pull her closer to me and a shiver runs down my spine. Happy. It's because I'm happy. God, I'm a lucky bastard.

39

SOPHIE

In the morning, I wake feeling like I've slept for days. I'm refreshed and warm and snuggled up next to the sexiest man on the planet. He's snoring loudly. *Hungry bear* comes to mind when I hear him. I giggle at the thought. He is big enough to be a bear, and he *is* always hungry.

Just then, my stomach growls, and I realize I'm hungry too. I think it's my turn to cook. I slide out from beneath his arms and out from under the sheet. I'm still in my tee and sleep shorts as I tiptoe down the stairs to the kitchen. I make a pot of coffee in my tiny pot. I need to get a bigger one. *A coffee pot for two.* That thought gives me goose bumps up and down my arms. There are two of us now. I should pinch myself, but that would be ludicrous. I do it anyway. I pull out the eggs, milk, and cheese to make us an omelet. *Us.* No amount of pinching will help me get past the feeling that this is unbelievable. The hottest guy I've ever met, or even seen, is up in *my* bed. *And he loves me.*

I shake my head in disbelief again.

"What are you shaking your head about now, beautiful?" he asks as he kisses the back of my neck.

Embarrassed, I say, "Nothing. Just thinking about everything."

"You mean like the book and stuff?"

"Um, yeah. The book. It's unbelievable."

"Maybe we have an email from the guy today. You also need to call the attorney back this morning," he reminds me.

"I will. You could check the email to see if we have a response."

He jogs back upstairs to retrieve his phone. As he enters the kitchen, he says, "Yeah. He wants to meet. He thinks it could be the real deal."

"Is he going to come here?"

"Not sure. Let me write him back and ask."

As Henry does that, I whip up the eggs and milk for the omelet and pop in two slices of wheat bread to toast.

"What's cookin', good lookin'?"

I snort a laugh out at that. "Omelets, you dork."

He wraps his arm around my waist as he buries his face in my hair.

I hear him sniff. "Are you sniffing me?"

"Yeah. You always smell so delicious," he says in a husky voice. His mouth moves to the spot below my ear that makes my nipples stand at attention.

"Henry, I'm cooking," I whine. But I've put the spatula down, and I've turned my head to the side so he can get to that spot easier.

He slides his hand up to run over my breast. "You turned on, babe?"

I know he knows I am. My nipples are rock-hard. I don't reply, but I nod.

"You feeling better?"

"Yeah. I feel good."

"You do feel good, Sophie. So fucking good," he says, sliding his hand down into my sleep shorts. "You're wet."

I knew that. He didn't need to tell me.

"I don't think you're ready yet. It's too soon. But I can make you feel good."

"I can make you feel good too, Henry." I turn off the stove and slide around to face him, lacing one of my hands in his shaggy hair while the other slides into to his pajama pants. I pull him down for a kiss.

He chuckles. "Jesus. You're turned on, aren't you?"

"Shut up and let me pleasure my man, Hanky."

"Henry. Call me Henry when you've got your hand on my dick, babe."

"Henry," I breathe. "Does this feel good?"

"Hell yeah, you only have to look at me to make me feel good." When she squeezes me and runs her hand over the head of my dick, I moan loudly. "Don't stop. Squeeze harder. You won't hurt me. Take off your top, Soph. Let me look at your tits while you get me off."

I stop to pull off my tee and then use both hands to push his pajama pants down to his midthigh. "You're so big, Henry."

"Not too big. We fit perfectly together. You and, ahh, yeah, like that. Keep doing that. Faster, Sophie. Goddamn you've got magic fingers."

"Good. Come for me," I say, pressing a hot kiss on him.

"Fuck!" He throws his head back and moans his release. "Wow, Soph." He sucks in a few deep breaths. "Wow."

"I'm glad you liked it." I turn to the sink and pump some hand soap into my palm. "Now, go get cleaned up. Breakfast is almost ready."

Henry does as he's told and heads upstairs to wash up. After breakfast, he goes into work to catch up on the latest. I call

Sharon Thompson, Sarah's attorney friend. Might as well get it over with.

"Sharon? It's me, Sophie Kincaid."

"Hello, Sophie. Thanks for calling me back. Let me update you on my dealings with Brooke Bellamy."

"Okay," I say, worried.

"First, she's not a nice woman," Sharon says with a chuckle.

"Uh-huh. I know."

"I told her I represented you and asked her if she had an attorney. She said she did but wanted to know what this was in reference to."

"Yeah, did she act surprised?" Brooke liked to act dumb. She could get away with a lot by acting stupid.

"She did. Brooke was shocked you'd even think of seeking damages."

"That's not a surprise."

"After I spoke with Brooke, I called her attorney, who was equally shocked, and told them we'd be suing Brooke and Bridal Belles LLC if she didn't provide you with a settlement."

I wait for the rest because I know more is coming.

"Friday afternoon, I received word they are filing a counter-suit against you."

"I heard that on your message. For the life of me, I can't figure out what grounds there would be to sue *me*?"

"She claims you were negligent when you locked yourself into the closet."

"But I didn't lock myself in the closet! There was a chair blocking my exit!"

"She claims you had no business going into that closet in the first place."

"She *told* me to refill all the order forms and paper before I left for the day!" I screech. "Ask Ashley. She was there."

"I have a call into Ashley. I hope she can corroborate our side of this."

"God, she's such a lying snake," I hiss. "If Ashley doesn't back me up, where are we?"

"We still have her for not changing the access codes. So that's good."

"Will you call me once you talk to Ashley?"

"I will. Take care, Sophie."

I hang up the phone and put my head in my hands. I think Henry was right. Brooke is a bitch. Just as I'm about to get up and get on with my day, my phone rings. "Hello?"

I wait for a second until I hear a hushed voice say, "Sophie?"

"Yes, this is Sophie. Who's this?"

"It's me, Ashley," she whispers.

"Ashley? Are you okay?"

"Yeah, I can't let Brooke hear me. I need to talk to you—like today!"

"Okay. Do you want to meet?"

"No. I'll go over to the Coffee Bean and call you back. This is super important so pick up. I'll call you back in five."

I wait by the phone until I hear it ring seven minutes later. "Hello?"

"Hi. It's me," Ashley says in a rushed voice. Her volume is back to normal, though. "I know your attorney called me, and I will call her back right after this, but you need to be careful."

"Why?"

"I heard Brooke on the phone with her attorney. She's pissed, girl. Like super-duper pissed."

"I can imagine."

"She's bailing out Ari."

"What? Are you kidding me?" *What the hell is she thinking?*

"Yeah, she hates your guts, and she wants Ari out. I don't

know if she's hoping Ari tries to get to you again or what, but she's up to something."

"Did she say that to her attorney?"

"No. Brooke was sickly sweet about Ari to her lawyer. She said things like, 'She's like a daughter to me. She just made some bad choices.' Shit like that."

"Bad choices?" I snort. "Attempted murder should be called a *worst* choice."

Ashley giggles. "Sorry. I didn't mean to laugh at that."

"It's fine. It was funny. Ashley, why are you telling me this? It's gonna get you fired."

"I'm quitting later today. I'm moving in with Mike. He'll help me go back to school. I can't stand that place. Brooke Bellamy is fucking crazy."

Now it's my turn to laugh. "She may be." I don't want to say anything that could come back to haunt me.

"I'll tell your lawyer that Brooke asked you to get that stuff from the closet. She thinks I'll lie for her because she warned if I didn't keep my mouth shut I'd be fired. So quitting needs to happen no matter what."

"Ashley, I'm sorry."

"This is not your fault. None of this is your fault, Sophie. You're innocent in all of this."

"I suppose."

"Okay. I've only got a couple more minutes. I'm calling your lawyer next. I'll talk to you soon, okay? Oh, and tell that man of yours about Brooke bailing out psycho bitch."

"Oh, I will. He'll be thrilled with that news."

40

HENRY

In the middle of Kent's long-ass bitch session about the fucking feds, my phone buzzes. I know I should ignore it, but I pull it out of my pocket to see Sophie's name flash on the screen. I tell the cop next to me I've got to take this.

I step out of the conference room and hit Talk. "Sophie? Is everything okay?" I hope we get to the point in all of this when my first question for her isn't asking if she's hurt, sick, or something worse.

"No."

"Fuck, what's wrong?"

"It's Brooke. She's bailing out Ari."

"What? How? Why?"

"My lawyer told her about the suit. She claims I was negligent when I went into the closet—she can't win that—but to get back at me, she's bailing Ari out."

"When?"

"I assume today, but I'm not sure."

"Who told you this?"

"Ashley. She overheard Brooke on the phone with her attorney."

"The bond for Arianna is big. She'd probably have to put her shop up as collateral to bond her out unless she's got a lot of money in the bank."

"I don't know. She's always dressed in expensive clothes and going to spas and things, but I don't know if she's wealthy."

"Let me do some checking. I'll be home soon. Sit tight. Stay in the house. Make sure the doors are locked."

"I was just going to work at Willy's place—"

"No! Stay in the house. Please, Sophie." *For the love of Christ, say you'll stay in the damn house.*

"Okay. I'll stay in the house. I'll hide out upstairs with a book until you get here."

"Good. Thank you, baby."

"Hurry home, Henry. This all makes me nervous."

"I know. I will. Love you."

"Love you too."

I press End, then dial Joel Peters.

"What's up, asshole?" Peters says in answer.

"Brooke Bellamy is bailing out Arianna Templeton."

"What the fuck? No way! Why?"

"Sophie's lawyer called Brooke about the lawsuit. She turned around and started the process of bailing out Templeton. Can you verify any of that for me?"

"Call you back as soon as I know something."

"Thanks, man." I hang up the phone. I keep it out as I walk back into the debriefing just in time to hear the captain give us the bad news.

"The Chicago PD is no longer working the William Gibbons case. The FBI has solid proof of Christopher Collins's embezzlement. They're working on murder for hire, but they aren't convinced they can get him on that. William's notes and other evidence is enough to send him away for a while. Not long enough, though."

We all grunt, acknowledging that eternity is not long enough time for a murderer.

Cap continues, "The FBI has the resources needed to see if there's a money trail for the hit. We do not have those resources. So, even though I hate giving it up, I'm glad that fucker will get something. William did a good thing. It's too bad he had to die for a scumbag like that."

"What about MacClenny in HR? Is she part of their investigation?" Kent has it out for MacClenny after all the bullshit she put us through. I'm sure he'd love to see her pulled into all of this.

"I wasn't briefed on that, but I would hope they would look at her as well—at the very least for conspiracy dealing with the embezzlement. Any changes to the payroll documents had to go through her. Unless she's a complete idiot, she'd have to have known he was up to something," says the cap.

My phone buzzes in my pocket. I'm pulled out of the meeting once again as Peters calls me back. "Hank?"

"Yeah. What do you got?"

"I wish I had better news for you, man. She's out."

"Ari?"

"Yeah, Ari's out."

"Already?"

"Yep. Bailed out at 12:35 p.m. today."

I look at my watch. 2:47 p.m. Two hours ago. "Was it Bellamy?"

"Yep. She must have deep-ass pockets. She'd better hope little Ari doesn't run away."

"I'd rather have her run away than go after Sophie again."

"I know, Hank. I know."

"I've called in a favor to one of our retired guys. He's tracking down Templeton. He'll tail her for us."

"Keep me posted."

"Will do."

I hang up the phone and send Kent a text telling him Arianna is out on bail and that I'm heading home.

I run to my car and race out of the lot. Traffic is thick as fuck. I honk my horn at anyone in my way. It feels like it takes hours, but I finally make it home.

I dash up the front steps, unlock the door, close it, and lock it behind me, then take the steps upstairs two at a time.

"Sophie?" I say breathlessly. "Sophie?" I yell as I run down her hallway. When I enter our bedroom, she's not there. Her book is there, but she's nowhere to be seen. I look under the bed and then yank open the closet door. *Nothing.* "Fuck!"

I do the same thing in the bathroom and the spare rooms. No Sophie. I sprint down the stairs, looking at the living room, and as soon as I hit the kitchen, I see the glass. The back window is broken. "Fuck!"

I cover my hands with my shirttail and pull that asshole fucking door open. I will get that fucking thing fixed as soon as I know Sophie is safe. I launch myself out the door and hurdle the cracked back steps. I'm at Willy's door in two seconds. The door is ajar, and I pull the gun out of my ankle holster. I place my back against the outer wall, turn, and kick the door open.

"Police!" I shout.

Nothing—no one is there. I run back to the house and launch myself into the kitchen just as Sophie walks into the room holding a laundry basket. Nearly mowing her down, I stop in time.

"Sophie? What the ever-loving fuck? Where were you?"

She pulls the earbuds from her ears and says, "What? Why is your gun out? Is Ari here?"

I ignore her questions, so I can get mine answered. "Where the hell *were* you? I was scared shitless."

"In the basement. I had to get laundry done. It's been a while."

I set the gun on top of the fridge and wrap my arms around her. "I was so scared, Sophie."

"I'm sorry. I locked up." She turns and looks at the door. "Henry, you broke my door?"

"No, I didn't. You did."

"No. I didn't," she whispers.

I grab my gun again and pull out my phone. I'd call Kent, but this will be a hell of a lot faster.

"Nine-one-one. What is your emergency?"

"This is Detective Henry Flynn. We have a possible break in at 1511 West Highland. Need backup. Now!"

"Officers en route, Detective Flynn. Three minutes out."

I hang up the phone, grab Sophie's hand, and pull her toward the front door. Since I don't know if Ari made it into the house, I want to get to my car so we can get the fuck out of here as soon as the cops arrive. I unlock the front door and wrap my arm around her waist to get her to safety faster.

I parked like a crazy person, backward and at a weird angle so I could get into the house. I press the buttons on my key fob that unlocks the doors and start the process of them opening. My mind moves to mundane thoughts to keep calm—like how I really need to trade this thing in on something more practical. It's not just me that'll be using this car now. We may need an SUV if we have a little Sophie or Henry someday.

The passenger door opens, and as I'm ushering Sophie in, I hear the cry of a screaming banshee. I look over just in time to see one Arianna Templeton running toward us, holding the biggest fucking knife I've ever seen. It looks like a Bowie knife from here. Those are used for hunting, and I suppose in this instance Sophie and I are the prey. She's at least twenty yards away by the time I get Sophie's door closed.

I draw my gun, and I'm about to yell, "Stop! Police! Drop your weapon," when a car whips around the corner at a high rate of speed. I don't think they see Ari running in the middle of the road because, before I can do anything, the car makes direct contact with Arianna Templeton.

Her slim body is launched into the air. Still clutching that knife, her body lands ten feet from my car, the knife having gone straight through her chest when she hit the ground. "Goddamn, that's disgusting." I swear I'll never get used to death.

The car that hit her stops, and a woman about Sophie's age jumps out and runs over to the body. She looks at me, holding my gun, and then at Sophie. "I didn't see her. I'm so sorry. What was she doing?"

"Trying to kill us," I say, deadpan. "She was running at us with that big-ass knife. You saved our lives."

"I did?" She looks at Ari and then at me. "So can I go?"

I chuckle. "No. You can't go. I'm a cop, and you're a witness to all of this. I'll vouch for you, though."

"Is she okay?" the woman asks, pointing at Sophie.

Damn it. Sophie. I turn to see a look of pure shock on her face. I open her door, and she jumps into my arms. "Oh my God, Henry. She... she was going to kill us."

"Yes, I think she was going to try, anyway. This nice woman saved our lives."

"You did! You saved our lives," Sophie says, awestruck. "Thank you so much!" Sophie walks over to the driver and hugs her. "You're so brave. You had to have been terrified when you saw her with that knife. Thank you so much."

The woman knows a good thing when she sees it. "I was! I was terrified, but I had to do *something*."

I wink at the woman as she peers back at me. I should feel bad, but I don't. It's a case of survival of the fittest, and Ari lost.

Finally, the cops swarm the place. Three minutes, my ass. When the uniforms descend on the body and the three of us, I do the talking. The woman who killed Arianna, Jill Fennelly, repeats my story verbatim. She may get a ticket, but I'll be sure she doesn't get charged. I mean, I was about to shoot Ari myself.

41
———————

SOPHIE

Five weeks have passed since Ari's death, and there have been no trips to the emergency room, no one has tried to kill me, and Henry hasn't lost his marbles and left me. He still loves me and tries almost every day to impregnate me. I guess I should be worried about it all, but after my near-death experiences, I've concluded that I need to just let go and embrace life.

I turn thirty in a few days, and thirty is a great age to have a baby. Okay, I've got a secret. It worked. I took a pregnancy test this morning, and it came back positive. I'm not sure when I'll tell Henry, but it'll be soon. I'm seriously worried he'll flee, but if he does, his mom Sarah will talk him down if I can't. Maybe I'll tell him today at the Flynn family dinner. It's Sunday, and those dinners have become an important part of our week—my week, in particular, because I love the Flynn family. Don't get me wrong. My family was perfect. I adored my dad, and my gran was the best sort of grandmother. But the Flynn clan is full of life, humor, and love.

Well, most of them are full of love. Mick is more brooding, almost angry. If the guy weren't so incredibly good looking, he wouldn't get away with being such a jackass. Besides Henry,

Mick is probably the best looking of the bunch—yeah, I'm biased. His sandy-blond hair is much longer than mine, and he's got a scruff of a beard that he keeps nicely trimmed. When he puts his hair into one of those man-buns, he takes your breath away. Mick is Liam Hemsworth to Henry's Chris Hemsworth. Can you picture it?

Mick is only a year younger than I am, but he acts like he's closer to twenty-one. He's a loyal brother to his siblings, just not as friendly as the rest, nor is he very trusting. I'm not sure where that comes from, but he has a way of saying inappropriate things to people he's not sure about. Case in point, last Sunday as we sat down to eat, there was a knock on the door. Everyone looked around the table, maybe taking inventory. Since everyone was there, they remained seated.

The knock sounded again, and Mick stood up. "I'll get it."

We all waited silently for him to return with the visitor, but all we heard was, "What the hell are you doing here?"

Then we heard a feminine voice speak.

"No one wants to see you," Mick replied.

More sounds came from the unknown woman. Then we all heard, "Just let me by, Mick. I need to talk to Hank."

I turned to Henry just has he muttered, "*Fuck.*"

"Language," Sarah said, quieter than usual.

What the heck is going on? Those were my thoughts when I saw the most stunning woman I've ever seen in person walk into the dining room.

"Angela, what the fuck are you doing here?" growled Henry.

Angela? "That's Angela? She's gorgeous. She's like a unicorn," I muttered.

"No, she's got two horns instead of one. She can't be a unicorn," added Sandy. "She's fucking Satan."

I'm not sure Henry heard us, but Emily did and spit out the

drink of milk she'd just taken. "Unicorn?" She laughed. "Sophie, you're funny."

"Yeah, it's *hilarious*," I said.

"I asked you a question. What are you doing here, Angela?" Henry demanded.

The unicorn spoke. "I knew you'd be here. You're *always* here," she said dramatically as she rolled her eyes. "I need to talk to you in *private*."

"No. If you have something to say, you can say it here. You know everyone, and they certainly know you."

She turned and glared. "I don't know *her*." She pointed angrily.

Sandy added to the flame. "That's Hank's girlfriend. She's awesome. We all love her so, so much. Don't we?"

There were mutterings of affirmatives around the table but nothing outright. It's okay. I know they like me.

"This is a private matter," Angela repeated, glaring at me. "Private. As in for your eyes only, Hank."

"Ears. I think you mean ears," I corrected her.

"I'm not talking to *you*." She glared at me again.

"Do not talk to Sophie like that. No. Don't talk to her at all. Fine, you've got two minutes," Henry said, standing up. "Keith, time this."

"Got it, chief," he said, pulling out his smartphone. "Go."

"Wait," Angela screeched. "I'm not ready yet."

"One minute thirty left," mocked Keith.

Everyone at the table got silent. We all wanted to hear what this was about. I had my suspicions.

Thankfully, Henry stopped walking the minute he was outside of the dining room, which meant he was close enough for all of us to listen in. It was then we hear Angela's simpering voice but couldn't tell what she was saying.

"No. No fucking way!" shouted Henry.

"Please? I'm desperate," whined Angela.

"Too fucking bad. Go see one of your hookups. You're not getting another cent out of me."

While the drama unfolded in the foyer, I peered around the room. I noticed that Jen, David's new wife, had her head down. Why did she look like she'd like to be somewhere, anywhere else? I then looked at Mick, who was seated to Jen's right. He reached out and grabbed her cell phone from the table. "Well, let's see how good ole Ang found out that Hank came to dinner," he said aloud, pressing buttons on her phone.

Jen attempted to grab it, but Mick stood up, taking the phone with him, turning his big body away from her.

"Goddamn it, Mick. Give Jen her phone back," yelled David.

"Here it is." Mick cleared his throat and read, "Angela. Hank is here at his parent's with some fat chick. If you want to see him, you'd better come now."

Everyone turned and looked at Jen. Then they looked at me. Why did they have to draw me into this? So she called me fat. I am fat. I know it's not nice, but I've dealt with worse, obviously.

"Jennifer? Why'd you do that?" her husband asked. "And why would you say anything like that about Sophie? She's been nothing but nice to you."

"Sophie this and Sophie that. Jesus. She's nothing special. You guys fawn all over her like she's the second coming!" Jen spit.

"Wow, you're one jealous bitch," Mick barked. "We've all welcomed you into this family even though we knew you were another Angela. You proved us all right."

"Mick. Goddamn it, shut up!" David yelled.

Without a word, Sarah stood up from the table and shouted, "Enough! Enough. I've heard enough. Michael and David, sit down and shush up." She turned to Jennifer. "Jennifer, darling, there's something you need to know about this family you apparently haven't figured out. We protect our own, and we are loyal. If you can't remember that, then perhaps you should stay home."

The table gasped. Sarah Flynn isn't the type to ban people from her dinner table.

Sarah wasn't finished yet. "Angela has no business here, and Sophie is a wonderful addition to our family. I'm saddened that you've resorted to name-calling."

Jen looked like she was about to cry. They might've even been real tears. "Sarah, I'm sorry. Angela, she's... she wouldn't give up."

"I understand. She's a piece of work, that one. But that doesn't excuse you saying something so hurtful about Sophie."

"I'm sorry," she whispered. She looked at me, but I could tell it wasn't a sincere apology.

Since I wanted no more drama, I said, "It's okay. I am fat."

I heard the usual responses to that, but I ignored them and looked out into the hallway, willing Henry to return soon.

We heard Angela whispering, but couldn't tell what she was saying until we heard Henry say, "Fine. Get a lawyer. You'll never get another penny from me. You got me? Now leave!"

Crying. She was crying. I bet that worked well for her because he's a sucker for a good cry. Or I thought he was. When *I* cry, Henry melts, but I don't use crying like Angela is right now, "Go ahead and cry, Angela. I'm immune to your fucking fake tears. Go home. You're interrupting my family time."

We heard him before we saw him as he stomped back into the dining room. The front door slammed shut as he took his seat next to mine.

"Sorry, everybody. She won't be back." He leaned over and kissed my cheek. "Sorry, baby," he whispered in my ear.

"How much?" Keith asked.

"Ten grand."

"Jesus!" Sarah exclaimed, surprising everyone at the table.

"Language, Mom!" shouted Sandy.

That caused everyone to laugh, and the dinner fun returned. With Henry on my left, I didn't notice when Emily leaned in and whispered in his left ear.

"What?" shouted Henry. "Jen? What the fuck?"

Oh great. Henry knew what she called me. "You let Angela know I was here and said disparaging things about my *woman?*"

This time, I thought Jen was nervous.

"Hank, I'm—"

"You're what? A *bitch?* I've had enough of women like you to last me a lifetime. If this is how you're going to treat Sophie, we won't come to dinner on Sundays."

"Henry, now don't say that. Jen is sorry. Aren't you, dear?" Sarah said in a stern voice.

"Yes. I'm sorry. I already apologized."

Mick snorted at that. I guess he could see right through it too. That's Mick in a nutshell, cynical, brooding, and immensely perceptive.

"Whatever," grunted Henry. "We'll see how sincere you are, Jen. Time will tell. Time will tell."

No matter. I love the Flynns, and I can't wait to spend holidays with them, the first of which will be my thirtieth *surprise* birthday party. Yeah, I know about it. Henry was right; they can't keep a secret. He'd kill Keith if he knew he's the one that blew it. The important thing is that Henry still thinks I don't know. He's worked hard planning everything, and if he thinks the surprise is ruined, he'll go on a murderous rampage.

No, not really.

Oh! I almost forgot. We met with the book expert last week at Henry's old place. Keith was in attendance because Henry felt the more people there, the better. The good news is that our expert is positive it's a rare first edition with the typo on the back.

He's estimating that we could get as much as $500,000. Maybe even more. The bad news is it won't go to auction for another six months because he wants to advertise the book worldwide to draw in the biggest pool of bidders. The other negative is that he'll get 40 percent of the sale. That stinks, but I guess it's part of the auction world. Still, if I end up with 60 percent out of the sale, I can fix up my house and go back to school. The baby will change things a little, but I'm happy to work around that—very happy.

Brooke settled with me. She needed to do something because she was about to be named as an accessory to Ari's attempt on our lives that last time. The Bowie knife Ari was wielding was Brooke's. It even had her initials on it. Who has a big hunting knife with "B. B." on the handle? Apparently, one of Brooke's ex-lovers bought it for her. Seriously? A knife? The police couldn't prove that Brooke gave the knife to Arianna, but we all know she did. Brittney has been released from jail. She's on probation with a stern warning not to get into any trouble or they will prosecute her for all of Ari's actions. I haven't heard a word from her, and I don't think I will. Brooke offered me $75,000 as a cash settlement plus she worked with the insurance company to pay my hospital bill. It was a good deal for me, so I took it. My attorney thinks I could have gotten a lot more, but I wanted to be done with her, with the bridal shop, with everything related to that episode in my life.

My life with Henry couldn't be happier. He's the kindest, most generous, and sexiest man in the entire world. I know I'm biased, but I feel so lucky. He keeps offering to pay for the home repairs, but I won't let him. We're not legally tied together, so it doesn't feel right to have him pay for something like that.

He wants to sell his place, but I've talked him into renting it to Keith and Beth. We found out last week that Beth is pregnant, so they're going to need the extra space. The rent is super cheap, as it should be because it's family. Well, time to get ready for dinner at the Flynn's. I hope there's no more drama. I don't think I could take it.

42

HENRY

It's been just over five weeks since that psycho bitch tried to knife us. A bunch of bullshit took place after that. Sophie and I were questioned, as was the woman who killed her. We all gave a similar statement, after which no charges were filed against Jill Fennelly.

Sophie has kept in touch with Jill. She's a nice lady. She didn't set out to run Ari over that day, but fate is a strange thing. When fate is good, it's very, very good. Out of the bad, there can be good. Take Jill for example. She and Sophie are now friends. So much so that Jill is coming to Sophie's surprise party tonight.

As for the case against Collins and MacClenny? It's moving along. TSA caught Collins at O'Hare attempting to flee the country, leaving MacClenny holding the bag. When MacClenny found out about that, she talked. Her testimony along with William's notes and computer records should be enough to get them both on embezzlement.

Word on the street is that MacClenny had no knowledge of the murder. I find it hard to believe she didn't suspect Christopher Collins when William was found dead, but I'm not privy to most of the background there. I'm just glad they'll both be behind bars for a while. The feds tracked down the money in the Caymans. I haven't heard whether the Luciph employees will see their money returned, but it's doubtful.

Tyrex checked into those fraudulent charges, and it turns out that Collins was still getting money from them. They had no clue about the additional fees for "Trading and Maintenance." They've removed the charges and estimate that he'd taken over thirty million dollars. Damn, the guy knew what he was doing. He got sloppy when he murdered someone. He could have just retired somewhere tropical and been done with it. Greedy asshole. No matter. I'm glad there's closure for Sophie relating to Willy's case. I'm also glad she's finally safe.

I'm having a surprise party for my girl tonight, and I'm almost positive that Sophie knows about it already. My fucking sisters can't keep a damn secret to save their lives. But that's okay because the real surprise isn't the birthday party. You can guess what it is, but I'll wait to surprise you too. It's almost time to go. I've told Sophie I wanted to take her out to a fancy restaurant for her big three-oh. She's getting all dolled up for that. I need her to hurry her ass up, though.

"Sophie? You about ready? We'll be late for our reservation?"

"Yeah, one sec," she yells in reply.

I stand at the bottom of the stairs with hands in my dress slacks. I'm wearing my nicest suit. It's dark gray with a tiny pinstripe, pairing it with a white dress shirt and a tie of blues and browns. Sophie picked it out because she said it's the blue of my eyes and the brown from hers. I'll never wear another tie again. I smile, thinking about my girl. She is the sweetest, kindest, sexiest woman I've ever met. I don't deserve her, but I want to keep her forever. I'm selfish that way.

When I hear movement above me, I look up, and it takes my breath away. "Jesus, Soph. You look beautiful."

She laughs from the top of the stairs. I watch her descend and step up so close, I feel her body touch mine. Running her hand over my now, clean-shaven jaw, she smiles. "I liked the beard, but you look amazing all cleaned up like this." Her fingers slide touch my hair and I close my eyes relishing in the feel of her hands on me. "And did you get a haircut?"

"I did. I wanted to look good for you, babe."

"Oh, Henry, you always look good but that's sweet of you to say. You're so good for my ego."

"Nothing egotistical about it. You deserve my best. You're fucking gorgeous and if we didn't have a reservation, I'd have you out of that dress in ten seconds."

She chuckles again. "Thank you."

The dress is navy blue. It wraps around her body like a present I can't wait to unwrap. It hugs her waist and dips to reveal some impressive cleavage. It hits her right above her knees and swings around her legs as she steps down the stairs. She's got on silver sandals with a heel that brings her up a couple of inches.

My mind keeps going back to that tie at the side of her waist. I wonder what she's got on under there. "I can't wait to see what you've got on under that little dress later tonight, babe."

"Who says I'm wearing anything?"

Holy fuck. She's killing me. "Soph, that's not nice. Now I'll wonder all night."

"Don't worry, baby. I'll show you later." She smiles devilishly.

"Baby? You called me baby?"

"I know. Did you like it?"

"Yeah. Almost as much as I like it when you call me Henry," I whisper in her ear. "Come on. We need to get going." I grab her hand and lead her out to my Range Rover HSE.

I said goodbye to my i8 the day after Ari died. The car was

sick as hell, but those butterfly doors were a pain in the ass. Plus, my girl needed a safe ride. I let her choose the color, and she chose *Montalcino red metallic*. It's a beautiful color. It would have been my first choice too.

Sliding into the driver's seat, I press start and listen to the truck purr to life.

"I love your car, *Hanky*," she coos.

Every once in a while, she loves to remind me of my past mistakes. It's not fun, but this time I laugh it off because I know she's just toying with me. "Thanks, babe. I bought it for my woman." I wink.

She beams at me and takes my hand in hers. "Wow, she's one lucky lady. It's a gorgeous car."

"I'm the lucky one," I say, smiling as I back out into the alley behind the house. I've created a parking spot back there, taking up only a small portion of the yard. My sister Emily doesn't care. She doesn't have a car anyway.

Oh, I guess you didn't know about that. After we finished cleaning out Willy's place, a large donation truck backed up to the door and took everything we didn't toss. My little sister is starting med school and needed a place to live. Sophie graciously offered the place to Emily, letting her live there for free, only paying for her own cable and internet. But don't worry. I'll make it up to Soph.

We make it to the restaurant right on time. I toss my keys to the valet with a warning look in my eye. As I pass the guy, I flash my badge. He should get the hint not to fuck with my ride. I wave the other guy away from Sophie's door as I open it for her and reach my hand out. "Ready to celebrate?"

"I am! I wasn't very excited about turning thirty, but you're making it fun. Thanks, Henry." She leans up and kisses me.

I lead her into the restaurant and straight to the back of the building where they have banquet rooms.

"Where are we going?" she asks.

"I reserved a private room for us."

"Oh?"

She's doing a great job acting like she knows nothing about this. Bless her. Once we reach the entrance to the room, I wrap my arm around her waist, and we walk in side by side.

As soon as they all see her, they jump out and scream, "Surprise!"

She is startled backward and nearly falls on her ass.

Maybe she didn't know. That'd be cool.

She puts her hands on her face and turns bright pink.

I'll be damned. She is truly surprised. Maybe it's because I flew in her best friend, Tracy, from Iowa that is getting to her, because she's crying.

"Trace? Is that really you?" She launches herself into her friend's arms and cries so hard she shakes.

"It's me, honey. It's really me. Gosh, I've missed you so much, Soph."

"How? Why?"

"Your boyfriend flew me in. He thought you'd want me here."

"I-I do," she says through the tears. "I do!" She turns. "Henry, thank you so much. You have no idea. No idea how much I've missed her."

"I had an idea. You talk about her a lot."

She takes hold of Tracy's hand and leads her around the small room. Since that's all she has, that's all that I invited. Well, I invited Kent, Joel Peters, and a couple of other guys from the force. They got to know her pretty well during the murder investigation.

Once dinner is served and eaten, they bring out a huge birthday cake. We all sing to her, which makes her cry again. I wonder when she last celebrated her birthday? The cake is served, and I lean over and suggest that Sophie say a few words. She stands and lifts her untouched glass of champagne. She must not like it.

"Um, excuse me," she says, waiting for people to quiet down. My family is damn loud. "I wanted to thank all of you for coming tonight. I was really, truly surprised."

My brother Mick snickers.

"Shut it, Mick," I yell.

"Anyway, thank you for coming out tonight and helping me celebrate. I'd like to thank Henry" she says. She looks at my seat, but I'm not there. It's then she looks down and sees me on one knee. "Hank? What are y—"

"Sophie, baby. I love you so goddamn much."

"Language, Henry!" my mother yells.

Everyone cracks up laughing.

"Mom, shut it," I yell. Then there's silence. "Sorry, Mom. Let me start over. And no interruptions, fuckers! Not you, Mom."

Sophie giggles, and it becomes a full-blown laughing fit. Tears are in her eyes from laughing, but I can tell they've turned into something more.

"Sophie, baby, I love you so much. You've turned my life upside down and inside out, and I'm so happy about that. Before you, I only existed. Now I live. I love. I look forward to my days and nights with you. To quote my little brother, 'I give my heart. I promise from this day forward you shall not walk alone. May my heart be your shelter and my arms be your home.'" I stop for a second and reach into my pocket for a tissue. I thought she might cry.

"Thank you," she says as she wipes her cheeks.

I clear my throat to continue. "I look forward to starting our family. I miss you when I'm gone. I can't wait to get home to you, angel. Please make me the happiest man in the world, Katherine Sophia Kincaid, and say you'll marry me?"

I pop open the box that holds her ring. I searched high and low for one that was good enough for her. I finally designed one myself. It's a three-carat princess-cut diamond with two square cut chocolate diamonds on either side set in platinum. The chocolate diamonds reminded me of her beautiful eyes.

"Oh my God, Henry. It's... it's beautiful," she says breathlessly.

I pull the ring out of the box and hold it up to her. "Will you marry me, baby?"

"Yes, of course. I love you so much, Henry. Yes!"

I slide the ring on her tiny finger. I had to steal one from her jewelry box to get the right size. She holds the ring up in front of her. "It's huge!"

"That's what she said," yells one of my brothers.

"Shut it, Mick," Sophie yells.

My family bursts out into laughter.

Mick looks like he got slapped, which makes it even funnier.

Once they quiet down, she smiles at me and says the fucking funniest thing. "It really pays to be a gold digger, Henry."

I lose my shit then and there. I fall over onto my back and laugh so hard I nearly piss my pants.

My sister Sandy stands up and high-fives her, saying, "That's what I'm talking about, bitch."

Sophie laughs hysterically right along with the rest of my family.

Once calm has set in and I've returned to my seat with my fiancée in my lap, my favorite spot for her, my mom stands up and holds up her glass. "To Sophie and Henry."

Everyone follows suit.

Then my mom says one more thing. "So, Sophia, when are you going to tell us all you're pregnant?"

Sophie's eyes get as round as baseballs. I turn to Mom, then back to Sophie. "Soph?"

"Um, surprise?" she says with a weak smile. "I'm pregnant."

"How did Mom know before me?"

"Henry, don't get all pissy. I guessed. She hasn't had a drop to drink all night. Call it women's intuition. I'm sorry I outed you in front of everyone, sweetie, but I wanted to know for sure. I've got plans to make." She laughs.

"Are you happy about it, Henry?" Sophie asks, obviously nervous.

I wrap my hands around her waist and then place my palm on her stomach. "Sophie, I've never been happier in my entire life. We're getting married and starting a family. I never thought I'd have that. It's because of you I will. I thank you." I kiss her without caring who sees, tongue and all.

Catcalls (Emily) along with words like "gross" (Mick), "get a room" (Mom?), and

knock it off" (Dad) don't stop the momentum. Time to take my woman home and consummate the engagement. "Let's go home, babe."

"What about Tracy?"

"She's staying at Keith and Beth's. She'll be here for two more days. She'll move over to our place tomorrow. I wanted tonight with just the two of us. Okay?"

"Okay."

"We're out of here, assholes. Not you Mom and Dad," I quickly correct. "Tracy, you're not an asshole either."

She laughs and then says, "I can be."

"It's true," says Sophie. "It's why I love her."

I carry my woman out of the restaurant and hand the valet my ticket. He pulls around and opens the door for us. I set

Sophie inside and lean in for a kiss. "Thank you for saying yes tonight. I'd be lost without you, Sophie."

"Thank you for asking. And thank you for my party. I haven't had a birthday celebration for five years. I loved it."

We kiss one more time. I jog around the car, hop in, and drive home. *Home.* Thanks to Sophie, I'm finally home.

43

EPILOGUE: HENRY

One Year Later: Henry

I FUCKING LOVE MY LIFE. I'm married to the most beautiful woman on the planet, and now I'm holding the most precious gift any man could ask for, Katherine Sarah Flynn. Our tiny angel was born only four months ago on June 1, weighing in at a whopping eight pounds six ounces and twenty inches long. My brave wife was a champ giving birth to our baby girl after having been in labor for twenty-three hours. I am in awe of her strength.

Katie is the perfect combination of both Sophie and me. She has my blond hair and brown eyes just like her mama's. She's got Sophie's nose and my mouth. When she's angry, she takes after me, but most of the time, she's like her mommy, always smiling and giggling. She's so joyous I have a perpetual smile on my face. It's impossible to be in a bad mood with my two girls nearby.

Sophie and I married a couple of weeks after her thirtieth

birthday party. She didn't want a big wedding and definitely didn't want to buy a wedding dress—I can't blame her. Even though my first wedding and marriage was a circus, I would have given her a big, expensive wedding if she'd wanted one. But she chose something small and private with just our family and friends. Her best friend, Tracy, was her maid of honor and my two sisters, Sandy and Emily, were her bridesmaids. I had my brother Keith as my best man. Dave was slightly put out I didn't ask him, but what can I say? Keith is my best friend. It had to be him.

Speaking of Keith—he and Beth gave birth to a beautiful baby girl a month before Katie was born. Her name is Abigail Sarah Flynn. Now our Katie will have a built-in best friend with a cousin the same age, and my mom now has two namesakes. It's cool. She deserves it. She's a doting grandmother, and my dad is so proud of his two granddaughters he wears two buttons with their pictures on them every day everywhere. It's a little embarrassing.

The person who has surprised me the most after we brought Katie home was Uncle Mick. He's almost a changed man—at least he is when he's holding our daughter. He seems almost happy. He sings to her (Who knew he could sing?); he rocks her to sleep, feeds her when Sophie can't nurse, and talks to her. He even babysits when Mom or Dad aren't available. Mick is still a moody asshole around the rest of us, but there's a bond between Katie and Mick that is hard to deny. Even at four months, she gets excited when Mick picks her up and talks to her.

Keith's and my daughter are both spoiled rotten whenever they visit my folks' house, which happens a lot. Sophie loves my family and wants to spend as much time with them as I do. Angela, my first wife, hated spending time with my family. That should have been enough to let me know the relationship was doomed. That my Sophie loves my family as much as I do makes me so fucking happy. Family means everything.

When we aren't at my parents' house, they are at ours watching our girl while we work on the house. Over the past year, we've made a lot of progress on Sophie's Victorian. We've replaced the roof and the boiler system. I refinished the hardwood floors throughout with the help of my brother and dad. The three of us added a bath off the kitchen with a small shower stall, a toilet, and a pedestal sink, which was a much-needed addition to our home. Now, we're renovating the bathroom upstairs. Sophie wanted to retain as much of the original bathroom as possible, but once we tore into the walls and saw the rot and water damage caused by leaky pipes, the only thing we could salvage was her claw-foot bathtub. It had to be gutted and the plumbing replaced.

While she was disappointed about it, I promised her I'd find tiles and fixtures that closely resembled her originals. We're almost finished with it, and it looks amazing and a lot like the original bathroom with the white subway tiles and the black-and-white hex-shaped porcelain floor tiles we chose. My added shower is just as updated as the ones in my old house, with multiple showerheads and temperature controls, but we've used retro fixtures and the same tiles as the rest of the bathroom. I've even added a towel warmer. I know, I'm a pansy ass.

I've offered to pay for all the renovations, but Sophie is adamant she pays. She's got the money now after her copy of *The Great Gatsby* sold at auction for over $750,000 thanks to an insane bidding war. Her cut was $450,000 before taxes. Now, she has a nice nest egg. She still wants to finish her degree, and I want that for her too, but for now, she wants to be home with Katie full-time.

Emily is still living in the carriage house. She's been in medical school for about nine months now and seems to be doing well. I'm not sure what goes on in that small garage apartment. I see people going in and out of her place at all hours of the day and night, and while I want to go find out what the hell she's doing in there, Sophie has made me promise to keep my nose out of it. Emily's not having noisy parties over there, but still. My baby sister is entertaining people, and one of those people is a man with a Harley motorcycle. I don't like it. It takes every bit of willpower I've got to keep from storming over there. Willpower and Sophie, that is.

Work is going well for me. Unfortunately, I've worked several more murder cases since Willy's. As for his case, Christopher Collins was indicted and convicted on embezzlement and money laundering charges. Evidently, they weren't able to get him on the murder for hire, which sucks. Janet MacClenny was also charged, but she made a deal with the feds and testified against Collins. Collins was sentenced to twenty years in a federal penitentiary and fined over $400k. MacClenny is on probation. That still chaps my ass. I'm positive she was involved, but the big fish was Collins, and the feds must have decided it was worth letting her walk if it meant getting him. That's how it works sometimes. I've gotta live with that outcome along with knowing I helped catch them and put Collins behind bars.

Ashley, from Bridal Belles, has become a fixture in Sophie's life. After Arianna died, Ashley stopped in to check on Soph, and their friendship slowly blossomed. She's also kept us up to date on Brooke and Brittany. Brooke's store is now closed. She sold the shop to a competitor so she could travel. It's utter bullshit. Brooke should be rotting behind bars too. Brittany still works at the donut shop as an assistant manager now. She should be incarcerated too, but maybe working at the donut shop is punishment enough.

While I would prefer those two women were prosecuted, if

it weren't for Brooke's store, I would never have met Sophie. If it weren't for Brittany and Arianna, I never would have needed to get close to Sophie to keep her safe. So as disturbing as this sounds, for that, I thank them. Fate and circumstance brought us together. Love and family will keep us together. Forever, if I have anything to do with it.

BOOKS BY KAYT MILLER

The Palmer Sisters

Lainie

Agatha

Sadie

Cortland

Keely

Violet

Molly

Standalones

The Art of the Game

The Virginia Chronicles

One of a Kind

The Portrait Painter

Game Changer

Bedhead

It's All Thanks to Santa

Coming Soon: Farm Boy

Coming Soon: Redhead

The Flynns

Out of the Blue

Mick'sology

Vested Interest

The Importance of Being Ernie with Bonus Book The Importance of
Being Kennedy's

Quirky Girl

For a complete list of Kayt's books, visit:

Kayt's Website: kaytmiller.com

ACKNOWLEDGMENTS

Thank you to Virginia from Hot Tree Editing for editing this book from start to finish.

And an extra special thank you to Becky at Hot Tree Promotions for your advice, expertise, and her positivity.

And to my beta readers. Your feedback is essential to this process. Thank you!

*Many thanks and adoration to Colleen Galligan for re-designing
the The Flynn series for me. She read the books twice to get them
just right. Thank you, Colleen!
Contact Colleen: galligancolleen@gmail.com
<3 KM*

ABOUT THE AUTHOR

How did it all start? Well, I love reading and one day I was searching for a book. A book about a certain type of woman and a specific kind of man and I couldn't find it so, I wrote it. I called it Game Changer and it couldn't have been a more appropriate title. It changed my life in many ways. While my real job is teaching young people, my fun job is conjuring up characters and situations to write about.

My goal, as a writer, is to write stories that relate to all of us, to make readers laugh and maybe cry sometimes. I hope my readers can escape into a fantasy, one that's actually possible. Sure, some of the stories could be dubbed "Insta-love" stories but that's okay. I fell in love with my husband pretty damn fast and with my daughter the second I saw her. So, it's a thing, I swear.

Please Follow Me on these social media sites. Following on BookBub to learn about special book deals.

I love hearing from you!

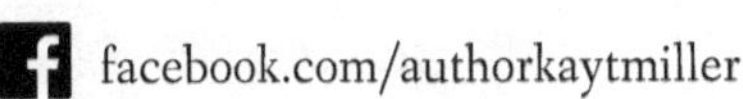

facebook.com/authorkaytmiller

twitter.com/kaytmiller1

instagram.com/kaytmiller1

bookbub.com/profile/kayt-miller

Thank you so much for reading Sophie and Hank's story! When I start a story, it begins with an outline, notes, and lots of crazy thoughts running through my head. When I actually start writing, the characters take over, leading me through the story like they're holding my hand—guiding me. The process is exciting and cathartic. With that said, I hope you enjoy the story.

If you did, please go to my website, www.kaytmiller.com, and join my newsletter so you can be the first to know what's coming up next. And...

Please, leave a review!

Chapter 1: Mick

As I lean over to buckle her into the back seat of the Uber, I feel fingers and the scrape of fingernails as they run across the back of my head, catching on my knot of hair. I turn to look at her as she pulls my head closer. She's beautiful for a thicker girl. Her long blonde curls are sort of a mess now, after having worked all day and spent the evening drowning her sorrows at my bar. Her eyes are hooded. She looks a tad drowsy. They're surrounded by long eye lashes. She flutters them for a second and my eyes are drawn to her full, pink lips. Lips that are on mine before I can even utter a word. They taste sweet, like the drinks she had tonight—one too many drinks, apparently.

Bent over at the waist to get her into the cab, I turn my body and place my hand on the back of her seat. I move my head a little to the side to get serious about this kiss. Her tongue moves over my bottom lip, seeking mine. I oblige because that's the kind of guy I am. I learned early on, when a pretty girl pulls you into a kiss, you reciprocate.

When our tongues meet, we moan simultaneously. I pull

the hand from the back of the seat and slide it into her lustrous blonde curls to pull her even closer. It's the best fucking kiss I've ever had. My dick is hard as a rock, and all I want to do is get this girl naked. But, she's drunk, and I'm supposed to be the good guy here and not take advantage of her. I'm her fucking bartender, not her date.

I pull away and see that her eyes are still closed while her lips are open slightly. She licks her lips as her eyes flutter open. She's got the greenest eyes I've ever seen.

"Wow," she says. "That was some kiss. You're hot as hell, Mick the Barkeep."

"Thanks," I smirk, still close enough to smell her sweet, feminine scent.

"It's a shame," she adds.

"Why's that?"

"Because... we could have made beautiful babies together." Her head falls back on the seat, and seconds later she's snoring.

Fuck! Of all the things she could have said to me, that one made my dick flaccid. Beautiful *babies?* What the fuck?

The Uber driver interrupts my thoughts. "Mick, Jesus, dude, time to hit the road. Where does she live?"

"Oh, sorry, Sam. I didn't.... I was caught up with...."

"Obviously."

"She's out cold. I'll see if she's got ID in her purse. You're my witness, Sam. I'm not trying to roll her."

"Be kinda hard to do; she's a big girl."

That comment pisses me off. "Knock it off."

"Oh, sorry, Mick. She your girl?"

"No. It's... just... she's a nice girl." Okay, I know shit about her, but after years of being in the bartending business, you get a sense about people. My gut tells me she's a nice girl. Too nice for the likes of me.

"Gotcha. Address?" Sam asks impatiently.

"Ah, here it is. Oh, Jesus." I snort out a laugh. "She said her name was Roni, but that must be a nickname. It's no wonder she has a good sense of humor. You'd have to with a name like that."

Sam chuckles. "I can't wait. What's her name?"

"Veronica Sue McGonigall."

"Veronica McGonigall? Shit, say that three times fast. Not possible," Sam says, laughing hard.

I can't help myself, but I laugh out loud and startle Sleeping Beauty. Not for long, though. She turns her head to the other side and starts snoring again.

"Today, Mick. What's her frigging address?"

I read it off and realize that she lives in Lincoln Square, which is the neighborhood just to the east of mine, North Park. We're neighbors. I put her ID back in her tiny purse and pull myself out of the car, wincing when I straighten my back. I shut her door and tap the roof, letting Sam know he can take off.

Sam is the guy I call when one of our patrons needs a ride. He's a good guy, a family guy with six kids, just like my family. Well, not my family, my mom and dad's. I have five siblings. That's what I'm trying to say. In any case, I like helping him out when I can.

I turn back to the entrance of Chrome and nod to our head bouncer, Steve.

Steve raises his hand up for a high five and says, "She's not your usual type, kinda a blonde Ashley Graham. She had nice tits. Way to go."

I can't leave him hangin', so I slap his hand. He smirks at me as I walk back inside. What can I say? She did have nice tits. The rest of her was pretty good too. Long blonde hair, full pink lips, plump round ass, and expressive green eyes. Remembering that kiss and the rest of her curves makes my dick twitch. Damn, she was all woman.

The end of my day sure beats the shit out of the way it

started. I was off last night, so I had come in early to get a jump on paperwork. When I walked into the bar, the first thing I saw was a fucking disaster. It looked like no one did any goddamn closing work. There were empties all over the place; the counters were sticky. They left dirty dishes in the sink, and the chairs were still on the floor, which means no one mopped the floors last night.

I stomped into my office and picked up the phone. I called every single one of those assholes that worked last night and told them to get their ass to Chrome, or they're fired. I thought about firing them anyway. Twenty minutes later, I had seven people in front of me who knew exactly what the fuck they didn't do last night.

"You've got thirty minutes to get this bar in order. If I ever see this place like this again, you're all fucking fired," I shout. Then I turn to the person who was supposed to be in charge last night. "Stacy, my office now!"

She follows me back, head hanging low. She knows what's coming. I slam my door shut after she enters and say, "If you ever leave my bar like that again, you're not only fired, you can kiss any recommendation from me goodbye. We clear?"

"We're clear," she says sadly.

"When I'm not fucking livid, I'll ask you what happened last night. Until then, get out there and get that shit cleaned up!"

"Okay. Yeah, thanks, Mick." She scurries out the door like the room is on fire.

I know I should feel guilty for being such a prick, but fuck that shit.

When I walk back out to the bar forty minutes later, the place is now spotless, and those worthless sacks of shit are gone. Good thing. I feel like yelling all over again. I turn to go back to my office but stop when I catch a glimpse of a guest at the bar. Emily. She's smiling at me, but I can tell she's tired. Still in her scrubs from, no doubt, a long shift at the hospital, she's got her dirty blonde hair pulled back in a tight ponytail and it doesn't look like she's got on any makeup. Not surprising, my little sister isn't girly. She's pretty but not overtly feminine.

"Em? What are you doing here?"

"Biding my time. I thought I'd let you cool off before I knocked on your office door."

"Yeah, so you heard that?"

"The tail end of it."

"So, what can I do for you, baby sister?" I love Emily. She and I are tight. We're just over two years apart, which means we were thrown together a lot when we were kids. As the two youngest in a family of six, we had to be a united front against the tyranny of our older, meaner siblings.

Em follows me into my office. I sit in my chair, and she plops her ass down in the chair in front of my desk.

"Well, I haven't seen you in a couple of weeks, so I thought I'd stop by to catch up. Maybe I shouldn't have come unannounced, though." Emily throws her feet up on top of my desk, getting comfortable. "From the scene out there, I was fearful I'd get caught up in the crossfire." Using her thumb, she points toward the bar. "What's up with you? You've been miserable for months." She arches her brow at me. "So, when are you gonna get happy, Mick?"

"What do you mean? I'm perfectly happy." No, I'm not.

"You're not happy. The Mick I know and love wouldn't have lashed out at everyone out there just now. Sure, he would have been pissed, but he wouldn't have been so harsh."

"Emily, you didn't see this place. It was a fucking dump."

"Stacy's dad died last night."

"What? Why didn't she tell me?" I pick up my phone and see my voice mail icon shows several missed messages. I click on it and see three from Stacy. "Shit."

"Did she leave you a message?"

"Three." Jesus, I feel like shit now.

"She had to get out of here last night to get to the hospital. The other people dropped the ball. Not her."

"How do you know that?"

"I sat at the bar and listened while they worked. They were careful not to say too much about you, but the consensus was: — you're a cranky, old bastard."

"I'm not old," I grumble even though I feel about a thousand years old right now. I stand to move around and sit on the front of my desk, the action pushing Emily's dirty sneakers off.

She huffs in irritation. "Older than most of them," she says with a smirk. "So, when are you gonna let your anger at Lauren go? It's been over a year."

"I may never get over the shit with Lauren. Look, Em, I'm doing the best I can."

"No, you're not. I mean, you've always been a moody asshole, but this last year you've become... completely unfun."

"Unfun? That's not even a word."

"It fits, though, doesn't it? You used to laugh with me, tell jokes, make fun of our older siblings, but whenever we're together, you're sullen and angry. It sucks. I want my fun-loving brother Mick back."

I sigh, knowing it's true. I haven't been able to shake the anger and sadness from all the shit that went down with my ex, Lauren Sly. Fuck, her last name fits her perfectly. She's a deceitful bitch. "Yeah, I know. I just didn't realize how far I'd slipped. Now that I know, I can make a conscious effort to do a better job. I can try to fake it."

"Jesus, Mick. I don't want you to fake happiness. Just get happy. Maybe it's time you met someone."

"No way. No fucking way. I'm never gonna be in a relationship again. I'll just stick with hookups."

"Having sex with these stupid barflies is a bad idea. You need a good woman. Look at what a difference Sophie's made in Hank's life. He's actually a joy to be around now, and we both know that's a miracle."

My brother Hank fell head over heels in love, and it shocked the shit out of all of us. He'd divorced his bitch of an ex-wife a long time ago and swore he'd never remarry or even have a serious relationship. But then he met Sophie, and all of that shit went out the window.

"Sophie's different."

"I know. She's cool. She's sweet, funny, and she loves all of us probably as much as Hank does. I never thought he'd get remarried after she-who-shall-not-be-named," she says ominously. Emily loves Harry Potter. She uses quotes from those books on a daily basis.

I chuckle. Lauren deserves that moniker too. "I'll think about it. Okay? That's all I can give you right now. I'll think about it."

"I guess that's all I can ask of you. I love you, big brother. We all do. You deserve to be happy, and you're selling yourself short if you let what Lauren did to you keep you from finding a good woman."

"Jesus, did Mom send you? You sound just like her."

"I know. It scares the living crap out of me too." She laughs. "But she has a point. She and Dad have been happy for decades. They've set an example for the rest of us—that it's possible to be in a healthy, long-term relationship and be friends as well as lovers."

"Please, do not say the word 'lovers' when referring to Mom and Dad." I exaggerate a shiver. "While I'm at it, what made you all Miss Fucking Romantic? Is there something you need to tell me? Did you meet 'the one'?" I say sarcastically.

"Maybe. But I'm not saying a word about it to anyone, and

neither are you." She points at me and looks serious. "What you and I talk about stays between us, or have you forgotten?"

"Of course, I haven't forgotten. I still have a scar on my thumb from when we made that stupid blood oath. You're such a bitch. I can't believe I let you talk me into that stupid ceremony and got me to let you use a knife on me."

"I was practicing," she smirks.

"Well, it's a good thing you're going to medical school. At least now if you cut someone open, you can sew them back up."

"True dat, bro. True dat. All right, I'm out. I've got a date with a textbook."

I stand up and walk around my desk to give her a hug. "I love you, Emily. When you're ready, I want to hear about the love of your life," I say sarcastically.

But she's serious. "I will. When you get fun again, I'll tell you about him."

Jesus, she's met someone? Damn. "Okay. That's a deal. Love you."

"Love you too," she says walking out of my office.

Stop being "unfun"? "Good luck with that," I mutter, picking up the phone to call Stacy so I can tell her how sorry I am about her dad.